Also by Cecilia Randell

The Adventures of Blue Faust

A Girl Named Blue

Behind These Blue Eyes - A Between the Adventures Novella

Beyond Blue Frontiers

For a Pixie in Blue

A Blue Star Rising

Wild is the Blue *(coming May 2019)*

The Forgotten Trilogy

A Forgotten Goddess

The Legends That Remain

The Final Melody

Stand Alone Novels and Novellas

Blinded Beauty

THE LEGENDS THAT REMAIN

Cecilia Randell

Book Two of The Forgotten Trilogy

eBook Published 2018
ISBN Print: 978-1-7339745-1-6

Front cover image by Covers by Combs

Published by Blue Wren Publishing

author@ceciliarandell.com

This is for the forgotten, the misfits, the ones who just do their own thing.
You're beautiful.

Contents

Chapter One

Dear Bastet,
Is it possible to be both wonderfully happy and extremely
frustrated at the same time?
- Bat, the goddess of the pub

Bat,
Yes. Tell me again why you're not doing something about
this frustration?
- Bastet, the goddess who is gonna go out there and make
something happen if you don't

BAT SITRU

*B*at placed a pint on the bar before Old Mike, a will o' the wisp regular. He came in every afternoon and stayed until dusk, when he would make his way back to the Keelogyboy Bogs and attempt to lead any travelers astray. It was an interesting purpose to have, and per the wisp, he was simply trying to show those travelers a new adventure, *"for didn't Lost hold hands with Fate and between them create adventure and wonder, the very reason for living?"* The words echoed in her mind in the wisp's deep brogue and she smiled at him. She loved that she was coming to know these people so well.

He returned her smile, his teeth bright against the faded gray of his beard and skin. A delicate swirl of pastel light passed under the flesh of his cheeks—a reaction she'd learned was a wisp's version of a blush. "Appreciate it, goddess."

She patted his hand. "I have told you, Mike. Bat. My name is Bat."

He ducked his head and shrugged. It was a reaction she was used to seeing from the immortals that came to The Dubros. No matter how she instructed them, many wouldn't, or couldn't, address her simply as Bat.

There were a few exceptions of course.

Mell O'Loinsigh—one of those exceptions—entered from the back hall, Killer at his heels and two plates of hot sandwiches in his hands. He flashed her a quick smile then focused on the table of banshees who'd come in for an early dinner. The Dubros didn't serve anything fancy, never had, but since she'd come they'd added a few simple items to the menu, on top of the basic crisps and pretzels and munching foods—as she liked to call them— which had already been offered.

Killer's big brown eyes stared up that the food, then flicked to her, to Mell, and to the banshees. He gave off a little whine, ducked his head, then pawed the flagstone floor.

Her puppy was a mooch.

"No." Mell pointed a finger at the pup then flicked it toward Bat, as though the animal would understand just from that.

Killer did understand. Giving another pathetic whine that didn't sway the Fomoiri or the banshees, Killer slunk around the end of the bar and came to sit beside Bat.

"That one's gonna be trouble," Old Mike said. He sipped his beer as he shifted to peer over the bar. "Ya should train him to growl at the humans. Troublesome lot those are. Never let themselves be drawn away, do they? Got that GPS and those genius phones and those apps that're always telling them where they are. Take the fun from living, those gadgets. It's enough to discourage a wisp into crossing over, it is." He sighed and shook his head, then took another sip of his Guinness.

Bat listened patiently and made soothing noises, both for the wisp and the puppy. A low rumble came from the other end of the bar, where Dub dealt with a tourist who'd just come in. "So, who should growl, the Fomoiri or the puppy?" she asked, unable to resist the tease.

Old Mike's eyes sparked in mirth and waved a hand to Dub at the end of the bar nearest the door. "Oh, the pup for sure. We already have a Fomoiri who growls at the humans. But do ya really think ya could train him?"

Deciding to play a bit, she leaned forward and tilted her head conspiratorially toward Old Mike then cast a glance at the Fomoiri in question. The tourist was asking for "a glass of that famous Irish beer." "With that one, the trick is to get him in a good mood before we open the doors."

Old Mike grinned then turned to gaze at Dub. "And have ya figured out how to do that, goddess?"

She pulled back. "No. It is a shame too. Killer is easier to keep in line."

He was. Her pup, an easy if squirmy handful when she had received him, now came up to her knee. According to Ciara, whose own hound was Killer's mother, he would grow to be just as large as his dam, his shoulder coming up to Bat's waist. And she would get to keep him forever and ever, as the pixie put it. A special breed combining the mortal wolfhounds and the Cu Sidhe of the Irish otherworld of the dead, these dogs could blend with the modern world, but wouldn't die of age. Bat had been relieved to hear it. Already, a mere two months after the brothers offered him to her, she couldn't imagine her life without him as a companion.

There were also others she couldn't envision her life without—but they came with their own set of worms.

Old Mike chuckled. "Well, let the world know when ya do figure it out, goddess. It'll save some bashed heads."

She twisted her head just in time to see Dub slam a half-poured pint down on the bar before the human tourist. Oh no. It took time to pull a proper pint. This man must have complained it was taking too long. "I'll be back." She hurried to where Dub stood, Killer on her heels, just as the pub door opened and a new annoyance —*person*—entered.

Finn, out of his guardi uniform, took it all in with a glance, the human who crowded in next to his own seat at the end of the bar, the scowling Dub, and the frowning goddess. He hesitated for just a moment then sighed, wedging himself into his stool. "A pint, please," he said. "And do it proper, will you?" He flicked a teasing finger at the cloudy glass.

Dub growled. Yes, she had been teasing with the wisp a moment ago, but that really was the best word for the sound that rumbled its way from her grumpy not-man and into the air. "Fine," he shot out.

Bat sent an admonishing look at Finn, then turned to the human. "A piece of advice. The Irish take their beer very seriously, as is only proper. Do not rush the pulling of a pint." She poked Dub's side. "You. Take Killer out and see if Shar is done in the garden." She paused. "Please." That should do it. Please-s were very powerful with this particular not-man, almost as effective as thank you-s. She'd learned to use them sparingly, but in the interest of keeping a troublesome human whole, she would use one now.

Dub pulled in a breath. "Fine," he repeated. He snapped his fingers at Killer and strode from behind the bar and through the doorway that led to the kitchen and storeroom. Her puppy followed behind obediently, knowing that signal meant he would get to go outside for a romp, or even a ride in the truck.

Her puppy was so smart. Why had she not gotten one earlier in her existence?

She started on Finn's pint, ignoring the grumblings of the tourist. She'd made humans leave before, she could do it again if this one got too out of hand.

"So, Finn. How is your work going?" A safe enough

5

question, and something to break the silence. "Will you stay tonight and play something with us?" He'd become more of a fixture recently, stopping by at least a few times a week to play a tune, or enjoy a pint. He'd also begun to mellow, as Ailis called the softening of his stiff mien.

Finn was another she was coming to think of as intrinsic in her new life.

He shook his head. "I'll be staying for a bit, but not to play."

There was an edge to his tone that told her there was more behind his words, but he wouldn't say anything with the tourist there. Her heart gave two hard beats and her fingers tingled, though no vision came.

"That's a shame," she finally said. Silence settled over them as she waited for the first pull to settle then topped off the pint glass.

Mell joined her behind the bar just as she set the finished pint in front of Finn, and stood a little too close to her. She shifted, unsure if she wanted to draw closer or pull away from the not-man beside her. Finn's gaze darted between the two of them and his lips tipped up. "Something I should know here?"

Bat frowned. "No." And *that* was the problem. There wasn't anything to know. The last two months, since she had agreed to stay, the brothers had, in a way, withdrawn. There were no more spontaneous and angry kisses in the kitchen, no more embraces, no more moments of revelation late at night or lingering touches. There were no more grand declarations of almost love. She told herself it was for the best, that there *were* good reasons for the lack.

6

It didn't matter what she longed for at night—and occasionally during the day. Just because the brothers offered her protection and companionship didn't mean it needed to be of a physical nature. Grainne and Diarmuid had shown her that she needed to tread carefully with the immortals when it came to sex, or love of that nature, so she allowed the distance. Dub had also insisted that, until the meeting with his father was concluded, she shouldn't draw any attention to herself, or let others know she planned to stay permanently in Ireland. He didn't explain, and she didn't press, since it was old business—business from before she came here to Ireland.

But sometimes, every once in a while, one of them would look at her, and the early heat would build. They'd stand close, as Mell did now, and her heart would pound like a girl in the first stages of maturity. It only ever lasted long enough to tease, and it always made her want more.

It had become clear to her a few weeks ago that there was a subtle boundary between her and the brothers. Not just her own self-imposed reservation, but an actual emotional boundary. It popped up every time they strayed into that teasing territory, like a protective construct.

It is for the best, though. She had found a balance with the brothers, with her life here, and she didn't want to upset it, to have to give up this new home—which was exactly what would happen if she broke that emotional barrier. Though, the brothers *had* once claimed she had brought that balance *with* her, and into their lives, their actions told her they were worried about that very balance. Already it was unsteady. Sometimes she thought if she could just sit them all down, tell them she wanted each of them, and could kiss them to her heart's content, it would all sort itself out.

It was a strange circular logic that didn't seem to have a resolution.

And what about the brothers themselves? Was the upcoming O'Loinsigh clan gathering simply an excuse for them to keep their distance because they couldn't figure out a way to tell her they'd changed their minds? Or were they afraid she'd end up treating them like Grainne did? What would happen when that gathering was over? Would they find another reason to keep her status as a newly permanent resident secret?

And all those questions simply fed into her resolve not to breach the distance they'd established. *Love and comfort and companionship doesn't need to involve sex.* She'd tell herself that as many times as it was needed for her to fully accept it.

Sighing, she brought herself from her musings and back to the present. She'd already decided many times over that she wouldn't do anything, would never cross the line they had made clear. There was no reason to dwell on it further. But it *was* still frustrating.

Mell shifted, pressing his muscled arm to her shoulder and she leaned in, just a little. Just to feel that reassuring pressure. *The comfort of touch doesn't need to be sexual. Sometimes a touch was just a touch...*

"No," Mell finally said, a beat too late. He pulled away from her and her shoulders sagged.

Finn frowned, his brows drawing together in puzzlement. Then he shrugged and wiped the expression away, resuming the more neutral lines he usually wore.

"Well, if I can steal you and your brothers for a moment, I've got something I'd like to run by you," he said to Mell.

Mell's gaze went from Finn, to Bat, to the human—who had watched the entire byplay with narrowed eyes. "Sure," he said. "Shar and Dub are out back, I'm sure." He waved at the beer. "Ya can bring the pint. Don't want to waste it."

Finn stood from his stool, inclined his head to her, and disappeared through the rear doorway with Mell. Her senses stirred and she braced her hands on the bar counter, wondering if a vision was coming. They'd tapered off for the most part after the soul blade had been recovered, and she usually only received the briefest glimpses of the immortals who frequented the bar; hints of where a wisp could find a human in search of adventure, places a banshee could go to find a new family to wail of, or gardens in need of the care of a pixie.

She strained, trying to capture the elusive feeling.

"Hey lady." The human's voice was rough. "Can you get me another one of these that's done right?" He held up the pint glass, eyes still narrowed.

Pulling her attention once more to the here and now, she tilted her head and studied the human. Was he one who would cause trouble, or was he simply tired and hungry and therefore easily upset? Hangry, she'd heard it called. His face was pale under his blond hair, with a faintly gray cast, which was not usual for a human. His gray eyes were bloodshot. Was he ill?

"Would you like something to eat as well?" she asked. "We don't have much on the menu, mostly sandwiches, but I do believe there is a stew being prepared. It may be a good idea to have something in addition to the alcohol."

His stilled, then relaxed. His expression eased and he nodded. "That would be good. I've been travelling for a few days now. A lady I ran into downtown recommended the place, said it had real local color. I thought I'd check it out before finding my hotel."

Bat suppressed a smile. "Did this lady have green hair?"

"Uh. No."

"Oh. Well, I do understand the travails of travel." She pulled out a glass and began the pint. "We should have a sing-song going later, if you can stay. We have them most nights, if you want to come again." She released the tap and set the pint aside. "You have to let it settle, and then top it off. I learned this a few months ago. It really does make it better."

The man nodded. "Um. I'm sorry about earlier. With the other guy. I was just…"

She gave him a smile of understanding. "You were tired, and he was rude. Dub is like that. If you come often enough, you will learn his frowns. I am Bat, by the way."

His brows rose. "Like the animal?"

She waved a hand. "It is an old, and traditional, Egyptian name. Though, yes, it is spelled and pronounced the same as the flying rodent."

"Sorry," he said again. He watched as she topped off the pint then placed it before him. "I have a feeling I'll be saying that a lot around here. I can't seem to say or do anything right. I've been pissing people off since I stepped off the plane."

"Would you like to hear a secret?" She leaned in conspiratorially. "Buy the bar a round, and you'll be welcomed. You do not have to do it here, in The Dubros. It works in most pubs. I would also advise getting sleep, and proper food in you, before you interact with anyone else."

He took a sip of the beer and his brows rose. "This *is* good. Really good."

She crossed her arms again. "Of course."

"I'm Daniel, by the way. Daniel Corous. I'm here to research some old tales, kind of do a tour of the county."

"Well, then you have definitely come to the right place for old tales. Just be polite in your asking, Daniel Corous, or I will have to ask you to leave."

He smiled at that, and it transformed his face from tired and plain to strangely attractive. "And what would you do if I refused?" The tone was playful, flirtatious.

Old Mike chose that moment to see what the human was up to. "Goddess, are you all right?" He'd risen from his seat and traveled to their end of the bar, his own beer in hand.

"Mike, I told you not to call me that." She grinned. "But, I'd like you to meet Daniel Corous. He's here looking for old stories. Says he is going to tour the area. You might be able to help him with that."

The wisp pulled out the stool on Daniel's right. "Ya don't say."

"I'll check on the stew. If it's not ready, I'll get a sandwich started for you," she said to Daniel and shot Mike a grin. "Play nicely now."

"I will," they said together. Daniel's tone was sincere, while the wisp's was anything but.

She shook her head and, after a quick scan to be sure none of the other patrons needed anything from her, made her way toward the kitchen.

"You haven't told her about the Fomoiri?" Finn asked. The four not-men stood gathered around the wood topped island in the middle of the kitchen, their large frames dwarfing the small piece of furniture.

Chapter Two

Dear Bastet,
I really do hate secrets. And my not-men, they were keeping
them from me! I am so mad right now. It is not that they
lied, exactly, but… but, they lied!
- Bat, one who is thinking of coming home
p.s. – Not really.

BAT

*B*at drew away from the door opening. What
about the Fomoiri? She knew there were
tensions between the brothers and the rest of their
particular kind of immortal. It was clear from Shar's
reactions every time they or the mysterious brooch were
mentioned, or the severity of Dub's frown when the clan
gathering was discussed. Of course there were secrets she
didn't know—she still had much to learn of this land and

its history, and the brothers—but it seemed Finn thought she *should* know whatever this was…

"No," Dub replied, a clenched fist pressed to the island counter. "And we will not. This is not something she needs to be involved in. It's our business, and I will not allow it to touch her. We promised her a refuge, and our protection."

Finn bowed his head and took a breath, letting it out slowly, his own hands curled into fists. He straightened and locked his gaze on Dub. "I think that is something she should be allowed to decide for herself."

Bat's eyes narrowed as Finn's words echoed in her mind. They were similar to the words Dub had once offered her: *just what you care to give*. The gift of choice. Something Dub had once given her, and now, with his words of pseudo-protection, took away.

Her hands trembled as a mixture of anger, remorse and longing swept over her. *Had* she been fooling herself that this place was a home, that they were a sort of family? How could it be, if the brothers didn't trust her to handle the things that touched them, that affected them? Didn't they know she would do whatever was needed to ensure their future? Didn't they know she considered them hers?

Was she really so diminished in their eyes?

I have already allowed the distance. That cursed distance, which crept in over the last weeks. That insidious distance, which… she had only moments ago been determined to maintain. Trembling hands curled into fists. Maybe she couldn't form a sexual relationship with the brothers, but she still cared for them. And they cared for her. They had to.

They had to.

Flickers of a memory she didn't want to examine danced along the edges of her mind. There was another time she had had people she considered hers. Claws of loss attempted to dig into her heart, to shed the blood of her soul, as the image of a broad back filled her vision. It was not a proper vision, simply the echoes of a long past pain.

She wouldn't do that again. She would not stand still as those she cared about stepped away. She would *not* do that to herself again.

And Finn was correct. Whether to get involved was something she should be allowed to decide. Granting the brothers their privacy and past secrets... well, that was their right. But if those secrets were coming into the present, shouldn't she know them? If she was to truly have a life here, in this pub, with these people, she needed to *make* her place. Right?

All of this flew through her mind in fractions of a second, in a blink of time. The four men still stood at the island, their attention on the center of the island. They hadn't noticed her yet. Despite her renewed determination and resolve, a hollow sensation lingered. She stepped into the kitchen, her feet silent.

They do not trust me. The thought crept up on her, snaking past her barriers. Mell's head twisted sharply, the chocolate of his gaze landing on her with a mix of guilt, sorrow and longing. An answering yearning built in her, and it wasn't as easy to push down as before. She took another step forward.

"We are not dragging her int—" Shar broke off as Mell

gave a cutting motion with his hand then flicked a finger at her.

Dub's fist pressed into the wood and the crack that he'd made in the island top after Dano was killed spread. Shar's single eye widened as she approached, and Mell crossed his arms, looking away. The only one who didn't react was Finn.

Pushing aside the confusion of her emotions once more, she focused on the *now*. What *exactly* was going on? She crossed her arms and stared at Mell, waiting for an explanation.

Dub shifted, drawing her attention and revealing the center of the island. Resting there was a card, the stock thick, with scrolling gold leaf twining into a familiar mark. A stylized crane decorated the front of the paper, matching a tattoo that each brother bore on his shoulder.

Flash. A hand clutched around a gold brooch, the pattern matching the symbol on the card. Blood coated one side.

"Goddess?" Finn's face appeared before her, his hands gripping her upper arms. "Are you all right?"

A large arm wrapped around her from behind and pulled her against a hard chest. "I told ya, we're not letting her anywhere near them," Shar said from behind her.

My protective giant. It was sweet, infuriating, and oh so unnecessary. Tension uncurled within her. She needed this contact. She leaned back, just enough to feel the solid muscles of his chest. Warmth crept through her, though it was not quite enough to fill that hollow place inside her.

Finn released her arms and stepped back, one brow raised. Dub looked from her to the invitation, then back to her. "What did you see?" His tone was flat, the words tight.

She clutched her necklace through her lightweight sweater. "A golden brooch, and blood." Drawing in a breath, she gathered herself and straightened away from Shar. "What, *exactly*, is going on?"

A barrier slammed down, cutting her off from the vague tendrils of emotion Mell had been putting out. She gasped and glared at the middle brother over Finn's shoulder. That was definitely not the vague, subtle shield she'd been sensing. He shrugged, the movement tight, but didn't lower his gaze or the barrier.

Flash. Deep brown eyes in a young, and bruised, face. Blood dripping from a cut mouth. He stood on a plank wood deck that rocked with the motion of the waves. Behind him stood a woman with golden hair and green eyes, her gown a fine midnight wool. She stood blank-faced and made no move to comfort the child.

The vision cleared and she once more stared at Mell, the grown version of that boy. She attempted to erase the growing horror and sorrow the vision had brought from her mind, knowing he would sense it from her anyway. He wouldn't know exactly what she saw, but he would surely be able to guess from her reaction that it was not something he'd want known. She gave him a slight nod, telling him she would not share this one unless he wanted her to.

He gifted her with a crooked grin and shrugged again, but the movement was easier.

"She's already involved." Finn, who had stepped to the side at some point, pointed out. "If she's having the visions, she's entangled, and you're not going to be able to keep her out." His lips ticked up. "You O'Loinsighs really do need to learn a little more about goddesses."

Bat gifted him with a smile and nodded. "It is true. I do not have random visions, as you know. They may be a little hard to sort sometimes, but they are not without purpose." She allowed her gaze to settle on each brother in turn, even twisting to take in Shar, who still stood behind her. "Now, what is going on?" She would get that question answered.

Dub frowned, resigned, and opened his mouth to reply. Before he could speak, Ailis came rushing in from the pub's common area.

"Bat, ya need to get out there," she said, her green hair mussed and eyes wide.

Bat had never seen the fae in such a state, and was effectively distracted. "Is it the tourist? Is he asking for his sandwich? Wait—is the stew ready?" She looked at the timer set beside a large pot on the stovetop. No, at least an hour left. Bat turned back to Ailis. "Can you explain I've been delayed? Or, better, could you make him someth—"

Ailis shook her head, sending tendrils of green flying. "It's not a tourist. Well, not really. I think—" She swallowed. "I think a bomen just walked in. The glamour's thick, it's hard to tell, but he's chattering away in the old tongue, asking for ya, and he's scaring the others. An agitated bomen is no' a good thing to be having on your hands, or anywhere near anyone."

There was a scratching scramble at the back door, and the familiar sound of Killer's puppy growl filtered through the wood. The brothers must have put him out to get some fresh air.

Ailis's head twisted in that direction. "Ye're going to want to hold onto that one, but I wouldn't leave him outside, he'll end up tearing the door down," she said.

The men stood frozen for another second, then they were in motion. Shar hooked his arm around her shoulders and pulled her into him once again, Dub and Finn headed for the common room, and Mell went for the fridge. Shar steered her to the door.

The scratching increased on the other side of the door, and a slight whine was added to the growl. "Killer, baby, it'll be okay," Bat said through the door. "I'm a goddess remember? The bomen thing won't kill me." Though it would be nice if she knew *what* a bomen *was*.

The growl left her puppy's voice, but the whine remained. Shar opened the door and Killer barreled into Bat, nearly knocking her from her feet. The pup twisted, trying to get to the doorway and the pub beyond. Shar caught the back of the harness as Bat hung onto his middle.

"Hush. No attacking unless we say so, remember?" Bat kept her tone even and firm. Killer paused and looked back at her, though he still leaned toward the doorway. "That's right," she continued. "You have to *wait* to attack."

Shar snorted. "You keep saying that, you'll give the poor boy hope."

"Someone's got to have some," she muttered.

"Do I want to know what you mean by that?"

Bat's hand itched to leave Killer and clasp her necklace, but her baby was still nervous. The pup could bolt, despite his training. "I have no idea," she said. Then, lower, "There's a lot going unsaid recently."

"I've got the milk," Mell said from behind them. "We better get out there and see what's going on."

Killer's whines faded away as Bat scratched just behind his ears. "Milk?" she asked, eyeing the shallow bowl Mell held.

He shrugged. "Don't know much about the bomen, but tales say they like milk. Better safe than sorry."

"How do you not know about these bomen? Aren't they another immortal? A not-man?" Bat handed Killer's leash to Shar and stood. She had a feeling she'd need her hands free.

"They're more sluagh than fae," Finn said from the doorway. "We need you out here, goddess. He's refusing to move until he is able to speak with you, and the humans are getting too curious for my liking." He paused. "Please."

She took a step forward then stopped. "Will he harm the others? The patrons?" Technically, because of the Morrigan's restrictions, they weren't her worshipers to protect, but they were still hers in a way—and many of them were her *friends*. There was an aspect to that kind of offering which was much more powerful than the more traditional rituals. She was nowhere near as strong as she'd been in her prime, but in a mere couple of months she'd gained enough power to not exhaust herself with simple actions or scans. She was able to put more into her songs, and her visions—when they came—were stronger and clearer.

"We've got him over by the hearth." Finn avoided answering her question and gave a curt gesture for her to follow him. He was out of uniform, but he was definitely in guardi-mode at the moment.

Bat braced herself. From the hints and the vague way the other immortals spoke of the sluagh, and now the bomen, she wasn't sure what to expect. Maybe something from one of those horror movies Mell enjoyed, with slavering jaws and too many teeth. And tentacles. She shuddered. *I hope there are no tentacles.*

She stepped into the pub, Finn and Shar right behind her, the larger brother with a tight grip on Killer's leash. The patrons were strangely quiet. *I suppose, if there is a rare creature in their midst, the silence is not so strange.* She scanned the room, but didn't spot anything out of the ordinary, and there were certainly no tentacles.

Heaving a sigh of relief, she approached the hearth, still looking for their visitor. There was a child standing near Dub. The Fomoiri stood with arms crossed, partially blocking the small figure. Had someone brought...

Light shifted and the child's features changed. The freckled cheeks became a gnarled and pocked brown, with a trace of fur over the brow. The gray eyes grew and changed to bright red. Thin shoulders widened and the arms lengthened. The nose and jaw pushed out until they more resembled a muzzle, and the fingers... well, there was the horror movie aspect. There were more knuckles there than the more human immortals had, and the tips now sported razor claws that flicked in time to some music only the creature could hear. The image of the child still overlaid the true form, but it was thin, like a nighttime shadow that couldn't quite disguise the fearsome thing lurking in the corner.

She tilted her head, studying it. Killer strained against Shar grip on his short leash, trying to get in front of her, and she put a hand down to rest on his head, attempting to calm him. The bomen's fingers stilled as its gaze landed on her, and then it smiled, revealing needle teeth. It held its arms out to her and chittered, using words that were both familiar and not...

She gasped and then returned its smile. Killer looked up at her and cocked his head. Instinctively she knelt, nearly forgetting all those around her, and extended her arms in invitation. The bomen rushed to her, wrapping its too long arms around her and holding tight, all the while spitting out words that were a strange mix of ancient Egyptian flavored with Irish. "Easy," she said in her native language. "Easy. How have you come to be here, so far from home?"

It was a logical assumption. The bomen was a curious blend of the aapi that Thoth once used as messengers, and Seth's animal—the animal she had never seen, though men drew it. Add in the fact it spoke some form of Egyptian, and it was not so far of a stretch...

But that meant these bomen, these hidden creatures, had once travelled here from her old home. And that meant they had been here longer than she'd been in existence. Seth would have known, as would Isis and Horus. Bastet would have known...

Anger stirred at that last. Bastet had helped her plan her trip, had known just where Bat was planning to go. She should have been told of these bomen. What other secrets did this land hold? What other things had the older gods kept from her?

Another thought occurred to her and her arms stiffened around the creature. Had the *brothers* known the truth of these bomen? A quick peek at Mell's stunned face told her no. This at least had not been one of the secrets they were keeping. Some of the anger bled away.

The creature finally pulled away from her. Killer thrust his head into the bomen's face, sniffing. It frowned and pushed the pup away, and Bat laughed.

"Is she his mom? I thought the kid was lost?"

The low words, spoken by the tourist, pulled Bat's attention back to the patrons and customers in the pub. They had an audience. Dub stood over her, arms crossed, and scowled at the immortals and humans alike. Mell hovered beside him, the bowl of milk cradled in his hands. Finn and Ailis were doing their best to keep their expressions neutral, but were definitely failing. The rest of the patrons were a mixture of wide eyes, pinched mouths and hunched shoulders.

Caw.

Everyone jerked, even the bomen. A large raven stood in the doorway from the kitchen, partially mantled. It hopped forward a couple of feet and opened its beak again.

Caw.

23

A new figure stepped into the pub from behind the raven. He was large, at least as tall as Shar and nearly as wide. The blond of his beard contrasted sharply with the dark cloth of his guardi uniform, and afternoon light gleamed off his bald head.

"Did ya know ya left the back door open?" The newcomer's voice wound through the room in a surprisingly mellow tenor.

Is there not a saying about threes? What was happening to her simple little slice of life?

Chapter Three

Dear Bastet,
I am so mad at you right now. Did you know?
- Bat, the goddess who is going to come back and beat ALL
of you up

Bat,
Ummm… know what? I am afraid you are going to have to
be more specific.
- Bastet, the goddess who has no idea what you are talking
about

BAT

"Farking bollix." Ailis breathed the words out as her gaze darted from the new man, to Dub and then to where Bat still knelt near the bomen. The small immortal had shifted, putting itself between Bat and the new guardi. Killer had also adjusted his attention, lowering his head and growling at the bearded man.

Flash. The blond man, with a full head of hair, wielded a sword over a meter long. He faced another with dark hair and bright blue eyes. A feminine cry rang out as the swords clashed, and the dark-haired warrior twisted his head, distracted. The blond struck again, and the dark one was late defending. He kept the blade from piercing his brain, but couldn't save his eye.

Bat blinked. She didn't know this newcomer's name, but she now knew *who* he was. He was the one who took her giant's eye. If Killer, or the bomen, decided he should be attacked, she wouldn't stop them. But he also wore a guardi uniform, and was accompanied by a raven. An attack could become complicated for her and the brothers. Maybe it was best to hold off.

"You." Dub's knuckles were white, and his expression fierce.

Finn sighed. "And *this* is what I was trying to tell you all, before the other distractions entered into the equation."

Mell stepped in front of his brother, blocking him. "Oh, look, it's Cuchi. The *mighty* warrior." He gave a mocking bow, the bowl of milk still balanced in his hand.

A sucked in breath from the bar had Bat's gaze shooting to meet that of the tourist. "I think we should go back to the kitchen." She rose and waved her hand in the general direction of the bar and David. "I still have a sandwich to make, and we should get this little one something to eat as well." She smiled down at the bomen.

Light wavered and the picture of a small child strengthened. It smiled back, sharp teeth in an innocent face. "The food would be welcome, goddess. There is much to discuss." The low words were in a slow and careful English, the accent heavy. Then it added something in a rattle of Irish. Dub snorted, Mell grinned, and even Finn's lips twitched.

Bat let it go and rose. She walked directly for the bald man, daring him or the raven to bar her way. At the last moment they moved, allowing her just enough room to brush by. Killer and Shar were on her heels and the bomen right behind that. As the little creature passed this new guardi, there was a grunt and a sucked-in breath, followed by another snort.

She had a feeling one of the mysteries presented to her a couple months ago was about to be solved—or at least explained. Cuchi...

A nearly forgotten snippet of conversation returned to her. Cuchi was what Mell had called the warrior who stole away with Dub's intended. Who fought them for the girl Derbforgaill, and who that same girl betrayed them for.

Ignoring the instinctive resentment—both for Dub and of him—that balled in her chest at the reminder he'd once loved someone else enough to want to bind his life to hers, Bat headed directly for the fridge and started pulling out sandwich ingredients. Though she was currently swimming in secrets and mysteries, she still needed to feed the tourist—they definitely didn't want him coming back here in search of food. Bat paused and tilted her head at the bomen, who had climbed onto one of the stools at the island. "Would you like something?"

Its eyes widened even farther, so that they took up nearly all of its face. It nodded, the movement slow and deliberate.

"All right. I will make two then." She slid open the door on the bread bin and pulled out a loaf that had been delivered that very morning.

Her mind wandered to a thought that *should* have been the least of her worries. *Dub had loved before, enough to seek the woman in marriage.* She'd known that. She just hadn't thought about it. Was it bad that part of her was relieved his joining with this woman had been prevented, no matter the means? Guilt twisted and she pinched it off, shoving the thoughts from her mind.

It was a seed of chaos, and she could not afford to allow it to sprout.

No, she would not be glad for Dub's past misfortune, but she would be glad that he had escaped someone who so obviously hadn't been suited for him. For the woman to be lured away by the bald man... incomprehensible, really. This guardi was handsome, yes, but there was a lack in the substance of his soul...

"Not going to offer me anything?" The object of her musings crowded in next to her before Finn or Dub could block him.

Well, she didn't need the not-men to handle an annoying male. She kept her attention on arranging the ingredients on the counter before her. "And what will you give me, immortal?" Was he really going to importune a goddess in such a way? And for a *sandwich*? She could not imagine the Morrigan allowing such impertinence. Bat glanced at Cuchi from the corner of her eye as she pulled a knife from the block and began slicing the tomato.

"For a… BLT?" He eyed the ingredients laid out. "Not very traditional of ya, to be serving that in a pub. What about a nice coddle, or even a stew? You've got one going, don't ya?" He leaned over her and sent her what she was sure was supposed to be a charming smile.

It was not. Even if he had not been the one to maim her giant or steal Dub's love, she would not have cared for this man. There was something so… *entitled* about his demeanor. *That's what the unattractive aspect is, entitlement.* "Do you know what my favorite traditional Egyptian dish is? The koldala." She pasted on a dreamy expression. "It's very good, but fell out of popularity many years ago when the gods noted that the local worshippers protested too much the use of the ingredients." She held up the knife and examined the edge, afternoon light flashing off the metal. Then she cut her gaze back to the guardi. "I will make you a deal, immortal. If you offer me the ingredients I need for the koldala, I will make you a special stew. One just for you. I think that would be fair, do you not?"

His brows drew together and a muffled snort came from Mell's direction. Ailis, Finn and the brothers had backed away and gathered near the bomen, giving Bat space to handle the arrogant immortal, though the brothers appeared ready to intercede at any moment. Dub's scowl was firmly directed at Cuchi's back, promising pain and blood if given the chance. Ailis stared with wide and sparkling eyes, and a small smile tipped up the corners of Finn's lips.

"What are these ingredients?" the bald man asked, pulling her attention to him once more.

Bat waved the hand still clutching the knife, skimming the blade close to the newcomer's chest. "Let's see. Two pints of blood, the pinky finger of your left hand—it has the most tender meat—and one eye, for texture, of course," she finished with a bright smile.

He stepped back. "Now, no need to be like that," he said. "It's only polite to offer a guest something to eat, ya know."

She twisted to keep him in sight and in reach of the blade. "You are correct. And no one has offered me koldala until now. It is so kind of you, really. There is not much about this place that reminds me of my home, so the thought is quite comforting. Ireland's hospitality, except for a few exceptions, has been quite lacking until now." She pushed the knife forward until it rested against the bald man's chest and he went still, his eyes wide. She'd put some power behind those last words, wanting him to know that though she was diminished, she was still a goddess, and should be treated with at least a modicum of respect.

Ca-ca-ca-ca-ca.

The raven had hopped onto the island. It laughed, the beak wide open.

That will stop him for a bit, sister. I should apologize for him, but I do so enjoy him being put in his place. Unfortunately, he never stays there.

Bat tilted her head. The voice was a familiar one, though she'd only heard it a few times. "Morrigan?"

The raven bobbed its head. *I am sending you a messenger,*

and a representative. I suspect you may need her in the days to come. Einin is a clever girl, and will help you well. The annoying sidhe warrior is also very capable, if, well, annoying. He has been instructed to offer assistance.

"What is going on?" Bat asked.

"That's what I want to know," muttered Ailis.

The raven twisted its head, first one way, then the other, eying the strips of bacon on the counter behind Bat. There was no answer from the other goddess.

Mother sky, I hope I'm not that frustratingly cryptic. Bat had a feeling that at times she was, though. Waving her knife at the island, she said to Cuchi, "Stand over there while I finish these. Then we will all discuss what is going on."

Dub indicated the far wall, his lips twisted into a sneer. "No room now at the island. Ya can go stand over there, *Cuchi*."

The bald man's hands curled into fists and he stepped toward her grumpy not-man.

"Ah, ah. Koldala, remember? There will be no violence in my kitchen. Unless I sanction it, of course." A bit more power went into this, and Cuchi was propelled back into the wall Dub had indicated. Maybe it was an injudicious use of her carefully gathered strength, but… she didn't like this immortal.

She busied herself with the sandwiches, which, yes, were BLTs. Not traditional fare, but they were simple, and quick. She finished the first and handed the plate to Ailis. "Could you take this one out to the tourist? He was at the bar, near the door. Mike is keeping him company."

Ailis's brows rose, but she didn't comment on the

wisp's companionship. She took the plate then pointed at Bat. "I'll be right back. Don't start without me."

Bat finished up the other sandwich and placed it before the bomen. "We have crisps as well, if you would like some."

Cuchi shifted and opened his mouth, and Bat glared. He raised his hands and leaned against the wall.

The bomen tilted his head, much as Bat liked to do. "I would like that." This time he spoke in a rough and ancient Egyptian.

A smile spread across Bat's face as she once more heard words familiar and dear to her. She crossed to the pantry, pulled out a large bag of crisps and shook a few onto his plate. "There," she said as she set the bag on the counter. "Now, we will let you eat, and you can tell me what brought you here." *One thing at a time. First the bomen, then Cuchi, then the brothers.*

She was aware that putting the bothers last on the list was her way of avoiding a discussion she wasn't sure she wanted to have. Her hand went once more to her necklace as she gathered her scattered emotions. This pub *was* her refuge, and the brothers her companions. They would not have kept those secrets unless they thought it necessary, nor would they hurt her deliberately.

Deliberate or not, it still hurts. The hollow spot filled, but it was with nothing good. She needed to solve this, and soon. Maybe she should move it up the list.

The bomen opened its mouth, his jaw hinging wide, so his face was all teeth and eyes and mouth, and then the sandwich was gone. Two seconds later the crisps were as well, and the bomen stared down at an empty plate.

All of them stared at the empty plate.

"Do you need another?" Bat asked.

It shook its head. "No, goddess. Your hospitality has been more than enough."

Ailis chose that moment to enter the kitchen once again, and she resumed her place at the island. "What did I miss?"

"A demonstration on why you don't anger the bomen," Mell said, expression blank.

The little creature crossed his arms. "It is not bomen," it said in ancient Egyptian. "They have been getting that wrong for centuries. It is ba. We are the men of ba." It focused its red eyes on her. "And now you are here, and our wait is over."

What did *that* mean? "I do not—"

"English, please, *a stor*." Shar edged closer to her, hovering in a way that was much more appealing than the way the bald not-man had done it.

"Well, you all have been calling them the wrong thing. They are the ba men, the men of ba, and they have been waiting for me." She stared into the red eyes of the creature. "And they speak my native language, which has been lost to all but the gods for centuries. These things are all very strange, I would say. Unless they are somehow from my land." The last she added for the benefit of getting answers. She had no doubts they were from Egypt. How they had ended up here in Ireland was another matter, and what she wanted to find out.

The brothers shifted and Shar somehow hovered even more without drawing closer.

Her gaze fell to the invitation still on the table, then

went to the bald guardi, the raven, and back to the ba man.

Flash. A stone cauldron, dark with age and use, stood nearly as tall as Shar. Around it gathered the sidhe, and around them were sun-dappled forest and rustling branches. Light rippled, and from the cauldron climbed a man, gray of skin and blank-faced. Another emerged after the first, and still another after that, until the forest filled with bodies possessed by the kas of those long dead. They were incomplete, though. The other half of the spirit was still missing.

Flash. A spear, the head shining golden even in partial dusk. A dark-haired man who stood with his back to her clasped it. Beneath him, a ship's deck swayed and around him, men scurried, while gray-green clouds gathered on the horizon. To either side more ships gathered, heading into that storm.

Flash. A blade, about a meter in length. The pommel bore a stone of deepest green, swirling with an opalescent light. From its tip poured shadow.

Flash. A harp—her harp—cradled in a pair of hands, brown and gnarled. They extended, holding the instrument out to someone.

"You see," the ba man said in rough English. "Come now, fix cauldron. Broken."

The raven twisted its head to stare at the ba man, and Cuchi straightened away from his wall. "The cauldron?" Something close to greed entered his expression.

The ba man—*I need to learn his name*—twisted and bared

his teeth at the guardi. "Is not for you, sidhe." It pointed at each of the men in turn. "The Fomoiri and sidhe broke it. Goddess fix it." It slid from the stool. "We go now."

"Wait." There was too much happening at once, and Bat swam in both her visions and the swirl of questions these new encounters had stirred. "Wait, please. I— *how?*"

The ba man sighed, nodded, and hopped back to his stool. "We were forgotten. Puchi suspected."

Shar wrapped his hand around her upper arm and tugged her toward the end of the island, shouldering aside Dub and Finn. "*A stor*. Sit. I will fix tea. This could… take a while."

Cuchi stepped forward. "These creatures have the cauldron, and you want to make tea?"

Though she'd used the word in her own thoughts, Bat didn't like the way Cuchi said "creature." There was no affection, no wonder, only contempt. "Go back to your wall, Cuchi," she said.

"My name is Cu Chulainn." His chest puffed out. "You will have heard of me, of course."

"Yes, in the idiot book." She didn't explain, and only just suppressed her grin at his slack expression. "And I will call you whatever I care to call you, arrogant not-man. Go back to your wall."

He stepped back, then shuddered. "The Morrigan sent me."

"I know. She said you could be of some use, but so far I have not seen it. Unless you have something to add to this conversation besides blustering and posturing, please stay by the wall." She emphasized her words with a finger pointed toward his place.

The raven cawed, as if agreeing with her. She turned away and focused once more on the ba man. "What is your name?"

It straightened. "I am Ari, eldest son of our band, and chief guard of Vessel of Creation."

"Well, Ari, I am Bat, and I am very pleased to meet you." Finally, a bit of order had been brought to this situation with the traditions of greeting.

Ari ducked its head. "You were no' there when we left."

"Left where?" She kept her voice gentle, coaxing. It was better if these things were said aloud instead of hinted and guessed at.

Dub made an aborted motion toward her, and Mell held up a hand. Something passed between the brothers and Dub sighed, frowning in resignation.

"The red lands," Ari said. "Seth asked us to go with vessel, to guard it. We travelled with the sea men. They, too, once served our lord of the thunder." He waved at the Fomoiri brothers.

His words at once confirmed her earlier assumptions, and broke a thin thread of trust she'd been holding onto. Her hand curled into a fist and her heart gave two sharp beats of anger before she reined in her emotions. This was *definitely* something she should have long ago been told. And *not* just by her not-men.

How could she not know these things? Immortals once lived in Egypt? The *Fomoiri* had lived there? *Had* the brothers known? It took one look at their averted gazes and hunched shoulders to tell her the answer. *Yes.*

She sucked in a breath and blew it out, slowly. There

were yet more questions to be asked and answered. *Patience.* She would get there.

Ari peeked up at her, his red eyes glinting. "How is he?"

Who? Oh. "Seth?"

The ba man nodded, the movement hesitant, almost shy.

She looked down. "Not the same god you probably remember."

"We heard some of the stories. The pixies chatter. But we didn't believe them." Ari bared his teeth. "Our Seth is a warrior, but he is also a guardian. He would never do the things he has been accused of."

Bat didn't know exactly what they had heard, and she wasn't comfortable with the direction the conversation had taken. Seth very well could have done whatever the rumors claimed. "When did you leave?"

"I do not know how many years it has been. Before the flood."

She knew the time he spoke of, though it was before she had come into existence. "And, you came with the... sea men?"

He nodded, and again waved his too-many-jointed fingers at the Fomoiri brothers. "These three were not yet there either," he switched to Egyptian. "But we travelled with their people. They left the red lands as well, charged with taking us to this new land. They were supposed to return to Seth, to continue the fight against Isfet, but they did not." Ari's lips pulled back from his needle teeth in a sneer. "They remained safe on their ships even as the waters rose. But it mattered not, our

Seth and the others prevailed, and Isfet did not find the vessel."

"The vessel?" A sense of memory swept over her, of having had just this type of conversation before, in this very room. *Déjà vu. It is called déjà vu.* Did deities experience such a thing?

Ari gazed at her with a grave expression. "Half of egg of creation," he said, switching back to English. "The giver of life. *They* call it cauldron, but it is not that. It *is*... creation. Life."

Shar pushed a stool under her just as her knees gave out. Even gods had their myths, and the egg of creation was one such. The egg that appeared on an island risen from the chaos waters of Nun, from which was born the first god. And these men of ba had been guarding it for centuries in an obscure forest on a northern island...

Awe filled her, crowding out the anger and frustration.

Bat looked to Dub, who shrugged. "As he said, we were not yet born. I have heard tales of that time, but they do not speak of the bomen—ba men, or the cauldron—vessel. And there is a much... different interpretation of the events that led us to leave the red lands."

Mell let out a laugh devoid of humor, and resentment wrapped its barbed tendrils around her. "And you really think our father would tell us the truth of it?"

Shar slid a steaming cup of tea in front of her. "He was not there either."

"There are only a handful of Fomoiri left who are old enough to speak of that time," Dub said, his tone carefully even. "The rest have fallen to the soul blades or chosen to move on."

Bat folded her hands around the teacup, allowing the warmth to seep into her fingers, and wished that one of her powers was that of emotion, like Mell. What was her grumpy Fomoiri thinking, feeling? What about Shar? Mell was a mess of dark and twisted anger and resentment, though she didn't think it was directed at her.

This was finally too much, too fast, and she needed a moment—just a moment—to think these things through. Meeting Ari's gaze, she tilted her head. "Will you allow me a minute, old friend? I am sure there is more to your tale, but I must gather my thoughts. Then we will continue?" She waited until the man of ba gave a hesitant nod—*and what exactly was his nature, that he was a man of* ba? —then she turned to the others gathered at the island. "I am going into the garden. I will be back shortly." She was careful to keep her voice steady and calm, even if her mind was anything but.

Leaving the steaming tea at the island, she rose and turned for the rear door. Shar silently handed her Killer's leash and she forced a small smile of appreciation, and reassurance. It must not have worked, because her giant's expression was pinched, his eyes filled with worry. No one stopped her as she opened the back door, not even the annoying bald man. No one protested as she walked down the steps. She drew even with the garden's gate and a small thought came to her. *If I were to keep walking, would no one protest then?*

She unhitched the latch and allowed Killer to pass her. They headed for the far corner, where red and pink blooms sat across from the dark leaves and bright red of strawberry bushes that were always in fruit.

Chapter Four

DUB O'LOINSIGH

*H*is hands curled into fists that he was careful to keep away from the island top. It would be a true inconvenience to have to replace it right now. Not that the island top was the most important thing at the moment.

How many things could go wrong? He glared at the bomen —no, the man of ba—then switched his ire to Cu Chulainn—who wore the uniform of a Ceilte Guardi Captain. And who was also now apparently stationed in Sligo.

Which Finn had neglected to mention. Dub's lips tightened as he suppressed a growl of displeasure.

Finn shifted beside him and stretched his head up, straining to see through the window over the sink. Bat passed in and out of their view, her dark hair swaying.

Dub's chest tightened and he forced his lungs to draw in a breath. He wanted to rush out, to take her away from what had tumbled into their lives today. The farking *cauldron*. And bomen. And messengers from deities who always had their own agendas.

Agendas that seemed to be focused on his goddess.

You are not blameless. The thought echoed in his mind as gold leaf and heavy parchment mocked him from the island top. Part of him wanted to ignore this invitation, though the summons—for that was what it was in truth—was something he himself had set in motion—hell, it was something he needed to have happen if his plans for the brooch were to move forward. He'd only anticipated three names being on the invitation, though, and this one held four...

Their own clan. He grasped onto the idea. This was the goal he and his brothers had talked of for centuries, but only in the last couple of decades had it seemed they could achieve such a thing. It started with a rumor of the Crane clan's brooch being sighted in a little shop all the way down in Cork. Dano had agreed to investigate, in return for a set of spelled cobbler's tools.

Then he'd been killed just a few days before Dub would have finished them. The tools were still tucked away in his workshop—Ciara hadn't wanted them.

The last two months had been the best of Dub's long life. He'd finally been... content. He'd been so sure he could get past this final barrier to their freedom without involving her, that he could negotiate around his father and keep Bat out of the damned politics. She was a simple tenant, after all. None of them had taken the relationship further than those first kisses, and everyone knew the restrictions laid down by the Morrigan. He couldn't do anything about the fact that she was playing the Uaithne, but they'd all been careful not to talk out in the open about Bat staying on permanently in Ireland. He'd also reinforced the wards after Scath had shown up at Dano's wake.

He'd done everything he could short of sending her back to Egypt—and there was no way he'd allow that to happen. All they'd needed to do was keep up the act another few weeks. Just another few weeks. That's all he would have needed. And then nothing his father did would touch them, or her.

That fourth name proved his strategies for the lies they were. He should have expected it—of *course* his father would investigate a newly arrived Egyptian goddess that Scath had seen in the pub with his own eyes.

Idiot. You've lived centuries and you're blind to the most basic strategies. His father was telling them that he knew Bat was important to his sons, despite how they'd attempted to disguise things. And that he would use that fact any way he could, whether she attended the gathering or not.

It's not as if you've done all that much to push her away. He hadn't been able to bring himself to do it, not after Mell's words to them that night. The most he'd managed was to keep his physical distance—and the last few secrets that, if she knew, would have burst the bubble on simple contentment she'd built around herself working at the pub and getting to know the patrons.

But, what just happened here in the kitchen? The words the man of ba had so casually uttered? The words she had heard the brothers utter themselves? Those had finally burst the bubble, and possibly broken something within her—the very thing he'd been trying to avoid. Even Dub, as dense as he knew he could be, was able to see the flash of betrayal she'd felt.

"Mell?" His voice came out tighter than he would like, especially with Cu Chulainn right there. The other immortal was definitely the type to pick up on weaknesses —and the goddess was one such, no matter how he continued to deny it to himself—and exploit them for his own sake.

Mell glanced at Cuchi and then shook his head. "Later, brother. We should deal with the more immediate, umm, issues. One thing at a time."

Right. They could decide what to do with the summons later, and they could try to fix their bungling efforts with Bat when she was done sorting her thoughts, but they could not neglect what the man of ba had just told them. The lost cauldron...

It had sustained the various clans through wars, and been a prize fought over not just for the prestige it offered, but the power as well. At one point, before the soul blades were confiscated and prevented from being used in the wars, the cauldron had been able to revive a lost immortal. It provided the ultimate advantage, and whoever held it held dominion over Ireland...

Then it was lost—or, hidden, he now suspected. Many of the old treasures had also disappeared after the second battle of Moy Tura and the Fomoiri had been driven out by the Tuatha de Danann. That time.

Dub turned his attention to the man of ba, Ari. What

other lies had the elder Fomoiri told? What other secrets were still being kept? *Am I really one to get angry over kept secrets?*

The small immortal's red eyes met his gaze, and Ari bared his teeth. "I will not talk of this with you, sea man. I owe you nothing, and I will not fix your ignorance. It is for the goddess to decide what you know."

Dub raised his hands in surrender. The words were not ones he could argue against, despite the gathering tension in his shoulders that begged to be released with a good punch at the nearest asshole.

Cu Chulainn stepped forward, his chin set in an arrogant tilt that invited Dub to relieve his frustrations against it. "The cauldron will, of course, be returned to its rightful owners."

More needle teeth appeared in Ari's brown face. "I do not doubt that, sidhe."

Why had the Morrigan ever thought it would be a good idea to send the oaf *here*? The reputation he'd built for himself was formidable, yes, but most was formed from half-truths and boasts. What did that goddess hope to gain from shoving this particular immortal in the O'Loinsighs' faces?

Dub braced himself and met Cu Chulainn's cool gray gaze. He waited for the tightening of his stomach and the familiar sour taste of resentment.

It didn't come. There was the all too familiar anger, but the sick twist in his chest that thoughts of Cu Chulainn and Derbforgaill had brought for centuries was no longer there. Even the vague ache of her loss had faded.

Something new had taken their place. Star-filled eyes and round warmth. The comfort of a teasing smile and a soft melody on the harp. And the image of a sharp knife held to a uniformed chest as Bat threatened to chop off a man's pinky.

The snort escaped before he could keep in it. "I wonder what koldala tastes like. It must not be a very large dish, what with only using a pinky and one eye." Dub bared his teeth in a savage smile. Part of him hoped Bat hadn't actually been joking. Not that he wanted to eat Cuchi...

Ari bobbed his head. "It is a delicacy." The ba man's red eyes sparked, but Dub wasn't sure if it was in mirth or anticipation.

Shar fingered the delicate teacup Bat had left behind, then met Dub's gaze. The message was clear. *We fucked up.* Mell had warned them. They had known they needed to sort their emotions and settle things with her. That they would need to tell her—eventually—about the Fomoiri's history, about how Egyptian deities were regarded by most of the immortals in Ireland. It was Dub who'd insisted they needed to resolve things with their father *first,* to get that straightened out so that Alatrom wouldn't be able to have any sort of leverage or grip on their goddess—and wouldn't have any influence or right of the brothers themselves.

He hadn't wanted her to hurt. The patrons at the pub were different from the Fomoiri and the other older immortals. They had welcomed her, and he'd wanted to keep her safe in that sphere of acceptance and warmth.

Just her, the three of them, the pup, the pub, and warmth and laughter and music.

It was a pretty fiction.

Finn, who hadn't taken his attention from the window, started for the back door. "I'm just going to check on her." He shook his head and mumbled as he pulled the door open, "I can't believe you didn't tell her what was going on. Ya knew the invitation was coming, and ya had to know she'd be on it. And ta have this other thrown at her like this…" The words trailed off as he pulled the door closed behind him.

Dub flinched at the quiet snick of the latch and met Mell's gaze, even as remorse kept his feet glued in place.

FINN

His fingers beat an unsteady rhythm against his jean-clad legs as he paused at the gate to Shar's garden. Bat stood at the far end, Killer at her heels, gazing at the strawberry bushes. She stood partially turned away, and he couldn't make out her expression, but there was a slump to her shoulders he didn't like.

Over the last couple months, he'd studied her. When the pub regulars told their stories, her smile grew. When she played her harp—and it was *hers*, he didn't think it would respond to even the Dagda now—she smiled. When the Fomoiri brothers touched her, or showed her a kindness, she smiled the widest.

Sometimes she even smiled at him.

And when had a goddess's smile become a prize worth fighting for?

Earlier, when Mell had denied a growing connection to her, he'd seen the struggle in her. Yes, she had denied it first, but Finn suspected that if the brothers—any of them—gave her the slightest indication that they would welcome a deeper relationship, she would respond with that same glorious smile, and open her arms in welcome.

Finn suspected something more was going on other than the brothers' ignorance and stupidity, but he wasn't sure what. It was suspicious that they'd given her the pup. Then the time for her to return to Egypt had come and gone, with no words spoken of an extended rental agreement. Her occasional assistance in the pub had grown until most patrons looked for her rather than the brothers.

She was truly making herself a home here. And the most suspicious thing was the fact the Morrigan hadn't come to kick her out. Had, in fact, just today sent a damn *representative.*

He'd known the gods were up to something ever since the Morrigan involved herself in the hunt for a leprechaun's murderer, but neither he, Oisin or his team had been able to figure out just what it was, or what was coming. And it seemed the brothers and Bat were just as clueless.

Anticipation thrilled through him. A battle was coming, and the warrior in him was eager.

Bat sighed, bringing him back to the present and his most immediate concern. Finn's lips tightened. The lack of respect the brothers had shown... He understood wanting to protect her, she elicited the impulse in him as well, but this was not how you went about protecting a goddess. In fact, goddesses protected themselves, and they went where they willed. You simply supported them, and obeyed them, or you got out of their way and avoided them.

She stretched, her light jumper pulling tight against the outline of her shape, and his heart gave one hard pound. So different from Grainne, and yet beautiful. Bat twisted to face him and their gazes met. Silver flashed in her eyes, then faded back to deep brown. What did she see in that instant?

He unlatched the gate and stepped through. When he reached her side, he pulled in a deep breath, unable to resist, and tasted a mixture of heat, crisp air, the subtle bite of pepper and the light fragrance of cornflowers. Below that was the tang of magic, a note particular to deities.

It was her unique scent, what he had first sensed on the day he'd come to inspect Dano's body. It grew when she felt something intensely, or exerted her power. Right now it nearly overwhelmed the natural flowers of Shar's garden.

"Are ya all right, then?" He kept his tone even. His hand rose and landed on her shoulder, the fingers squeezing gently. He stared at it, wondering when he'd become so forward with a goddess.

Or maybe it's just this one.

She shrugged, pulled in a breath, and let it out in a carefully released exhalation. "I do not know. Did they send you out thinking I would be less angry with you?"

"No." He wanted to add that he'd simply wanted to comfort her, but the words stuck in his throat. She'd seen him at his worst, had called him out as the coward he was. What comfort would she want from him?

"I am not angry, exactly," she said. "Or, not at them, not really. Imagine, the egg of creation is real, and has been here all this time." She stretched out a hand and ran a gentle finger over a leaf of the strawberry bush. The damned thing waved at her. "They didn't say anything when I first came here. We were in the kitchen, speaking of soul blades and immortals and gods. They never mentioned they'd originally come from my homeland. Maybe they assumed I knew and was playing at ignorance?" She faced him then, eyes wide.

He licked his lips. How was he supposed to respond to that? "I... don't think they would play at such a thing with you. And I can guarantee none of us knew our cauldron was this vessel-egg thing. The bomen—men of ba... well, many things can be lost to the stretches of time."

A muscle in her cheek ticked. "Seth knew." There was anger in those two words. "The older gods of my land knew." She paused. "*Your* gods would have known."

He bowed his head in acknowledgment. "The gods do not confide in me."

"Not even your Morrigan?"

He nearly snorted, but he had not lost all his sense. "Not even my Morrigan. It is true she heads the guardi, but I doubt any but those who directly serve the Tribunal know even a fraction of her secrets."

Bat's gaze roved over him, and his spine stiffened. Then she lowered her eyes. "I knew there were things the brothers kept from me. I assumed they would tell me when they were ready, that these secrets were things of the past that no longer mattered. This... I do not know what to think, and therefore do not know if I am all right, as you asked. Do—" there was a small hitch to her voice and Finn suppressed the urge to storm back into the kitchen and beat Mell silly. *He* should have known better at least. "Do you think they didn't trust me, to not tell me these things?"

"No." He didn't hesitate in this answer. "No, I think they were being foolish men who thought to protect a goddess, and went about it in exactly the wrong manner."

Her gaze shot back to his and a smile formed. "Protect me?" Her laughter rang out and her eyes flashed. "They still do not understand, do they?"

He returned her smile, unable to help himself. "No, goddess."

Her head tilted. "And do you? Understand?"

"That I would never presume to do, goddess."

She gave another laugh, this one short and a little rueful. "I will tell you a secret. Sometimes I do not understand either."

Killer, who'd been silent up to that point, let out a low bark, and trotted to the garden gate, his leash trailing on the ground behind him. The brothers stood there, lined up oldest to youngest, and wore matching expressions of apology, even Dub.

Bat looked back at them, longing and resolve flashing across her expression.

"Give them a chance to explain, to make it right," Finn urged. He wasn't sure why.

Her hand went to the pendant hidden under her jumper and her head tilted, sending the silk of her hair sliding over her shoulder. "Sometimes, I think I would give them all the chances they needed." The words were soft, uttered as though she didn't expect—or want—him to hear.

In that moment Finn *did* understand at least one thing. She loved them. Whether she realized it or not, she loved them, and would continue to love them in any way they would allow.

He also understood that, whatever else was happening, she had not been pushing the relationships forward, not for fear of hurting herself, but for fear of hurting *them*. The brothers would need to be the ones to act in that regard.

He'd had that love, once, long before Grainne. If the O'Loinsighs were foolish enough to allow that to slip from them...

Finn leaned in, close enough his lips brushed against her ear. "If you need anything, if you need *me*, never hesitate, goddess. I will be there, *whatever* it is." His blood rushed as images crowded in on him, of soft skin and rounded flesh. He wasn't sure he could love properly, after Grainne, but he could do this for her. He *wanted* to do this, he realized. The goddess was hurting, and he knew at least one thing that could ease that hurt. Finn drew in one last breath of her essence, and stepped back.

Bat swallowed, a delicate flush riding her cheeks, then gave him the slightest of nods. "I... appreciate the offer. But right now, we should concentrate on the vessel." Stars entered her eyes once more, a soft glow. "Imagine, it's real."

How can she seem so innocent? According to her, she did not come into existence until after the floods. It made her young for a deity, but it was still a very long time to live. He was younger than that, and sometimes speculated if he'd ever held such wonder in himself.

His first thought on realizing the cauldron had resurfaced? *Crap*. That was all. If the cauldron came back into their world it would set off a new power struggle, and he would have to deal with it. Bat's reaction was all childlike delight and awe.

"I should caution you," he said, placing a hand on her forearm. "Many will seek to use the– the vessel for themselves. Now that its location is known—"

"Those greedy for power will always strive for more. I know this. We have one such already in our midst, I saw it in him earlier. But the Morrigan sent him, and I cannot turn him away without a very good reason. I, too, have to trust she has her reasons and knows what she is about." The last was said with a rueful smile.

Finn released her and stepped back, chastised. So, not innocent, simply willing to allow a bit of reverence into her own mind. It was an interesting thought: *what did the gods revere?*

She set off through the neat rows of growing things, toward the O'Loinsigh brothers.

Lucky farking bastards.

Chapter Five

Bastie,

*I am still mad at you, but I had to tell you—I think Finn,
the one who reminded me of Seth, wants me. He came after
me in the garden. I... there are not many who have ever
come after me.*

*And... I think I want him back. Maybe this is the perfect
solution to my frustrations?*

- Bat, a confused goddess

BAT

*T*he heat of her flush still rode her cheeks. Finn
had surprised her, but not in a completely
bad way.

She supposed the sidhe was truly done with his
obsession with Grainne? And he was attractive, especially
when he smiled...

Maybe it was the perfect solution. She could remain with the brothers, in her home with them, and use Finn for her physical needs, for that comfort of touch.

Or maybe she wouldn't need to go that route? Now that she'd been invited to the gathering along with the brothers, was there really a need for them to keep secret the fact that she planned to stay? And if that no longer needed to be hidden, could they not openly show affection?

That is not the only problem. No, being named in that invitation only handled one of the barriers. The other was the brothers themselves, and her refusal to choose one over the others.

The three O'Loinsigh brothers waited for her in the alley, and the closer she drew to them her thoughts both stilled and fell further into confusion. As she'd told Finn, she would give them as many chances as they needed. Maybe it was because she'd finally found something here, with them, that she hadn't had in centuries. These immortals delighted her, confused her, and warmed her. She was not ready to give that up.

Immortals from *Egypt*. Her thoughts circled back around to that particular fact. Egypt. This was not a small secret they had kept. This was not something that would fade into the past. This was something she should have known all along.

They were also part of a clan the brothers had distanced themselves from for a reason. A mysterious brooch that belonged to their father and that Dub and Mell had sought before she ever came to Ireland.

But, she *had* stumbled into their unfinished business, a

part of their life they no longer wanted, and that she had no part of. Put like that, she could understand. They were not part of her life back in Egypt, had no part in the deities and people she had left behind. Her break had simply been much cleaner than theirs.

She shoved aside these circular thoughts that tumbled over each other in a never-ending spiral of confusion. There was no use in getting mired. All she could do was attempt to move forward. And handle the immediate situation that confronted her: A man of ba asking for help in restoring the broken vessel of creation. She could worry about the rest after that.

Holy jumping gods. The egg had been real.

Bat stopped just on the other side of the gate, but made no move to open it. Dub shifted restlessly then crossed his arms, causing the muscles to bunch, and her gaze lingered there.

That early heat returned. She wanted so much to reach out and touch the grumpy not-man, to let her hand linger just as her gaze did. She wanted to kiss away the pinched skin between Mell's brows, and slip into bed with Shar so he could wrap his arms around her and pull her close. But to do that…

Yes, maybe Finn was the perfect solution. But later. She firmed her resolve.

Mell's brows rose. "What are you thinking?" The words were clipped.

"Nothing that we should talk about now." She opened the gate and stepped through, brushing against the middle brother. Restless warmth filled her. "Let us see what we can do about the man of ba's distress. And later, we will discuss the… invitation." A kernel of anger and confusion returned, burning in her chest.

"Goddess. I ride with you, and explain what I know of vessel, what happened to it." Ari stood on the bottom step of the rear stoop.

Cu Chulainn had taken a place in the open kitchen door, filling the whole space. A muffled voice came from behind him. "Move out a' my way, ya oaf."

"No." The guardi captain didn't budge even as a slim arm reached around him and waved. "This is no business for a mere trooping fae. Go back to your shop and—"

The arm had withdrawn, and a booted foot appeared at his groin, between his legs. Cuchi grunted but didn't move. His face turned red, and he blew out a breath.

"Fine." Ailis's foot disappeared and stomps sounded from the kitchen, moving into the pub.

Bat held her hand out to Ari, who now wore a wide grin. All the men did, though Finn's looked a bit pained. "We'll go to the truck. I am sure Ailis will meet us there. She has probably gone around the front of the pub."

Cuchi scowled and his face turned near purple. "You're going to all go? Who will watch the pub?"

The raven appeared on his shoulder and cawed.

"Don't drive any of the customers away, will ya? And the stew needs to come off in about forty minutes." Mell waved and spun on his heel.

Bat hesitated. The bald not-man had a point. "Do you want to leave our home in his care?"

Dub hooked his arm over her shoulder. Bat stilled, wary. The move was more something Mell would have done, when he was in a mischievous or gregarious mood.

"He'll be fine, won't you Cuchi? Besides, he's got a watch-raven. The Morrigan will see every move he makes." Then he scowled. "You can borrow some of my clothes," Dub said. "Can't have you keeping the bar in your uniform."

"Or I can go with you, and Finn can stay here."

Flash. Cu Chulainn beside the stone vessel. Blood poured from a wound on his head. He reached up and wiped his fingers through it, then smeared the red substance over the lip of the stone. It glowed, light turning the blood to rubies. There were four other similar stains, ranging around the circumference of the vessel. Ailis, Finn, Dub, and she herself stood beside them.

She sighed. "He needs to be there. I am not sure why exactly, but we will need his blood. And it will need to be freely given. So, no—" she held up her hand to Dub, who had growled. "We cannot just take it from him. And we will need Ailis, Finn and you." She poked his side.

Mell and Shar exchanged a look, and for a moment she was afraid they would argue. "Paper, rock, scissors?" Mell finally asked.

Shar sighed. "Fine. Whoever wins will accompany the goddess."

"Who said we were playing to see who got to go give up their blood? Maybe I want to stay here."

Shar raised a brow.

"Fine. Yes, I want to go play in the blood." Mell grinned, and it was different from any she had seen from him up to this point, far from the broken expression he'd worn after she'd been shot, and it lifted her heart.

Bat waved her hand. An urgency was building in her,

though there was no flash of vision. They needed to get to the vessel. "Please decide. Or you will both stay."

They both shot her narrow-eyed looks. *Did I stumble on some sort of obscure ritual they hold sacred?*

Then they did something with their hands, making different shapes, and Mell groaned.

"If you would cease always picking 'rock' first, you would sometimes win," Dub admonished Mell. "You must adjust your strategy."

"It is decided?" Bat looked between the brothers, brows raised. They nodded and Mell stepped back, toward the pub. She pointed at Cuchi, then to the end of the alley where both the brothers' truck and Ailis now waited. "Then let us go play with the blood."

They'd taken a few steps when a sharp fear sped her heart and churned her stomach. She waited for the flash, but it didn't come. She turned back, Dub's arm still over her shoulders, and looked at Mell. "I do not like to leave you here."

"Maybe we could wait until the morning when we can all go? The cauldron has been lost so long, what's one more day?"

"No," Ari said.

"No," she said a fraction of a second after the man of ba. The word slipped out, though Mell's suggestion had merit. Urgency to go with the man of ba filled her, warring with the flash of apprehension, and yet there were still no visions. Was it simply her eagerness to see the vessel itself? It *was* an exciting thing...

Then why the reluctance to leave Mell? So that she would have all the brothers beside her? She *did* want them with her, despite her recent frustrations and the latest almost-revelations, but this didn't feel like a simple want.

Flash. Bat stood in a spacious, open-air court.

She struggled to shove this vision away. She knew what it showed, and she did not need to think on it, not now.

Flash. Hathor approached, her golden skin nearly glittering in the Egyptian sunlight. Horus stood just behind her, a gentle hand on her shoulder. He looked at Hathor as though she were all he needed, all he wanted.
He looked at Hathor as he had never looked at Bat.
Light shifted and Seth stepped from a doorway that led into the palace. He took in the scene, frowned, shook his head, and walked away, mumbling under his breath, too low for her to hear.
Hathor gave her a brilliant smile. "Bat, you are here. I am so glad." The other goddess took her hands. "We wanted to tell you together. Horus and I have decided to join." Hathor twisted back and looked at Horus with the same devotion he showed her.
Horus tore his gaze from Hathor and focused on Bat. "The unification has been secured for a few centuries now. Seth and I are getting along just fine. You will no longer need to travel to Memphis so frequently, or try to mediate. I know how much you've been longing for a freedom from your duties."
Bat wanted to argue. She didn't want to be free of her duties. She wanted to be free to choose her duties. There was such a big difference…
But she saw the way Horus looked at Hathor. He had never once

looked at Bat that way, even when they'd been twined together in
passion. And Hathor had never been a goddess good at sharing.
Horus skimmed a hand down Hathor's shoulder, along her arm,
and gripped her hand.

He'd never done that for Bat. Maybe he, too, wanted the freedom
to choose his duty?

And Seth must have seen this happening in the decades since Bat's
last visit. For all she knew, it had been going on for longer than
that. Why else would neither of them want her to join them in
residence here at the palace?

Something inside her broke. There was no choice here, not for her.
She swallowed, then inclined her head. Her mind was blank. There
were no visions, nothing to guide her on what she should do. Was
this truly the end of her purpose, her usefulness?

No. She had her temple, her home in the seventh nome. The people
there relied on her. And so Bat nodded once more, turned on her
heel, and left the lovers to their love.

She blinked. This vision had passed in a fraction of a second. Did they even know she'd seen something?

But she had her answer. These thoughts she'd been having... they were much too similar to the confusion and hurt she'd experienced when she'd walked away from Horus and Seth. Or, when they had walked away from her. And she'd already promised herself she wouldn't let that happen again.

Bat shrugged out from under Dub and propelled herself into Mell, squeezing her arm tight around his waist. "You had better be in good condition when we return."

Mell returned her embrace, wrapping his arms around

her as though he would never let go, like they would have to live the rest of their existence locked together.

She tucked the moment away in her memory. This was one she'd pull out over and over again.

Dub drew her away and the raven flew to Mell's shoulder and cawed. *I will help watch over him, sister.*

Does the other goddess know something I do not? She nearly snorted. Of course the Morrigan knew more than she was saying. *I need to learn more of the local deities.* It was something she'd neglected, wanting to enjoy the slice of peace and home she'd found, but she couldn't avoid it indefinitely. Had the brothers simply been following her lead in ignoring the world outside the pub and keeping it away from her? It was something else to think upon, later.

"Thank you," Bat told the other goddess.

The raven bobbed its head.

Dub placed his arm over her shoulder once more. "He'll be all right, *storeen*. Mell is a much better fighter than he is a musician. If anything happens in our absence, I have no doubt he can handle it."

"He is a very good musician."

"Precisely."

It wasn't a long drive, maybe fifteen minutes, to the turn-off toward Benbulben. Then another twenty minutes to reach the end of the marked path. The shadows deepened as they hiked, but there was still plenty of light to see by.

At the foot of the mountain was a small forest—or, more like a large copse. It was this they headed toward.

They walked single file, Ari in the lead, Ailis and Finn behind him. Bat walked in the middle. Then came Cu Chulainn and finally Dub. Killer trotted along beside her, head up, tongue lolling in a happy grin.

Trunks, limbs, and leaves loomed before them, and light wavered. As they passed through the tree line there was a pressure, similar to the first time she'd entered the pub, and then a pop.

"Damn, those are some strong wards." Cu Chulainn shuddered and rolled his shoulders.

Bat didn't disagree.

"Not far," Ari said, and his short legs became a blur in his eagerness to reach his people.

The men of ba. Ari had filled her in on some of their history on the ride over. They'd been born of the egg of creation, not long after humanity was created, to help guide the pieces of the soul together for their final journey. Ari said the men of ba's appearance was fearsome so as to encourage those spirits who were reluctant to make their journey to judgement, usually the wicked. What he told her was very similar to one of her own powers. It was very telling to her that her existence had come about *after* the men of ba had left Egypt.

They were kindred.

According to Ari, there had been a grand battle between Isfet and Ma'at. Most of the gods had fought for Ma'at, but Apep and a few others had sided with Isfet. When Apep learned that Seth had sent the egg of creation out of their reach, he let out a mighty roar that shook the world, and Isfet caused the waters of Nun to rise and churn, in an effort to stop the escape. But the sea men, gifted long life and powers from Seth, were skilled, and they made it safely to this new land. There were other creatures who were sent away as well, the beloved of the various gods, in an effort to save them from the chaos.

Her mind whirled with the images Ari's tale had conjured. She'd seen a few battles in her time, but nothing on that scale. And how had she never learned of the immortals that had been sent away? She kept coming back to that fact, and the kernel of anger in her chest grew into a bag full of popped rage. The older gods had a lot to answer, especially Seth, and Bastet.

Maybe it's like the brothers? Or my time as the Unifier? An era long done, that has no bearing on the current existence, something to be put away and not contemplated or discussed? She wanted to make sense of what she could only see as her friends' betrayal. *It does have bearing, though. I'm being led to the very vessel Chaos has been seeking, and it is apparently* broken.

Ari couldn't tell her why it wasn't working properly, only that the Fomoiri had lost it to the Fir Bolg, then taken it back, then lost it again to the Tuatha, this time for a few centuries. They regained it, and kept it for quite a while, then once more lost it in the same battle where their leader, Balor, had been killed.

After that, the men of ba had stolen away with the vessel and hidden it.

Ahead of them Ari drew to a halt. He twisted and held a hand out to her. "I need to take you across this one. We are very skilled with twisting the points of the spirit, and while I am sure you could navigate the pathways eventually, goddess, I am just as sure you do not want to take the time." He spoke in wonderfully fluid Egyptian, the words themselves music to her.

She took his hand. "Take me." The words were harsher than the creature deserved, but anger still rode her hard.

"*A stor.*" Shar stepped up to her, one hand outstretched as though to stop her, and she twisted to glare.

"Do not." She held back her power, but he halted nevertheless, palms facing her. "Not yet, not right now." Pressure built within her, and she needed to move, to get to the vessel. "We will talk later, but you need to not 'protect' me right now."

He gave her a slow nod and took a step back. His expression was neutral, oh so carefully arranged, and her chest tightened in something other than anger.

We will fix it later. Right now there is something much more important. She gave Ari's hand a gentle squeeze, and he pulled her forward.

Chapter Six

Dearest Bastet,

There is too much to tell you. So much has happened today, and I have learned so many things. Things you did not tell me, yes, but also things I only thought legend and myth myself.

If you get this, please answer. I… need to talk to someone. Please.

- Bat, your friend

p.s. – I laid a curse today! It was upon a very annoying not-man. He definitely deserved it.

BAT

*A*ri was correct—the men of ba were very good at twisting the paths of the soul. In the step it took to cross the threshold of their protections, she caught a glimpse of shining roads and beacons, each tugging at a part of her.

Where she ended when they crossed the wards was... beautiful. She could think of no other word. Ari dropped her hand and stepped back, leaving her to stare in wonder at his home.

The trees were massive, larger than any she had ever seen outside of photographs. Some bore rough, dark brown bark, and others had smooth silver. There were dark green leaves and feathered fronds. The prettiest sported fluffy white flowers that were so numerous the branches seemed to be pulled down.

Built into the sides of these trees were small huts. They blended so well it took Bat a few seconds to spot them, and even then she wasn't sure if she was seeing them correctly. A stream glinted in the distance, and the gentle sound of water acted as a soothing music. Shadows and sun played a game of chase on the path before her... It really was quite pretty... A patch of sunlit grass caught her eye. It looked like the perfect place for a nap... and she was so tired...

"Do not be fooled." Shar stepped up beside her as Ari disappeared once more.

Bat shook her head, and the forest became once more just a forest, the enticement fading away. "It is a very good trick." She took a breath and looked up to study her giant. He gazed at the flower-adorned trees, his good eye wide and shining.

"The rowans..." he breathed. "I thought they were lost."

"No. Just hidden from the bunglings of men like you."

Ari popped up beside them, Finn in tow. "I'm bringing the bald one over next, he's started poking at the frowning one, and the green haired fae is not helping matters." He disappeared once more.

Shar barely acknowledged those words, his gaze still trained on the trees. Bat took his hand, her earlier anger forgotten for the moment. "Are you becoming lost in them as well?"

He shook his head. "No. But they are a beautiful sight, are they not?"

She squeezed his fingers and Killer leaned into him. "They are."

Finn stepped up beside her, not touching, but close enough to tell her he was there. In another minute, Ari had crossed everyone over the wards. He started out once more, leading the way over a barely-there path.

"Why do you say the vessel is broken? Not, what broke it, I know you do not have that answer, but why? What is it doing, or not doing?" she finally asked. She had been letting instinct guide her up to this point, but if she was to truly fix it, she would need more than a vision and a few pieces of vague information.

Ari partially twisted back to peer at her without even pausing on the path. "It no longer offers true life. Those who come from it no longer have their full soul, but are mere shadows of themselves."

That fit with her vision.

"It is true. Near the end of the last true war between the immortals, those revived by the cauldron were no more than animated corpses, used as meat and fodder for the fields of battle." Finn's quiet voice echoed with remembered horror. "When the final fight against Balor was won, we had to use the daggers…"

Bat stopped and dropped Shar's hand. The others stopped around her, and even the air stilled, holding itself in anticipation of her reaction. But as with the gold embossed card that still lay on the island in the pub's kitchen, she did not know how she felt about this news. To kill someone in battle was different from murdering them to steal power that did not belong to you, true. And the blades had a purpose other than to kill. But using them in such a manner did not sit well with her. Nor did reviving a corpse without true life. Her stomach churned with both anger and disgust. Those blades… She needed to ask the Morrigan about them. *All those lives lost, those souls unable to move on…*

She closed her eyes and sucked in a breath as her power surged in response to her roiling anger, seeking an outlet. No one moved, not even Cuchi, and for that at least she was grateful. Another breath. It was centuries past, there was nothing she could do about it now. A breath. She had ensured the one still at large in the world had been confiscated and locked away. And another inhale. She was about to do what she could to restore the vessel. One more breath.

Bat opened her eyes and locked her gaze on Finn, the last one to speak. "We will see what we can do about fixing the vessel." She turned her head and pinned Cuchi with a glare. "And then the men of ba will hide it away once more. It will not be used. Is that understood?"

Each of them nodded, eyes wide. Ailis, of course, wore

a savage grin. The fae bounded over to Bat and took her hand. "If they use it, will you smite them?"

Bat relaxed and allowed a small smile to pull up her lips. Her friend was trying to lighten the tension, and she could appreciate it, to a degree. But Bat also wanted to make her wishes, and her opinion, very clear on this subject. "I will. I do not care what the Morrigan, or the other deities have to say. This is not a thing to be played with, or used for the whims of power. That it was abused so…" She shook her head as her power surged, pressing against them all. She pulled it in again, not wanting to waste it on something as simple as making a point.

"We understand, goddess." Finn bowed to her, a gesture of respect and even reverence. "I will ensure your words are carried to the Morrigan."

"I am here as her messenger, Cumhaill." Cu Chulainn crossed his arms and glared at the other guardi, though Bat noted he was careful to avoid her gaze.

"Then please act like it," Bat said.

Cu Chulainn opened his mouth, paused, then closed it again and nodded.

Hmmm… maybe he could be managed.

"Goddess, please." Ari darted a glance back over his shoulder, the direction they'd been going. "We must hurry." His long fingers clenched then uncurled, then clenched again.

She took a step forward then stopped. This man of ba had come into the pub and refused to leave. Then he had insisted they must go right that instant, only relenting briefly, and she herself had been swept up in the urge, but with no visions. Now, he was once more hurrying them along. The vessel had been hidden and broken for centuries. Why did one more day make a difference?

And why am I only now thinking of this? Some of her urgency eased at the thought and she narrowed her eyes at the man of ba. "What do you know that you have not told us, Ari?" *And how have you clouded my mind so effectively?*

Ari slumped. "You figured it out, didn't you? I told Puchi it would not work, that we should not attempt to trick a goddess so, but he insisted…"

"Tell me the rest. Now, Ari." She kept her voice gentle on the last. There was something more than guilt lurking in his darting gaze and hunched shoulders. There was fear as well, but not of her.

"There is not much more. Puchi woke this morning and said something was coming. That we had to be ready and the vessel needed to be fixed before it arrived. But he didn't know what *it* was, exactly, or when it would come, so he insisted we had to bring you right away." Ari kicked at the ground in front of him and lowered his gaze, for all the world like the child he cloaked himself as at the pub.

Killer went to the ba man and sniffed at his neck, whining a little. The pup twisted back, looking up at Bat with the big begging-eyes he loved to use, and her heart melted.

"I understand," she said. Then she held up a finger. "But you will not do it again."

Ari nodded rapidly. "Yes, goddess. Of course. Not again." He hunched further, so that his too-many-knuckled hands nearly dragged on the forest floor.

Dub's fists curled. "You forgive too easily."

She glanced at him from the corner of her eye. "And you will be glad for it, I suspect."

Dub grunted but didn't say anything else.

"Who is Puchi?" Finn asked, bringing them back to the topic. His arms were crossed over his chest and feet planted at shoulder width. He didn't look to be moving any time soon.

Had they *all* been taken in by this trick of glamour? Bat caught Ailis's gaze, and the fae shrugged then gave her a small grin as if to say, *I was just along for the ride*. The others shifted, and Shar moved close to her once more, as they waited for Ari's answer.

"He is the chief of our band. He was chosen because he has the gift of future-seeing, though it is not a reliable ability. But we always listen."

Bat nodded. "Yes, you should always listen to those with the gift of the future, and of the past. I will accept this. Is there anything else we should know?"

Ari shook his head.

"Then—"

"Bat, *storeen*, I do not trust—"

She spun to face Dub, the anger that had waned a moment ago boiling up once more. "I am not your *little treasure*—" She regretted the words as soon as they left her mouth. She knew better than to speak out in senseless anger, for it always twisted the mind and poisoned words. And her swings of emotion were too hectic to be anything but senseless.

But didn't she also have the right to be mad at them? Did she always have to be reasonable, and forgiving?

They'd been keeping secrets, even after telling her their home was *hers*.

It was as though she was on one of those contraptions in the amusement parks. *Roller coaster. I am riding a roller coaster of emotions*.

Dub's expression closed off and he crossed his arms, matching Finn's stance. "Goddess, then. I still do not trust that we have been told everything. He has led five immortals and one goddess about as though we were humans. Who is to say he is not still doing so with you?"

She sucked in a breath as Dub's words found their mark. She *was* very weak for a goddess.

Shar hit the back of his brother's head and Dub twisted to glare at him.

"You don't get to talk to her like that." Shar's tone was steel. "Nobody gets to talk to her like that." He switched his glare to Cuchi, then Finn, before settling back on Dub.

"I didn't actually say anything," Cuchi protested.

Shar took a step toward him and stopped. He pulled in a breath and let it out, rolling his shoulders. "There's a lot that's happened today. Let's just... get this done, then we can go back to the pub and sort out the rest, okay?" He turned his dark eyes on Bat. "Ye're not the only one angry."

With his words, she once more got her own emotions under control. Shar edged closer to her and, after only a brief hesitation, wrapped an arm around her shoulders, careful to keep the touch light. She leaned into him, trying to tell her giant that she still welcomed him. She still welcomed all of them, she was just... frustrated. There was that word again. And the feeling was bleeding out through the holes that Finn and Ari and the brothers had poked in her contentment.

She focused on Ari. The poor creature didn't deserve to be admonished for her mess, or her weakness. "Lead on, Ari. Let us see what we can do for the vessel."

He turned and headed down the path once more, no longer quite as assured, but still with a speed that told Bat he did not lie about this Puchi's urgency in sending Ari to get her. Dub fell in just behind her and Shar, and she could feel the weight of his gaze on her back.

She thought back once again to the day two months ago when the brothers had come to her, and asked her to stay. To make this place her home.

Home. She latched onto the idea. *I am not ready to give this up, nor will I throw it away.* She held onto the idea. It was what would steer her through the confusion. She and Dub, and the other brothers, would sort this out.

After nearly ten minutes of walking, Shar pulled her to a halt. Lost in her thoughts, she'd failed to take full note of her surroundings. A figure lay in a shallow dip in the ground, partially obscured by shadow. Beyond it was another, half hidden in the trees. Blood pooled beneath them both.

Whimpering reached her ears as Shar swept her into his arms and spun, putting their backs to the bodies.

"What—?"

Flash. A man with dark hair bound back in a braid, shadow hounds playing at his feet, bent over a clear bowl of water. In the water was their kitchen, and in the middle of the kitchen was the invitation, and it whispered their own words to the shadow man.

She was half turned into him, and his broad shoulders prevented her from seeing more than a few tree trunks and tufts of grass. Her giant cupped the side of her head and pressed her cheek to his chest as figures sped past them in near silence.

"Puchi, Puchi, can you hear me?" Ari's voice carried to her seemingly from a long distance. "Who did this to you? Who?"

"Do not look, *a stor*." Shar's heart thundered in her ear.

"Shar—"

"No. He said if we came now, then we avoided whatever his elder saw. If you did not see this in your visions, you should not see it now." His arms tightened on her, lifting her from the ground, and she squeaked at the pressure.

"Shar, my giant, I cannot breathe. Let me down." She hugged the arms wrapped around her, making a lie of her order.

His grip eased, but he did not put her down, and her legs dangled under her. She kicked a little, hoping to make her point gently. He either ignored the movement or did not notice.

"Brother." Dub appeared beside them. "Whoever was here has gone. I have searched. Finn has searched, as has Killer. All traces lead away." He placed a hand on Shar's shoulder. "Let her down, the elder wants to speak to her."

"You may come with me if you like," she offered as she eased up on her own hug.

"Brother. *Goddess*, remember?" But the word lacked Dub's earlier stiff tone.

Bat twisted her head and met the eldest brother's lapis gaze. He frowned, yes, but it was the frown of concern, and it was for his brother. This must be something like what happened to Mell when she was shot. What memories did Shar hold inside?

Half-surprised when there was no flash of vision, Bat turned her attention to calming the giant brother so they could investigate what had happened here. She stroked her hand over his forearm once, then again, setting up a soothing rhythm. "I have been alive for a very long time, my giant not-man. I have seen many things. I am no stranger to death."

She'd meant the words to be reassuring, but he stiffened against her, his muscles turning to stone. "We're going back to the pub." He shifted his grip, spinning her in his hold so that her front was cradled against him. Shar started down the path, then pulled up short.

"You are going nowhere until we have determined exactly what happened." Cu Chulainn's voice was flat, devoid of his earlier arrogance.

A low rumble built in Shar's chest. "Move, ya braggart."

"I beat you once before, I can do it again."

"Ya beat me because we were trying ta retreat, and I thought the woman had become injured."

"So you admit your cowardice." And the arrogance was back.

All the anger, all the frustration and pain and fear of what might be coming and what was already here surged to the front and found a target. "Let me down," she said to Shar, and the power leaking from her must have gotten through to him, because he slowly lowered her to her feet.

She spun and glared up at the bald man. "I have told you to behave. I have told you to maintain some respect around me." She stepped forward and Shar's warm hand brushed against her back in a gentle warning that she ignored. "Now I will tell you. I do not care about your Morrigan, or your gods, or your legends or myths or claim of this land. I do not care about what you may or may not have accomplished in your past."

Cuchi stepped back and she continued to close the distance between them, step by step. "You will not speak unless it is to offer something constructive. You will not speak at all to the O'Loinsigh brothers." As the words flowed from her, she wove her anger and frustration into them, twined it all together into something the Egyptians had always been very good at—a curse. "If you violate these strictures, there will be no second chances, and... you will not be *able* to lift your sword."

He opened his mouth and she held up her hand, cutting him off.

"No second chances," she said again, as the power settled in place and bound around his arm.

His eyes widened and he backed up another step. He opened his mouth again, closed it, and nodded. "I will patrol the bounds of the grove." Then he spun and stomped off.

Dub, his lapis eyes shining, appeared before her, grinning widely. "That was glorious, goddess."

Bat's cheeks heated. "You may call me *storeen*, if you truly want to," she muttered.

His grin slid away and his pupils dilated. *"Storeen."*

She swayed toward him, allowing the chaos and horror that surrounded them to be swept away for a moment by the lapis of his eyes. Then she pulled herself back. "Take me to the elder."

Dub held out a hand and she took it. As they passed him, she grabbed Shar's hand with her other and gave it a squeeze. "Let us resolve this. And then there are other things to discuss."

"About the invitation. I'm sorr—"

"No. Well, yes, but not about the secrets, though we will need to talk about those too." Now that she had let some of her anger out it no longer clouded her thoughts so extremely. "I am not sure the bar is secure. That is what we need to discuss." She paused. "Are you able to call Mell?"

Dub pulled his mobile from his back pocket and checked the screen. "No signal."

"Then we will need to fast indeed, and return to the pub as soon as possible." She sped her steps.

The two brothers allowed her to pull them along and soon they stood at the edge of the grove, the three of them lined up just inside the rowan trees. Ailis hovered over Ari and an older, gray-skinned ba man who lay propped in his arms. Finn prowled the edges of the clearing, kneeling occasionally to check on a crumpled figure. At the far edge of the clearing huddled a small group of the men of ba.

Ailis looked up and spotted them. She waved, urging them over. "Oh, thank the gods." She bit her lip. "The cauldron's gone. And..." She waved her hand around the clearing.

Fallen bodies and twisted limbs, crushed grass and broken tree branches met Bat's gaze. And... that was all she saw. "The vessel of creation is gone?" A hollow feeling opened in her chest as her stomach dropped. These bodies... there were so many. And that meant there was at least one more blade out there, and the creature who wielded it was ferocious enough to take on the men of ba, with their needle teeth and razor talons.

"Goddess." The gray-skinned ba man raised a hand toward her.

She knelt beside the older immortal and took his hand.

"We fought, but the shadows..."

She brushed a hand over the wrinkled brow and smiled. "I can see you fought very well."

"Puchi, you must tell her what you saw, what you know." Ari leaned in, his red eyes shining.

Puchi's eyes slid closed and he nodded. "I do not have much time. The vessel must be restored, and the shadows defeated. He comes, he of the evil-eye, and he seeks vengeance and restoration." His breathing grew ragged. "He wields the shining blade of Nuada, that may slay even the gods."

Shar shifted behind her and she held up a hand, stalling whatever he would say. Now was not the time. "Who is *he*?"

Red eyes dimmed as the older man of ba struggled to focus on her. "Balor. Find Tir Hudi." The red dimmed and the too-long fingers went slack in her grip.

The pieces of his soul separated from his body and she

wasted no time in gathering them to her, enveloping them in comfort, and the idea of a job well done. If she understood correctly, this not-man had guarded the vessel of creation for longer than she had been in existence. And an accomplishment such as that deserved a true reward and acknowledgment.

She held those pieces to her heart, and whispered to them of the Otherworld, the Land of Reeds, where the sun would always shine upon him, and the other gods would welcome him with open arms. The pieces danced in her hands, then fused together and sped away. She sent a silent plea to Nephthys and Anubis, to ask for mercy for this soul, and to ensure Puchi found his rightful place.

Her eyes slid closed and pressure built against her lids. She'd sensed the man of ba's longing for his home, one he had held all these years. And yet he'd stayed here, doing his duty. But, now, he could rest.

She opened her eyes to find her hands resting on his abdomen, just above a wide gash. Leaving one of them where it lay, she brought the other to Ari's shoulder. "He is going home, my friend."

Ari nodded, then stood, shrugging off her hand. "He held on as long as he could, and did not let the blade claim him. Now we must carry forward, and recover the vessel."

Did not let the blade claim him…

Bat surveyed the clearing once more, and opened her senses wider. There *were* souls lingering. She had not expected it because of the methods needed to slay an immortal, but—though their bodies held no life—many of the ba men had managed to avoid that fate. Though the number of souls did not match the number of bodies, a handful had remained free to move on. She stood and walked to the closest body and gathered the ba of the fallen warrior. She called out, pulling the not-man's ka to her from where it had fled to and, as she had with Puchi, tethered the pieces together and sent them on their journey.

She had no doubt the pieces would have eventually found their way to each other, but it was the least she could do for the fallen, to speed them on their way.

Body after body was gathered and brought to her. The other men of ba, who had stayed huddled at the far end of the clearing, slowly crept closer as they saw what she was doing. Ari encouraged them, waving them to his side. Finn and Dub brought the fallen, and Shar stayed steady at her other side. Eventually, Cuchi returned from his patrol and waited at the edge of the trees.

Finally, she'd moved on all she could, and she rose, dusting off the knees of her jeans where damp leaves and grass clung. The gathered immortals stared at her with wide eyes as she slumped against Shar, her limbs heavy, as though she'd been toiling away in the garden.

The moment hung there, no one willing to break the silence. Could Dub and Cuchi and Ailis tell what she had been doing? She had assumed so, but they also didn't really have a connection to emotions or the spirit... or she didn't think they did. What was Ailis's power exactly, and Cuchi's?

A cutting wind blasted through the clearing, as though the world had let out a heaving sigh of impatience, and she shivered.

Why didn't I pull on my coat? And how is May still so chilly?

Dub shifted. "We need to get back to the pub, and Mell, and regroup."

He was correct. She had lingered here too long already, distracted from her suspicions that the brother's protections on the bar had been compromised. Bat nodded then looked to the ba men—some of whom were women, she now saw. "I am sorry I could not provide them the proper rituals. Will you be well here?"

Most of them nodded. A few bowed their heads, hiding their red eyes, and three stepped forward, including Ari. "We are coming with you," he said in ancient Egyptian. "The vessel is our responsibility."

Bat almost nodded, then froze.

Flash. A familiar alleyway. Dark had fallen. A small body lay there, blood seeping from multiple wounds, limbs bent at weird angles. Beyond that was a trail of blood leading to a hunched figure, a patch covering one of his eyes. He gripped a hand... whose arm ended at the elbow. A piercing scream sounded.

Her chest tightened. She couldn't let that come to pass. "No."

Ari's shoulders hunched up and he bared his teeth. "It is our duty, goddess."

"If you come with us to the pub, you will die. And at least one of your companions will die with you. Others will be injured." She didn't know how else to put it.

He crossed his arms. "And how do you know that my presence, my death, does not prevent even more from coming to come to pass?"

83

She had no answer to that and shook her head. He had a point. But her visions showed her what she needed to *know*, not what needed to happen. Maybe that particular one would still not come to pass. If she kept Shar away from the men of ba, or kept them from the pub... Maybe—

"Bat, I found something." Ailis's voice cut through her thoughts.

Chapter Seven

Bastet,

Why are you not answering? This is why we began to use the texting, and why I signed up for the international usage you told me about. So we could communicate in this rapid manner.
I suppose I will email you later, when I have time.
But… I held a piece of creation in my palm, Bastie.
Creation.
Imagine.
- Bat, who was the clueless goddess

BAT

*A*ilis knelt a few meters behind where Bat and the others stood, her gaze focused on a patch of muddy and churned ground. Her hand hovered over a stone and her fingers twitched, as though she wanted to touch it but didn't quite dare.

Flash. A spear, plainer than the other and wrought from wood and iron and strips of fresh leather. Its head was made of a dark and opalescent stone tipped in shining steel. It rested on a stone anvil in a small forge.

Bat blinked and came back to herself. Though it had been but a moment for her, this particular vision must have taken longer. Most of the men were now gathered around Ailis, only Shar still stood beside her.

Anticipation thrilled through her. She knew what Ailis had found. Taking a breath, she brought her pounding heart under control. Excitement would not be appropriate in such a setting... But she couldn't suppress a slight bounce as she stepped forward.

She reached the circle of men, and Dub and Finn parted to allow her to see exactly what they and the others still stared at. A shard, shining and dark, protruded from the ground. Bat fell to her knees, matching Ailis, and extended her hand. She hesitated for the barest moment, then ran a finger along a protruding edge. There was a brief pain, and then the shard flared.

It reached for her. That was the only way she could define what happened. It reached for her, like a child seeking its mother, which was strange, as this was a piece of the egg that birthed creation.

Ari was right. There *was* something wrong with the vessel. She plucked the shard up and studied the way the light played over it. It was as though the heavens lived in that small piece of stone.

Transferring the shard to her left hand, she turned her right over and watched as the cut along the pad of her finger closed. Gentle waves of reassurance and worry came at her, and she realized that the shard was less like a child and more like a mother, who'd finally found a lost child of its own.

"Is that...?" Cu Chulainn shifted where he stood, a little apart from the others, just to the side of Ari.

"It is a broken piece of the vessel, yes." She studied him, but for the moment all she detected was wonder and a good bit of fear. Climbing to her feet, still carefully holding the shard, she stepped over the patch of mud separating them and held out her empty hand. "I would like to try something."

Killer, coming back from wherever he'd disappeared to, wiggled his way between the various legs and pressed against her thigh. He made not a sound, just stared up at her hand and Cuchi.

Cu Chulainn raised a hand but didn't give it to her. "What will you do?"

Her head tilted. "Feed the vessel, and reassure it that the children are all right."

When Cuchi continued to hesitate, Dub stepped to her side and nudged her shoulder. "Let me go first."

She turned her head and looked into those lapis eyes. Then his gaze fell to the smear of blood on her finger, all that was left of the earlier cut, and those eyes of his narrowed and his frown deepened. But he didn't say anything, instead holding out his own hand for her to take, and locking his gaze with hers once more.

Her chest swelled. He cared. That particular frown... it showed her he cared. She'd known he did, but... And he trusted her—he'd offered her his hand with no hesitation.

The universe held its breath and then exhaled, changing the direction of its course, just as it had when she stepped over the threshold of the bar for the first time, and then once again when she picked up the Uaithne. This moment was a turning point, for her, for the brothers, and for the trials yet to come their way.

Then the corner of his mouth ticked up. "Why do you hesitate? I would think you'd have been waiting for a chance to slice me open."

She let out a short laugh. Taking his hand, she pressed the shard to the thick meat just below his thumb, all the while whispering to the piece of creation she held. She needn't have bothered with the last. The shard recognized Dub—or, recognized the Fomoiri in him—and delicately sipped his blood. The cut was thin, clean, and when the shard had had its fill and reassured herself, a gentle power reached out to close the wound.

Dub's eyes slid closed and he let out a soft sigh, his expression easing into something she would have called wonder on anyone else.

Killer shifted against her and growled, his attention on a deeper patch of shadow on the edge of the trees. Bat blinked and it disappeared.

It reminded her, though, that they were no longer safe here, despite the many wards and protections the men of ba had put in place. And the pub was not safe. Not yet, not until they determined exactly what her vision meant. Where could they go…?

"I need to check in." Finn pulled his cell from his back pocket.

Yes. Perfect. Maybe his would have reception. "We will need to get Mell. And then we will need to go somewhere secure. I would also like to view your books of artifacts again." Shadows stretched across the ground as the sun held onto the last of its time for the day.

Finn grimaced and tucked his phone away. He must not have had reception either. "We can go to the guardi headquarters for now. It's probably got the best security outside of the Tribunal's headquarters."

"I think that is a sound plan," she said when no one spoke with an alternate idea.

Dub's gaze was trained on the place she had seen the shadow a moment ago. "I need to check something," he said, and started toward the spot, not waiting for an answer.

Bat gestured to her pup and Killer went after her not-man, ears forward and tail up. That, more than anything, told her Dub should be well. He disappeared briefly behind a thick trunk.

As soon as he was done, they really did need to leave. No more distraction. Everything that could be done in this place had been. She turned her attention to Ari. "Last chance. I would rather you stayed here, or moved to a new place until this was over."

Ari, his red eyes narrowed, shook his head. "No. I have a purpose too, goddess. And I will fulfill it."

A purpose. She understood that. "Very well." She

would not try to convince him again. "Will the rest of you be all right? I really would recommend locating to another area."

Ari glanced at the handful of survivors. "They will finish seeing to the bodies of the fallen and then find me. They, too, have a purpose."

Bat swallowed. "And maybe, when we are done, you may return home."

Ari turned his large eyes on her, the red glowing like the sun through a film of blood. "I would like that."

Bat, promising herself she would find a way to make that happen, wrapped the shard in the lower half of her sweater to keep it from cutting anyone else. It was a little awkward holding it there like that, but it would have to do for now. Shar grunted, shrugged out of his jacket, and handed it to her, gesturing to the bundle at her middle. She smiled and slipped the jacket on over her shoulders, knowing that wasn't what he had intended her to do. It was still toasty with the heat of her giant, though, and she needed that extra bit of warmth now that the sunlight was fading.

His lips twitched and he shrugged, but not before she caught a slight shaking of his shoulders.

Finn rolled his eyes and pulled off his sweater, revealing the t-shirt beneath. "Use it for the shard," he admonished as he handed it over.

Bat took the sweater, her gaze lingering on the clearly defined muscles of Finn's arms and chest.

"Right." Shar slung his arm over her shoulders and steered her to the tree line. "We need to get going.

Regroup." He pulled her into his side, not harshly, but definitely closer than before.

Dub, his lips pressed thin with anger, caught up with them, Killer at his side. He must have found whatever he looked for in the tree line. Something they had missed on the first inspection?

Finally, they wasted no more time in setting out, cramming themselves back in the truck. Ari and his fellows climbed into the back, pulling a strong glamour around themselves.

First stop, the pub to gather Mell and the raven Einin. Second stop, the guardi headquarters. Third stop? She had no idea.

Chapter Eight

MELL

*M*ell sighed as they entered the main floor of the guardi's open office. Though there were officers scattered through the room, the silence was heavy. Even the pixies had been subdued as their small group had crossed through the yard, only greeting his goddess briefly—with none of the usual exuberance—before returning to their shrubs. Killer had remained behind in the yard, setting himself to guard the entrance to the building. Bat had attempted to coax him inside but he'd refused. The pup had radiated determination, and she'd eventually relented.

Light from the clerestory windows flashed across his eyes as they crossed to the stairs leading to the library, and Oisin's territory. Finn and Cu Chulainn both had insisted that they needed to identify the objects Bat had seen in her recent visions as quickly as possible, before any other talk or planning could be done. She had agreed.

And now here they were.

Mell had kicked everyone out after receiving the call that they were on the way to pick him up. He didn't care if they lost business, or if the fae whispered. There would be no keeping something like this quiet. All that had mattered was seeing that she was all right, that his goddess was fine. He'd paced at the mouth of the alley, the Morrigan's raven perched on his shoulder, as he'd waited for them.

Dub had filled Mell in on what they'd found in the wood, and Shar's reaction. How the youngest brother had sought to keep Bat from the carnage, and how he had refused to put her down. Maybe it was the fact that the devastation had been amongst those precious rowans— and wasn't that another revelation, the sacred rowans weren't lost, just as the cauldron wasn't lost—or maybe it was the mention of Balor, but Shar's protective instincts had gone into overdrive. They'd managed to calm him, but they could not get him to leave her side. He'd even gone so far as to pull her into his lap to make room for Mell in the truck, tucking her against him, his shoulders partially hunched around her. Even now there was a tangle of fear, determination, and need radiating from his younger brother.

And... Mell's thoughts circled back to the one he couldn't escape from. The one that had been harder and harder to hide from Bat, and the one that had begun to trouble him over the last weeks to the point he'd needed to finally lock it away where he kept his memories of the Great War. Except it wouldn't *stay* there...

They'd farked things up with their goddess. *He'd* messed it up. They'd agreed none of them would pursue her until each brother was sure of his reactions and wants. He'd been the one to insist on it originally. He'd wanted her to heal, to have time to become certain that she was wanted no matter what. That they would not leave her, no matter what. He'd wanted her to know there were no demands or stipulations on the offer of a home.

It had backfired magnificently. And today it had blown up in their faces. He and Dub and Shar should have sorted this out with her sooner. They should have told her their plans for the brooch, how they planned to create their independence, and hers, with it. They should have included her in that. And they should have prepared her, told her of the Fomoiris' origins.

The last months had been a mixture of delight and frustration for Mell himself. He'd felt the changes in Bat, how her need for touch and physical comfort had grown. How the brothers' distance—though explained away by the need to keep her decision to stay a secret until the clan meeting was over—had begun to not only frustrate her, but hurt her. How her own decision to keep away for fear of hurting them had begun to tear her emotions in two—and Mell hadn't been able to do a damned thing about any of it, not without a consensus between the brothers. Eventually, he'd had to block himself from feeling her emotions, and that in turn had brought about even more confusion and frustration on her part.

His mistake? Not getting things resolved as soon as

she agreed to stay, two damned months ago. Shar had still been unsure of his reaction to seeing the goddess with someone else, and Dub had managed to focus all his attention on handling things with the clan. It was to the point of an obsession for his older brother. Mell had attempted to steer his brothers into facing the dilemma of what to do with the goddess, but both had either brushed him off or outright refused to listen. They were, the both of them, too stubborn for his and the goddess's good. And as a result, Mell had locked away his own growing frustration and left Bat hanging in the wind, so to speak.

Well, we're in it now. The trouble's found us and grabbed us but good. Not just the fact that Bat's name was on the invitation for the clan gathering—which was two weeks away, something everyone seemed to be conveniently forgetting—but all the emotional entanglements were coming to a head at the same time.

He grimaced, thinking of the sickening emptiness that had entered Bat as she stood in the kitchen doorway, listening to the brothers deny her a place among them. Because that's what their words, and actions, had amounted to. It was this that had finally broken through his self-imposed barriers, and it had hardened his own resolve to kick his brothers into some sort of decision.

But, it looked like he may not have to do much kicking. Dub and Shar, though they didn't have his emotional ability, must have seen some of that emptiness in her eyes, in the not-quite-there smile, the slumped shoulders. They had both been a mixture of guilt, remorse, and resolve.

They'd begun to wake up. Finally. He'd corner them soon, and they would sort this ridiculous situation.

Shar raised a hand to Bat's head as they neared the back stairs. It hung there, hovering just over where her dark hair fell in sleek sheets. Caution, longing, protectiveness, and a quiet fear radiated from his younger brother. Then the hand fell without making contact.

Mell himself wasn't immune to that protective instinct. He wanted to sweep Bat away and back to the pub, to hide her away from whatever they'd fallen into the middle of. His gut clenched as he remembered the expression she'd worn when he'd slid into the truck. In a remote voice, she'd told him of her suspicions regarding the invitation, that it had somehow been used to spy on them. From the emotions hitting him, it was obvious the others had already heard this from her. Bat herself was shrouded in a thin layer of shock, but under it, there was a seething tangle of loss, bewilderment, concern, and anger.

Mell stiffened as Finn laid a possessive hand on his goddess's lower back and ushered her into the library. Shar hunched his shoulders but didn't protest or pull her away. Dub, just behind Mell on the stairs, growled.

And, more than the rest, *that* was where he'd messed up. Had they missed their chance with her?

Reality hit him like a charging bull that afternoon as she stood out in the garden with Finn. Mell wasn't sure exactly what the sidhe had said to her, but her reaction was obvious. Longing and relief and desire.

And now Finn stood right where Mell wanted to be, touched her how he wanted to. All Mell sensed from his goddess at the tender gesture was… a warm acceptance, a bit of affection, and that same relief. She welcomed the touch.

He couldn't even be too upset about it. He just... wished he was the one who was finally giving her what she needed, and—

"Get yer head out of yer ass." Dub's growled words were low, his emotions locked down. "Now is no' the time ta lose yer thoughts because of a woman."

They'd just reached the doorway themselves, and Mell paused on the threshold to study his brother. Dub's shoulders were back and his brows drawn, but the usual scowl was missing. He gazed at where Bat now sat, flanked by Finn and Shar.

Then he focused on Mell. "She's no goin' anywhere." But his accent was still in full force, and there was a questioning tilt to the statement.

"No, brother. She's not going anywhere." Mell hoped he wasn't lying. His resolve wavered.

Dub gave a sharp nod and strode into the room, taking a seat across from Bat, and Mell followed. Ailis and Cu Chulainn, the raven on his shoulder once more, came in after them.

Oisin approached from the rear shelves as they found their seats. Ailis had been strangely silent since the wood, as had Cu Chulainn. The Morrigan's "back-up" took the seat farthest from Bat. The four men of ba also crowded at the end of the table.

Bat set the bundled jumper she'd been carrying on the table and unwrapped the treasure. Mell's breath caught as a rush of emotion hit him, coming from each person gathered at the table. And the strongest was from Bat herself, followed by Dub. Wonder and reverence.

"I need to tell you *all* of what I saw. And then we can work out the strategy," his goddess said, her fingers lingering on the shard. She told them of each vision she'd had that day, starting with the blood-covered brooch, and ending with the second spear. Only twice did she hesitate. She also left out whatever she'd seen of him, and for that he was grateful.

There was silence as she finished, each of them processing her words.

"Balor," Finn finally whispered. "The bomen said Balor was coming back."

"And to find Tir Hudi. Which is a myth even for us." Shar propped his elbows on the table and bent his head to his hands.

Bat looked at them all, eyes wide. Her gaze settled on him, shining and pleading. Fear reflected in those dark depths.

"We'll figure it out," Mell said, reassuring her and himself at the same time.

Oisin stood, his face blank. "Well, protocol and all that. I'll be back." He strode toward the back stacks, and no doubt to one of his books of weapons for identification.

The silence descended once more. It was ridiculous. Why was no one talking, planning, sorting things out? It was as though they were held is some weird suspended animation, just waiting for the next horrible thing to happen, the next axe to fall, or sword to swing. Even Bat. Where was the goddess who insisted she would help? The one who ran for her Idiot's Guide to Ireland, or dragged them to Ailis's shop downtown? The goddess who faced down a crazed Grainne under Benbulben?

"I'm sorry!" he burst out. All eyes turned to him, and he swallowed. Where were all his fancy words now? Why did they elude him? "We should have predicted you'd be included in the invitation, and prepared accordingly. Dub arranged for it before we knew you would stay. And, we should have told you about our plans for the brooch, and the history of the Fomoiri, and the banshees, and the bomen. Well, we didn't know about the bomen. Ba men." Focusing on Bat, he ignored the others gathered around the table, especially his brothers. "We should have told you so many things."

Her eyes widened and her lips trembled, then the corners lifted.

"There are still things we need to say. That I need to say." He tried to tell her, without telling her, just how he felt. He interjected his need to hold her, to see her happy and whole and smiling through her existence, no matter the reason. He couldn't let it go another minute, and screw his brothers.

She opened her mouth, closed it, and opened it again. "But now is not the time," she finally said. Her expression was soft, and she leaned forward, just a little. Shar's hand went to her neck—without hesitation this time—and cradled the delicate length in his palm. Finn's hand massaged her shoulder. She didn't pull away from either touch. In fact, she relaxed into it, and he could sense the comfort she took from the two men, and from Mell's own words.

Mell's stomach churned as he focused on the hands on

her. Again, it was not jealousy he felt, but a regret that he had blinded himself to what she truly needed. The O'Loinsigh brothers were not very good protectors of the goddess, not if they were going to be neglecting her in such a manner…

Her eyes narrowed. "Wait. Banshees? Meera? The others? They are from Egypt?" She blew out a breath. "They never said a word."

"The Egyptians don't have a great reputation in Ireland," Cu Chulainn said, the raven giving a caw of confirmation.

Mell glared at the guardi, still not quite believing the braggart was here. Anger and resentment flared. How Dub and Shar had not pounded the man into the ground, he didn't know. His hands curled into fists. They *were the ones who'd been wronged*…

A heavy hand landed on his shoulder and tightened. He flinched. His brother was barely suppressing his strength. Mell twisted his head and eyed Dub. The oldest brother had his gaze trained on Finn's hand, and his cool was cracking, leaking anger into the air.

Oh.

Mell gathered the scraps of his own control.

Bat looked down and bit her lip, unaware of the undercurrents around her. Or doing a very good job of ignoring them. "What is said of us?"

Everyone shifted. Her eyes flashed. "Do not think to continue 'protecting' me in such a way." She focused on Mell.

So he plunged in again. "I am not sure about the banshees, but generally, the Egyptian gods are considered selfish, greedy, and overgrown. They grab for power any way they can, and would think nothing of forcing other gods and immortals from their homes."

Her head tilted and she was silent, her gaze far away, but lacking stars. She was simply thinking. "Why? Oh, we can be all of those things, especially amongst each other, but I do not recall a time when we invaded another land. If anything, we have struggled against *being* invaded."

Mell had no answer to that. Not one that made sense, at least. After living with her these last months, he knew she was not like that. But her own people had also neglected her, so she may be the outlier. However, she was his *only* experience with the Egyptian deities. And the stories his father and the other Fomoiri had told…

"Stupid tales, passed down by so-called elders," Dub said, picking up the explanations. His hand was still hard on Mell's shoulder, but his tone reflected none of that. "That we were driven out, that we fled persecution, slavery, and even murder. That if the Egyptians ever came here, they would steal our greatest treasures."

Mell's eyes widened even as Bat's narrowed and the raven cawed. Everyone else remained still in their seats, fearing to draw attention to themselves in the moment. Pressure built in the air, and the goddess's emotions were a swirl, changing too fast for Mell to pinpoint.

And then she laughed. She threw her head back and nearly roared. She laughed so hard tears leaked from her eyes. There was astonishment there, and a little bitterness, but mostly he sensed her humor at the situation. When he thought she may be done, she peeked at the faces around her and started up again.

Oisin returned, an old leather volume held in one hand. "Um. What did I miss?"

It set Bat off again. Finn gave the other man a sheepish smile and shrugged.

"The Egyptian goddess has gone insane," Cuchi said.

And *that* was when *Dub* went off. But not in laughter. His anger swelled and finally burst from the fragile shields that had been holding it back.

He leapt from his chair, putting extra strength in his movements so that all Mell grasped when he tried to stop his brother was air. In a fraction of a second, Dub was at the other end of the table, the collar of Cuchi's shirt clutched in his fist. Then the guardi captain was across the room, tossed like he was nothing more than a doll stuffed with wool. He crashed into the wall as though he was stone.

Mell, Finn, and Ailis jumped to their feet as Dub sped to the dazed guardi, pulled back his fist, and struck. The crunch of Cu Chulainn's nose under his fist was loud as Bat's laughter faded.

"This is for me." Dub hit him again, easily avoiding the blocks Cuchi tried to throw up. "This is for my brother." Another hit, this one catching the other man's chin. With each blow, Dub's anger eased, though there was still enough of it to keep the beating going for some time. "This one is for your lies." Dub struck again, and Cuchi moving just in time to keep his jaw from breaking, though he was still dazed.

He must have hit his head on the wall. It was the only reason Mell could think of that the sidhe wasn't fighting back.

"This one is for Derbforgaill." Dub pulled his fist back once more and Cuchi stopped struggling.

"She begged me. If anyone lied in that situation, it was not me." Cuchi shot Dub a bloody smile, an asshole to the end.

Dub's anger swelled once more and he struck. "And this one. This one is for my goddess."

"Dub," Bat said, her tone indulgent but firm.

The eldest brother paused, his fist raised. Mell cut his attention back to Bat. She was still seated, Shar beside her, and a dark satisfaction flitted through her expression.

Dub pushed away from the guardi, leaving him slumped against the wall. There was something wrong with Cu Chulainn's right arm... He was trying to use it to straighten from the wall, but it hung limp against his side.

"It will even out in a little while," Bat said, her gaze on Cuchi. "You should be able to use it for most tasks, but do not try to use your sword. Oh, and you will want to begin practicing with your left arm."

Mell exchanged a look with Oisin, the only other person in the room who didn't seem to know what was going on. Ailis let out a sharp laugh, full of wicked mirth. Finn's eyes slid closed and he shook his head. Shar wore a pleased smile. The men of ba nodded knowingly, and Dub...

Well, Dub was headed straight for the goddess, heat in his eyes.

Finn shifted to partially block Bat and held up a hand. "Not in anger."

Mell snorted as Dub pushed Finn aside and leaned over Bat. "That's not anger."

Chapter Nine

Bastie,

He kissed me! My grumpy one kissed me again!

FINALLY.

- Bat, the goddess with a bit of hope, and who wishes you'd
answer

p.s. – this is not all the news. Things are moving too
quickly to fill you in this way. I will try calling in a
moment.

BAT

*D*ub's gaze pierced into her. Suddenly his hands were around her upper arms, and he pulled her up.

Then his lips were on hers. The kiss was hard, fierce, and his movements sharp. But the heat of him spread through her, and she softened, sinking into his hold. Bat opened her mouth beneath his and welcomed him into her.

This was what she'd been missing. He'd kissed her, the once, and then nothing.

Now he kissed her again, staking his claim. And that's what it was. He was showing the world, well, Cuchi, just who this goddess belonged to.

Bat lifted her hands and clutched at his sides. He still held her upper arms firmly, and she couldn't reach around him, but this was just fine as well.

She slid her tongue along his, and he pulled back to nip at her lower lip before diving back into her mouth. His hands slid up her arms and to her neck, cradling her, his thumbs brushing against her jaw. The strokes were short, smooth and enticing.

She wrapped her arms all the way around his waist and pressed against him, reveling in the firm muscles.

This. Yes, this.

"Guys."

A throat cleared.

Someone snickered.

"Guys."

A new heat appeared behind her, close enough she could sense it, but not so close she could feel the person's body. New hands gripped her arms and she moaned. How had they not done this for two months? Two whole months since they'd really touched her...

How she'd wanted them. Dub. Shar. Mell. And now Finn. The four of them, they would be perfect...

The four of them.

Grainne's visage flashed before her.

Four of them.

She crashed back to reality just as Mell succeeded in pulling her from his brother.

Oh, gods, what had she done? There was a reason she was holding back from them. She stared, eyes wide, at Dub. He was breathing heavily, his face drawn in tight lines. His hands still cradled her neck, the oh so careful strength there speeding her heart once more.

Mell stepped back, taking her with him, until they'd backed to the first row of bookshelves. She pulled her attention from the oldest brother and found Shar. Her giant stared at her, lips tight and cheeks flushed. Finn took a step toward her, swallowed, and stopped.

"Well, that happened." Ailis leaned back in her chair. "Thank goodness. Now we can all stop prancing around the issue." She pointed at Bat. "Ya all want her." She pointed at the brothers in turn, hesitated a moment, her expression thoughtful, then pointed at Finn. "And she wants all of ya." The pointing finger turned into a wave of her hand. "Ya need to all just go get this out of yer systems. Or at least settle it. But not now. Now we have ta figure out what the hell is going on."

Bat stared at her. Ailis was right. They should not be kissing or seducing or thinking of sex at a time like this. The men of ba had just been practically slaughtered, and she was worried about *kisses*...

"The goddess has her needs. We should not be impinging on them," Ari said, as though he sensed her thoughts.

Bat's cheeks heated. Dub sucked in a deep breath and uncurled his clenched fists. Mell soothed his hands over her arms. Shar, his face flushed, straightened her chair and waited for her to be seated.

Finn rolled his shoulders and nodded to Ailis. "The fae is correct." Heated green eyes met hers and he licked his lips. "I do want you. And we need to get on with our planning."

Dub jerked and closed his eyes. He was on the edge of his control.

Bat stepped forward. "I am being a wanker."

Shar and Dub's brows drew together, and the youngest brother opened his mouth, but she cut him off.

"I am. I am worried about my feelings, hiding in my anger and fear when there is something so much bigger confronting us."

Mell's hand settled against her back. "You deserve to be angry."

Did she? Maybe. *Yes.* But they could not afford it, not now. Not with the vessel stolen, a possible attack coming against the pub, and the O'Loinsighs' father most likely conspiring with Balor. "I will be." She focused on Dub. "Later." The word held a promise, not just of her anger, but of everything else still unsaid. "For now, we need a plan." She held her hand out to Dub. "Sit by me?"

As Dub stepped forward and slid his callused hand into her much smaller one, she came to a realization. She couldn't continue as she had. And she was unwilling to give up her new home, or any of the brothers or Finn. She didn't want just part of them, though. She didn't just want a warm room or the pub or friends. She didn't want a temple, refuge or supplicants. She didn't only want nights with music and Guinness and admittedly wonderful scenery in the form of wide shoulders and flashing eyes. She wanted the kisses and caresses and heated nights. She wanted to be able to hold them to her, and comfort them when they needed it. She wanted to be able to speak the words that Horus and Seth had never needed or wanted from her. She wanted... She wanted it all.

She deserved it all.

Finn glanced between the two of them, then pulled back his shoulders and rounded the table to take Dub's previous seat. Bat sent him a grateful smile, hoping he could see that this was not a rejection of him, merely what needed to happen in this moment.

As everyone resumed their seats, Dub leaned into her. "I will not be letting you go." The low words were a promise. "Ever. Know that."

His words settled into her and nestled next to the promise she had just made to herself. Her eyes slid closed and she took that moment to revel in the feeling of being wanted. "Thank you," she whispered. Then she pulled her back straight and focused on Oisin, who still stood near the head of the table. "Let us begin."

He set the book before her. She remembered how this went. She used the drawings to identify the weapons and artifacts from her visions. Oisin had the volume flipped to the beginning pages this time.

The Cauldron. It didn't look like half of an egg. It did look like a large pot, with a curved lip and everything. She thought back to her vision. There *had* been a slight difference between the body of the object and the rim.

Tracing a light finger over the drawing, she chose her

words. "It is this, the vessel. But someone disguised it. The rim is stone and iron, and false."

Oisin nodded and flipped a few pages.

She shook her head. The sword was close, but not quite what she had seen. This had a red stone in the pommel, and the blade was too thin.

Oisin turned to the next sheet.

"This one. With the green stone. A dark shadow flowed from the tip."

"It is Nuada's," Oisin said.

Cu Chulainn snorted but held his words.

The next picture showed the spear. "This is the first spear I saw, in the possession of the dark-haired man. I did not recognize him, and only saw him from the back, really. But his ship led others, and they headed into a storm."

"It could be metaphorical," Mell mused.

"Or literal, if it is one of the Fomoiri who holds it," Dub countered.

Finn leaned forward, hands clasped before him. "No one should hold it. The artifacts, other than the cauldron that was lost and the harp that was waiting, are locked away."

"Are they?" Bat cut her gaze to the crow. It had claimed the back of the chair nearest Ari.

Feathers ruffled and the raven twisted its head, but made no answer. Finn's and Cuchi's eyes narrowed and their lips thinned, the similarity of their expressions reminding her once again that they were both captains of the fae's guardi. They held their silence. They were, after all, under the Morrigan's command.

"If I ever become that cryptic and uncooperative, please shake me until I come to my senses," Bat murmured to Dub.

He raised a brow. "Okay."

She gave him a light slap. "You are supposed to protest."

"I will spank you, then."

Heat pooled and her lower belly tightened.

"Guys." Ailis waved a hand. "Focus."

Bat cleared her throat and kept her gaze on the drawings in front of her. "Yes. Well, I did not get the sense that these visions were too far removed in time."

Oisin tapped the book. "We have more to identify."

Bat laid her hand over his and met the man's too calm gaze. "We won't find the other in here. It has yet to be created."

"Someone is gathering the treasures and preparing for war. And we know who that someone is, or at least who is directing them. He is crafty." Cu Chulainn leaned back in his chair, frowning, gaze thoughtful.

They all stared.

"What? I am not always an idiot, as you all seem to believe. Some have even called me wise."

"He's right." Oisin drew the volume away from her and carefully closed it. "Unless these were visions of the past?" he asked Bat.

"No. Sometimes it is difficult to pinpoint an exact time, but most of these were not of the past. And I, too, believe Cuchi is correct. They are gather—" Her breath caught and it took her a moment to force the next question out. "Where was the harp when you left the pub?" she asked Mell.

He shot to his feet. "By the hearth. I didn't even think of it. No one has so much as touched it until you came."

"Farking bollix. He can't get his hands on the harp." Finn pushed back his chair. "I'll transport us. No time to take the truck. We'll grab the harp, come right back here, and then finish sorting out the next steps."

Bat rose as well, her heart pounding. She wasn't sure what exactly the harp did, other than enhance emotions, but those were powerful things indeed. If this Balor needed all the artifacts she had seen, then they needed to prevent him from acquiring this last one. "Can you take us—"

Dub pushed her back down into her seat. "No. We—" he gestured to Finn "—will go. I need you here, working with the ba men to see if you can figure out exactly how Balor—who is *dead*—plans to come back."

Caw.

The raven half flew, half glided to land in the space before Bat. *Let them go. It will give us time to discuss things.*

"I will not keep secrets." Bat was very clear on this. Secrets had gotten them into this mess.

The raven's head cocked. *Well, I will let you make that decision. But sometimes secrets are a kindness.*

Bat pressed her lips together, refusing to agree.

"Dub, Mell and I will go," Finn said. "Shar and the men of ba will remain here, and you may strategize with Oisin."

She noted he was leaving those she'd seen in her alleyway vision of death here with her, and that he carefully did not mention Cu Chulainn, who was now effectively hobbled. The other guardi sat in stony silence, his fists clenched on the table before him.

Ari stood. "We will go with you. As I told the goddess, we have a purpose."

"Which is to guard the cauldron, not the harp," Finn pointed out. "And the best way you can guard it, is to find it. Am I correct in thinking you have some kind of connection to it?"

Ari bared his teeth, but nodded. "You are correct, sidhe." He looked to his companions then nodded, slowly. "We will remain this time. As you said, our duty is to the cauldron."

Thank you. She thought the sentiment to Finn, sure he would not hear her, for that was not his power, but hopeful he would at least feel her gratitude.

Mell's brow rose. He at least had felt it. Good. Dub stepped toward the door, and she grabbed his wrist, tugging until he bent down. "You will bring them, and yourself, back in one piece. There will be no missing limbs, and no wounds that will hamper our mission." *Or your life.* "Do you understand?"

Dub pressed a hard kiss to her lips. "Yes, goddess. I will keep your playthings safe."

Mell snorted. "That sounds more like my line."

Dub straightened and glared at his brother. "Stop yapping." Then he headed for the door, Finn just behind him. Mell shrugged and went after the other two men. They had just opened the door when Bat called out.

"Wait." She focused on Cuchi and the power that wrapped around his right arm. "I am modifying your curse. You may lift your sword, but only in defense of the O'Loinsighs and Finn. None other, not even me." For another sword to defend her men, she was willing to do this.

Cu Chulainn's eyes widened as he flexed his arm. But he rose and joined the other three men at the door without a word.

"Are you sure about that?" Ailis asked on a whisper.

"I would think you, of all of us, would appreciate the irony," Bat replied as Mell closed the door behind him. She held onto her control. It would not do to go running after them. Finn and Dub were correct. It was smarter to divide their resources. Still, she didn't like that they were gone from her sight, even with the extra defense she'd provided in the form of an asshole.

Goddess of Egypt. The raven hopped closer to her. *They will be well. I do not have much time. The others are suspicious of me, and have started monitoring my actions.*

"Others?"

The other deities. The Tribunal. We have a seer. She has predicted some of what is to come. Know that, if I could have, I would have prevented all of this. But things were set in motion long before any of us were aware of Balor's plans. And now there is a very narrow path of success that you must travel. After observing you these last couple of months, I have to admit Ruith was correct —you are the one to handle this.

"What is 'this'?"

The raven twisted its head and ducked, eyeing her hungrily. Or what Bat thought was hunger. *Just what the elder man of ba told you. Balor seeks resurrection.*

"Is he in the blades?"

Oisin sucked in a breath and Ailis stared at her with wide eyes, any previous mischief wiped from her expression. Shar's hand crept to the nape of her neck and kneaded, slowly. Ari and his companions showed no sign of shock. But then, they knew so much the other immortals seemed to have forgotten.

He is in Nuada's sword. We think.

"Was he the one guarded?"

The Morrigan hesitated. *No. Or, not the only one. The being held by the smaller blades is secure, for now.*

"Who is it?"

That is a secret better left kept. You are a curious one, though.

"I've learned recently that there is much of this world kept from me, despite the fact I am a goddess."

Caw-aw-aw-aw-aw-aw. The goddess laughed.

"I am glad I can amuse you. Is there anything else you are willing to tell me?"

The raven mantled and hopped, but did not leave. *You will need to restore the cauldron. You will need the second spear. And you will need to bring back he of the evil eye before you may defeat him.*

"Why are you, and the other Irish deities, not handling this, if you know so much?" It seemed like they were doing this the hard way. If the Morrigan knew the cauldron would be taken, that the spear and the swords would be taken, why not simply stop it before it began?

You, more than anyone, should know the answer to that.

She ignored the non-answer. "When was the sword taken? I assume it has gone missing, along with the spear I saw."

Six months ago, before you arrived.

Also about the same time her visions of Ireland began. Even then things had been in motion. Had Finn known? Why did he not say anything when she first talked of the sword? His and Cuchi's tight expressions when the possibility had been mentioned came back to her. No, he had not known. The Morrigan, all the gods, were keeping secrets from their own.

We do not know everything. We do not know how he escaped in the first place, or how the sword went missing. All we can do is follow the paths laid down by she who is more powerful than any deity.

"I met her once. Fate. She seemed nice. Told me people blamed her for more than she deserved."

Caw. But it sounded as much like a snort as a raven could make. *I've met the bitch too, and believe me, she is a bitch.*

Bat held her silence on that. "Is there *anything* else you will tell me?"

It will get bloody, and there will be death. You can not allow this to deter you, and you must trust yourself. As you said, your visions are never without a reason.

There wasn't really anything she could say to that.

Trust yourself, the Morrigan repeated. *And your companions. The brothers, my Finn. The fae and the bomen and the banshees and pixies. Even Cuchi. And, oh, how I will use that name from this point.*

Bat didn't like the other goddess calling Finn *hers*, but let it go. "Did they all really come from my homeland?"

The raven shrugged. *Probably. It's not as if I ever stopped to have tea and a chat. I mostly tried to kill them. They only recently learned to play well with others. And before you ask, no, I do not know the truth of why they came to this land. But based on what dealings I did have with Balor before he was slain, I would trust the bomen over whatever tales are passed down in the Fomoiri clans.*

Bat thought over these words. Balor. A Fomoiri. Who was taxed by Seth to take the vessel from Egypt, but then never returned to the war. Who, from what Ari had said, had used the vessel for his own gain.

Maybe Isfet had not won the war in Egypt, but it seemed chaos had won at least one battle.

"Morrigan?" she asked. "Why me?"

The raven cawed, leapt to the air with wings stretched, and flew to the top of a nearby shelf. There was no answer.

Bat took a breath, gathered her thoughts, and turned to the men of ba. Shar was a reassuring bulk beside her, and Ailis and Oisin looked ready to leap to their feet and follow her merest whim.

"Ari. Tell me all you know of Balor." The shard had been pushed to a corner of the table at some point, still nestled in Finn's sweater. She pulled it in front of her and ran a careful finger down the length.

Chapter Ten

DUB

*A*s soon as they materialized at the mouth of the alley, Dub sketched a quick rune of hiding and opened his senses. He had no special power there, but he had been trained as a warrior by one of the best. Whatever he thought of his father as a father, or a man, he was undoubtedly a formidable fighter.

A warrior was always aware of his surroundings. He'd grown complacent, if Bat was correct in her assumptions of the invitation. He should have sensed the attached spell, and the wards should have averted it.

Beside him, Finn and Mell scanned the alley.

"Clear?" he asked.

"Wait." Mell stared at the far end, where the alley opened again onto Tobergal Lane. A shadow moved there.

Dub gathered strength and poised to attack. He'd

found no traces of Scath in the trees around the glade, but what he'd seen, combined with the shadow hounds Bat had glimpsed in her vision—and who the invitation had been sent by—were enough that he suspected his father's lieutenant—and his father as well—of deep involvement in this quest to revive Balor.

Both Mell and Shar were too young to remember the old bastard, but Dub had been unlucky enough to bear that particular privilege. Balor had been cruel, coarse, and power hungry. He'd stirred the men with promises of riches and freedom to do as they pleased, preached the mightiness of taking what you were due.

And Dub had followed him as well. For a time.

Balor had a quality about him, one that riled you, and teased and seduced you, into believing his way was the right way.

As soon as Puchi had mentioned his name, things had begun to come clear to Dub.

"Scath?" Dub asked.

Finn cocked his head, a hunter scenting prey, then shook his head. "No." He drew in a deep breath. "But he was here. And recently."

The shadows shifted yet again, and dissolved into a dark and stooped figure. It shuffled closer, tattered robes hanging from twisted shoulders. Its skin was rough, wrinkled like the ba men's, yet translucent like a wisp's. Instead of lights and pastels, though, this figure swirled with darkness. When it was half-way, it lifted its head, revealing blue lips and bright red eyes. Fangs flashed then disappeared back into the dark, and the robes shifted and bunched at the back, as though there were more limbs hidden under there than there should be.

Dub called his sword from the fold of space he stored it in and readied himself. A sluagh. If it had sided with Balor…

"Hold," Mell whispered.

The figure drew even with Shar's garden, stepping into a stay beam from the streetlights, and changed, pulling on a mask of humanity.

Was that…?

"Faolan?" Dub had never cared for this particular immortal, but he was fairly certain Faolan hadn't sided with anyone. This sluagh preferred to keep his allegiances free.

"Can ya get me ta the goddess?" Faolan shuffled forward another step, then stumbled, falling to one knee. "I saved it."

Dub looked to Mell who nodded, telling him Faolan was sincere. Dub went to the sluagh, Finn and Mell flanking him as Cu Chulainn, whose presence he'd been attempting to forget, remained at the mouth of the alley, facing out, ready for anything that came from that direction.

Dub knelt, matching the sluagh. "What did ya save?"

"The Uaithne. Bastards came for it, but its no theirs, now is it? None but the goddess should have it now. So I snuck in after them." He grinned his evil smile, then coughed. Blood speckled his lips and the sluagh licked it away. "Yer wards suck, Dub O'Loinsigh. Ya should fix tha'."

"Finn? Can you?" Dub asked. Whatever had injured the sluagh, it wasn't a soul blade, or even Nuada's sword. If it had been, the fae would be dead already. They needed him healed. If he passed out before they got all the information they could from him, who knew what they could miss.

Finn nodded and headed for the small hose tucked in a corner of the garden.

"Faolan," Dub said, his voice sharp. He needed the sluagh to focus. "What happened?"

"Well, ya closed too early, and I didn't get me pint. I was just waiting. A man's got to have his pint, now doesn't he? And then these shadows, no mine, mind ya, come sneaking around, prying at the door, at the locks, at the windows, till they finally went down the flue. If I'd know the pub was weak there..." He shook his head.

"Faolan, focus for me."

The sluagh rolled his head and it flopped back, another smile flashing fangs he usually kept hidden. He pulled his head forward as Finn stepped beside them, hands carefully cupped together. "I saved it," Faolan continued. "Me shadows are better. I hid it, but they got me. Not fatal, mind ya. Never fatal for me." The red of his eyes dimmed. "But it burns, it does, to hold it so. Only meant for the goddess."

"Finn."

The guardi knelt and held his hands to Faolan's mouth. "Drink, sluagh, and if you bite me, so help me I will sneak a lann de anam from the vaults of the gods and finish your misery."

Dim red eyes rolled, but Faolan stretched his head forward and slowly sipped from the sidhe's hands. A bit of light returned to his gaze and his shoulders straightened, though he didn't rise. "Ye'll take me to her? I'll not hand the harp to any but her."

Dub stiffened and moved his hand back to his sword. Was this a trick? Had Faolan chosen a side after all?

Mell's hand fell to his shoulder. "He tells the truth. All he wants is to give the harp back."

"He can give it to me."

"And how do I know ye'll take it ta her? No. None but her shall have it from my hands. I know who your father is, and who serves him."

"If you were so suspicious of us, why show yerself?" Did Faolan really think they would side with their father?

"Because I know ya as well." Faolan licked his lips, then licked Finn's lingers.

The sidhe jerked his hands away and stood. "I'm going to see what else I can find."

"I'm no taking the harp out till we're with her. My shadows hide it. My shadows are verra good."

"Good enough to penetrate the wood around Benbulben?" Dub didn't release his sword. Shadows. There were too many shadows.

Red eyes darted to his. "I'm not picking sides, Fomoiri. Some things just belong where they belong. And... she's played me a song, just for me. Can't have a power-hungry idjet go ruining something like that, now can we?"

Dub sighed. The sluagh's words rang with truth. Well, as much as it would ever hold. And, he knew the power of those songs, and her generous smiles. "Fine." He stood, gesturing for Faolan to rise as well. "We'll finish here, and then we'll make sure the harp gets to her, one way or the other."

Faolan stepped toward the mouth of the alley, and Dub settled the tip of his sword at the sluagh's throat. He needed to make sure he was understood. "There will be no pranks, no bargains, no tricks. You will return the harp to her."

The sluagh nodded and Dub lowered the sword. He looked to Finn. "I want to do a full sweep of the pub, and grab that invitation. I assume the guardi has a secure place we could trace the seeing spells?"

"Of course." He turned to the mouth of the alley. "Cu Chulainn, we have this side secure. Could you patrol the front, scan for any watchers, or traps laid?"

The other guardi captain gave a jerk of his head and disappeared back onto the street.

"You're asking him?" Dub wasn't sure how he felt about that. Finn was more the type to order, rather than request.

Finn shrugged. "He *is* a guardi captain, whatever you feel of his accomplishments."

Mell was at the back door, looking it over for more overt signs of tampering. He stepped back and looked over his shoulder. "Finn, could you check it? I don't see anything, but I don't have your tracking abilities."

"Are we going after them tonight?" Finn asked as he took Mell's place on the back stoop.

Dub's first instinct was to say yes. He wanted to find whoever had invaded his territory, hunt them down and make them pay for the violation. Not just of his home, but of his goddess's. How dare they come in, and seek her possessions, defile her sense of security? Put that look of fear into her beautiful eyes…

"Dub?" Mell appeared before him. "Ya need to pull it together." His brother placed a hand on either shoulder and shook. "We're not going anywhere but back to the guardi headquarters, and forming a plan."

Dub shook his head and blinked, focusing on Mell's wide brown eyes and the soothing waves he emitted. *Calm. Have to remain calm.*

"That's right. We just need to finish here, and then get back to her, all right?"

"We should get her coat. And those thick socks she likes." That was what he'd do. He'd pack up her favorite things while they were here, make sure no one would take them. He wasn't sure they'd be able to come back to the pub right away, at least not until they found someone who could lay stronger wards than he was capable of. He'd put back the basic ones before they left, to keep the riff-raff out, but those wouldn't be enough to keep his goddess truly safe, not now.

"Dub." Finn's sharp tone snapped him back to the current task.

Dammit to all the hells and afterworlds and lakes of brimstone in existence. Get your head in the game. Dub took a few more breaths to even his breathing. "Watch this one," he told Mell, gesturing to Faolan. "And keep your senses open."

His brother gave him a simple nod, and refrained from pointing out that Dub was the one who needed to keep his senses keen. Dub joined Finn on the stoop. "What do you have?"

"At least four, including Scath. I don't know the others,

but then, I haven't met all the Fomoiri. One of them does have the taste of a Fir Bolg, or one of their descendants. Possibly a sluagh, and not Faolan—I know his scent."

"So the neutrals *are* taking sides." That wasn't good news. There were many creatures who preferred to be left alone and out of the struggles of general power. It worked well for everyone that way. If Balor or his agents were bending those creatures to their side, this was going to be more difficult than tracking down a mythical island, fixing one of the lost treasures of the sidhe, and killing an immortal who was once considered as powerful as the gods.

Yeah, they were fucked.

"Which means we need to begin gathering our own allies." Finn stared intently at the door's lock for a few more seconds, then began scanning the edges of the jamb and trim. "We've got a good start."

Dub snorted. "One sluagh and a handful of bomen. And we don't know the enemy's forces."

"Don't forget the pixies. And whoever else Ailis knows. The leprechauns and the wisps. Hell, the guardi. I'm sure a few of the sidhe could be convinced to stir themselves."

"We're going to get ourselves killed."

Finn's lips twitched up. "But think of it. One more great battle." He stepped back. "That's it. Other than Faolan, and those of us who gathered earlier, I sense four others, much more recently."

Dub began probing at the pub's wards, looking for the weak point. Unless all four intruders had come down the flue, there must have been another way in. They seemed intact, which was more disturbing than finding them obliterated.

He traced a quick scanning rune. The lower level appeared clear. He was mid sketching a second one specifically for the upper level, when a crash sounded from the front door.

Dub aborted the scan. No sense in wasting the energy now. "Mell."

"On it." Mell ran to the street and cut left, toward the front of the pub.

Twisting the knob, Dub found the door locked. Of course it was.

He pushed, breaking the door frame and crushing the knob. He'd fix it later. "Hide," he shot over his shoulder to the sluagh. Shadows swept over Faolan and he faded into the night as Dub and Finn entered the kitchen.

Scuffs and muffled shouts came from the common room. Cuchi and Mell fought against three men. One, another sluagh, grinned and rushed them. This one was shirtless, and gave Dub a good view of what the creatures usually kept hidden under their clothes or wrapped in glamour—wings. The membranes were dark, but so thin what little light filtered in from the street turned them nearly translucent. The bones were delicate, and tipped in wicked claws.

The sluagh leapt, using his wings to propel himself into Finn.

Can't let him get to Faolan. They must have been watching, waiting for the other sluagh to show himself, and the harp. Dub didn't see Scath, but that also didn't mean he wasn't here.

Cu Chulainn let out a roar and swung his sword, fighting off a bald warrior the size of Shar. A second man, shorter but nearly as wide, charged Mell, propelling the two of them through the front window of the pub and out into the street.

Dub took a precious few seconds to sketch a silence rune, hoping none of the neighbors came to investigate. The last thing they needed was to involve the human guardi in this mess.

Finn cried out and Dub sprang toward the sluagh, who was just pulling a knife from the sidhe's shoulder. Dub's sword sliced through the left wing, shredding the membrane. The sluagh pulled away from Finn and jumped to the side, shrieking. The sound was piercing enough the fae could have passed for a banshee.

It slashed out and Dub caught the thing's wrist, twisting. Bone snapped with a sharp crack and it shrieked again.

I will make you scream forever. Dub swung his opponent around and into the stone hearth, relishing the crash and the smear of blood it left behind. As had happened earlier with Cu Chulainn, his anger surged forward and took control, and this time he allowed it to reign.

Stalking past broken chairs and splinters of wood, he snagged the thing's hair and, barely avoiding the flashing claws on the wings, flashed his sword into the pocket of space, freeing his fist. He wanted the hand to hand, to know his own flesh destroyed, and not a mere sword. Dub struck the sluagh across the check; teeth flew and more bone snapped. He hit again.

A hand landed on his shoulder and he spun, growling.

Finn stepped back from him, one hand raised in surrender. The other hung limp at his side. The sidhe grinned, small flecks of blood on his lower jaw and blending with his hair. His green eyes sparked. "It's out, Dub. You're not accomplishing anything anymore."

Dub looked back at the limp figure in his hold and grunted. Dropping it, he wrested control of himself. Mell and Cu Chulainn stood in the street outside, two more figures at their feet.

"Got yerself?" Finn asked.

Dub gave him a sharp nod. He didn't, not quite, but it was good enough.

Finn surveyed him a moment longer then spun away, opened the front door, and stepped up to the others, speaking low. Soon, the four of them were gathered in the pub's common room, three bodies sprawled before them.

The room was a wreck. The booths and the bar were pretty much the only things intact, and for that, at least, he was grateful. His blood still pumped, and his hands tingled. The fight hadn't been nearly long enough, not with only three opponents and four of them fighting.

"They're not going to like this," Finn said.

"Who?" Mell asked, a crazy grin firmly in place.

If only our goddess could see us now. What would she think? No doubt the Morrigan would have been munching popcorn and sipping minerals—fizzy drink, Bat would call it. But what would *Bat* think of this?

Finn pulled out his mobile with the good arm, keeping the other close to his side, and hit a button. "Criedne? Yeah, vacation is officially over. Need you to get the team over to the Dubros. There will be cleanup involved as well. May as well come with the patrol unit, flashing lights and all. We'll have the glamour in place in a few minutes." He listened for a few moments more, made affirmative sounding noises, and hung up.

"I'm going to go pack up some of our things." Dub couldn't stand there any longer, just waiting. He wasn't letting Bat anywhere near the place. She'd need a few jumpers, socks, her boots. Wait, had she been wearing her boots earlier? He couldn't remember. He set off for the stairs, scanning ahead of him just in case.

"Just pack it all up. We'll need to scan for any glamours or traps that may have been laid on the items before they go to her," Finn called to him. He didn't even pretend that Dub wasn't going only for Bat's things. "And are there any bandages around here? Dammit, this stings."

Mell let out a short laugh. "I'll get you something, then go help Dub. At this rate, the only person who will have anything to wear is the goddess."

"And grab that other sluagh!" Dub called down. "I'd rather him—and the harp—in here with us than out there!"

He paused outside her door, then crossed the hall to his own room. They couldn't stay at the guardi's headquarters indefinitely. He knew where they could go, but he'd need a few things of his own first.

Chapter Eleven

Bastie,

Well, things are beginning to move along with my immortals. My giant pirate confessed that he was afraid he'd be too jealous, which was what I was afraid of, of course. But he also confessed that he is willing to try. These men are not walking away from me.

But, you probably already knew that, did you not? There are also new updates on the situation that is developing here, but I am not sure I should text you. Please answer when I call.

- Bat, the floundering goddess

BAT

$\mathcal{B}$at stared at the shard, then glanced at Ari, who now sat across from her. The men of ba had shifted down the table and taken the places vacated by

Dub, Mell, and Finn. Shar was still beside her, one hand resting lightly on her hip, while Ailis remained in her own place as well. The green-haired woman had been strangely silent since Bat's conversation with the raven.

Ari's knowledge of Balor had been spotty. Puchi was the one who'd dealt with the Fomoiri leader most of the time, back in Egypt and then on the ship while on the way to Ireland. When they'd reached the new land, Balor had helped them unload, then lingered, saying he needed to make sure it was secure. When they discovered the Fir Bolg were already there, he said the Fomoiri needed to stay, that the men of ba would be insufficient to keep the vessel safe. Then he'd confiscated it. Ari and the others had followed, keeping track of the vessel, but they trusted Balor. He'd been Seth's right hand for so long that there was no reason to doubt him.

When the waters began to rise, he used that as an additional excuse to stay. And when they finally receded, he told the Fomoiri that Seth had sent word and instructed them to stay in this new land. But the stories from his mouth gradually changed, his version of events twisting until they didn't resemble the truth in any way. By that time, the men of ba were competing with both the Fomoiri, the de Danann and the Druids for possession of the vessel. Their band was not large, and until Balor was gone, they did not have the power to take and conceal the vessel.

Balor had been one of the strongest of Seth's children. His strength surpassed anything seen on Earth, his gaze could turn enemies to stone, and he could call the winds. He'd only been defeated at Mag Tuired because the Irish gods finally stepping in, gifting Nuada with a blade designed to kill anything.

Bat, of course, now knew those blades didn't kill, but trap.

She shifted her attention to the raven, who had gone back to simply being a raven. Did the Morrigan expect her to keep this other secret? Did it actually matter?

It did. Because escaping a prison was much different from returning from the otherworld.

She'd tell everyone when, well, when everyone was back.

In the meantime, they had a cauldron to find.

"Anything?" Oisin asked from the head of the table.

Bat ignored him. She reached out a finger and touched the shard, running the pad of her index finger over one of the flatter areas, where it had sheared from the main piece. There was a connection there, much fainter than when it had first cut her, but there. The small piece of creation welcomed her, though it was… distracted. It looked for the rest of itself, but more than that, it looked for its children.

She shook her head. "Anything?" she asked Ari, well aware she echoed Oisin's words.

The man of ba ducked his head, bringing it even with the edge of the tabletop. "No, goddess." His voice was muffled. "Only a general direction, to the northwest. Our connection is clouded."

"I think she is confused," Bat said. "She is looking for too much, and cannot focus on the larger part of herself."

"You speak as if it is alive," Shar said. His hand slid to her lower back and rubbed in slow circles.

"She is." Bat leaned back into his touch. Dub had kissed her. Shar still touched her. Mell had continued to smile at her, but his expression promised more. And Finn... he looked at her just the same as he had before Ailis's little revelation—he'd known those truths all along.

"What else is she looking for?" Ailis asked, leaning forward.

Bat ran her finger down the side. "Her children," she murmured.

"Well, then we have to help her find them." Ailis held out her hand. "I assume that's what the whole blood and cutting thing was about earlier?"

Understanding the gesture for the invitation it was, Bat picked up the shard and carefully, oh so carefully, pressed the tip to Ailis's palm. A drop of blood welled and was absorbed by the glimmering stone. Ailis's eyes widened, the green flashing nearly neon before fading back to her normal emerald.

"What—" She licked her lips. "What was that? It was as if..."

"I think it's everyone she had held within her."

"What is this thing? Really?"

Bat's cheeks heated. Had she been doing what the others did to her? Assuming they knew what her own Egyptian myths were? There was so much she hadn't known when she first came to Ireland, guided only by her Idiot's Guide.

Is there one for Egyptian history or mythology? Should I pick one up so they can use it? Would it even be accurate?

"I—"

Ari lifted his head. "I can tell it, goddess."

Bat sent him a grateful smile. "Please. I would just, ummm, balls this up, I am sure."

Shar snorted and Oisin made a choking sound.

Ari squinted, then nodded. He told the tale as she had heard it. How first all there existed were the chaos waters of Nun. And from those waters rose an island, and on the island was an egg. From the egg was born Atum, the first god, and from him the others gods were born—deities that were both the world and of the world, the originals. Shu, who was the air, and Tefnut who was moisture. Geb the Father Earth and Nut the Mother Sky. Osiris and Seth and Isis and Nephthys. And from them came all the rest. But, first, there was the egg. When he was done Ailis made a thoughtful noise in the back of her throat. Oisin stared at the ba man.

"That is fascinating," he said. "I wonder how much of that is universal, or if this was simply the origin of the Egyptian gods? The Greeks definitely have a different story, as do the Christians, though they really only believe in the one god. Hmmm…" He hurried off and returned with a pad of paper, scribbling hurriedly.

Bat stared. That was the most animated she'd seen this particular sidhe yet, even when they were hunting Grainne, or when Balor's name came up.

"Considering the cauldron—vessel—only seems to be seeking those with either Egyptian blood or those who were once—"

"Born from her." Bat nodded and bounced in her seat. That made sense. "When the bodies were placed within, and were given new life, that life came from the vessel. They, in essence, became her children. But it wouldn't work like that, because they already *had* life. They were not new creations."

"It did not always do that." Ari, too, was shifting excitedly. "Only new beings were born, at her own whim, or when she felt it was necessary. And after the first god, only we—the men of ba—and the fennecs were born."

"Foxes?" Ailis snorted out.

Ari's head bobbed. "I think she thought they would be cute."

A small pulse came from the shard, a warm contentment radiating out. Yes, the vessel had thought they would be cute.

"So, it's conscious?" Shar asked, leaning in a bit to eye the stone.

"Yes?" Bat wasn't sure how to answer. "She is aware. I do not think she… thinks as we do."

Oisin's hand hovered over the shard. "It wouldn't. It wouldn't think like us in any way."

"But someone convinced her to grant life in another way," Bat mused.

"Probably Balor. She would have known him," Ari said.

"So she tried to create, but she could not do a fresh creation, so she tried to restore…"

Ailis waved a hand. "I'm kind of sorry I asked the question, now. Back to the topic?"

Bat shifted in her seat. She wanted to jump up, run around the room, maybe do a dance, or maybe hit someone. It really was real. A piece of it sat right in front of her.

The egg, the vessel. It was real. And broken.

"Right. Back to the issue. I think we need to reassure

her that her 'children' are safe. She recognized me. So, I would represent the Egyptian side. Dub is Fomoiri. Mell or Shar could have just as easily done it as well. Maybe because he was the eldest he showed up in my vision?"

"So, because the de Danann fed their dead to the cauldron when they had possession, she considers them children as well?" Oisin speculated. "Would my blood work?"

Bat tilted her head. It had been Finn in her vision, but that was next to the whole vessel, not this piece. "We can try…"

"And why Cu Chulainn?" Shar leaned into her, pressing his shoulder to hers.

"Hmmmm…" Oisin didn't take his gaze from the shard. "He is rumored to be Lugh's descendant, but I don't know the truth of that. He is also rumored to have Fir Bolg ancestry."

Ari nodded. "Yes, the Fir Bolg once held the vessel. It was a brief time."

Trust her instincts. That's what the Morrigan said. And everything in her screamed that she needed to allow the shard to taste both Finn and Cuchi. And only Finn and Cuchi.

"We will wait for the others to return." There was something else her instincts were telling her, and her own emotions warred with. "I have a call I need to make." She stood, Shar's hand skimming over her hip. Her stomach balled into a tight stone.

Shar stood as well. "*A stor?*"

She tried to smile, but all she achieved was a twitch of her lips. "I will be fine. It is past time I did this."

"Who are you calling?" Ailis asked.

Bat waved her hand, impressed with herself that it was steady. "Someone who may be able to answer our questions."

"Right then," Oisin said. "I may be able to formulate a tracking spell, connecting the two pieces. It usually only works for living things—"

"Like people," Ailis interjected.

"But since the cauldron has a consciousness, it may work. I'll have to adjust some things..." He scribbled once more in the notebook he'd fetched.

"We will keep trying as well," Ari said.

Bat inclined her head and pulled her phone out. She wandered through the shelves and cases until she found a secluded corner of the library. There was a well stuffed chair and small side-table tucked there, perfect for some quiet reading.

Or a difficult conversation.

She'd just settled when Shar appeared. "I'm not leaving you alone."

"I will not leave the library. I'm safe."

He shook his head. "That's not what I mean. I can guess who you're calling. I'm not leaving you alone to do that." He crossed his arms and set his feet.

She gazed up at him, this giant who was determined to protect her in any way she would let him. A lump formed in her throat and her eyes burned. She wanted to throw herself at him, to snug her head into his chest, and hold on.

He made her feel safe, she realized. She teased them about wanting to protect a goddess, but the truth was she needed it. She needed to know they were there. That they weren't leaving her alone...

"Thank you." She cleared her throat. "Thank you, my giant."

His eye gleamed at her. "You are very welcome. Now make your call, and if you need me to maim something, you simply let me know." He looked down, then met her gaze again. "You really do not mind me listening?"

"No. I think you, and the others, will need to know these things, eventually."

"The 'others' being Dub, Mell, and... Finn."

"Yes," she said.

He nodded, once, a sharp movement. "Okay."

That was all. Okay. It seemed Ailis's words had indeed worked some kind of magic.

"Okay," she replied. Her lips twitched again, then curled up in a grin she couldn't control.

He thinned his own. "We will probably be wankers."

She stared, admiring the way the muscles in his jaw bunched.

"And I will probably hit them a few times, especially in the beginning. I will try to refrain, but make no promises."

He was sounding much too much like Dub, but... She really did like the eye-patch. He looked... dashing. That was the word, right?

"I won't like seeing them touch you. I already don't."

Oh, was he flexing? The muscles under his sweater bunched then released, performing a little dance of their own. She wanted to touch...

"But I will allow it, because I can see you need them as

well." His voice was clipped, a far cry from his normal gentleness.

Her fingers twitched, remembering the feel of his skin. It was smooth, and softer than she'd thought it would be.

"And there will be times when I need to be in my garden, or by myself."

She bit her lip.

"But I will make sure one of the others is with you. You will not be left alone."

The pressure in her eyes finally won, and a tear spilled over her cheek. Why was she crying? These words were beautiful to hear. And there really was no time for her to break down.

"We promised you a home, and companionship, did we not?"

She sucked in a breath and her smile grew. Yes, they had.

"Make your call. I'll wait."

Chapter Twelve

Bastet, you… you CAT. Answer. The. Phone.

BAT

Scrolling through the contacts in her phone, the ones Bastet had put there, she found the name she looked for.

Seth.

She hadn't spoken to him in centuries, not even in passing. The image of him walking away came back to her. Just as with Horus, they'd never made any promises. But she'd always thought of Seth as more of a friend, and the sight of his back turned to her hurt in a completely different way than Horus standing there with Hathor.

She hit the dial button. The little green phone image popped up, and she stared at it.

"*What?*"

The voice was harsh but faint and she hastily put the phone to her ear. "Hello?"

"*Who is this?*"

"It's Bat."

There was a heavy pause. "*Who?*"

She rolled her eyes. Seth really was an asshole. "Bat."

"*How did you get this number?*"

"The Cat gave it to me."

A snort. "*Of course she did.*"

What did that mean? "Seth, we need to talk."

"*We don't have anything to talk about. Haven't for centuries.*"

A dull pain stabbed through her. Then she paused. It didn't actually hurt as much as she'd thought it would. "No, we haven't, have we?"

Silence.

Fine. "I'm in Ireland."

Silence.

"I just met an intriguing creature named Ari."

Silence.

"And I gathered the pieces of Puchi's soul, cradling them until I sent them to Anubis." She was fishing for a reaction and she knew it.

"*They made it to him.*"

"Good." He still wasn't really giving her what she wanted. But he also wasn't hanging up. She'd half expected him to do just that as soon as she told him her name. "I fed my blood to a shard of the vessel of creation, one left over after it had been stolen and the men of ba were slaughtered."

A sucked in breath was her only answer.

"And Balor is trying to use it to resurrect himself, and for who knows what else."

"Well, fuck."

Hah! That was a reaction.

"So, why are you calling?"

Bat frowned. What did he mean by that? "What do you mean, why am I calling? The Fomoiri are your men! The ba men, the vessel, the egg of creation… It's all real! Why didn't anyone tell me? Does Hathor know? Of course Hathor knows. She knows everything, because everyone loves her. You had to know I was heading to Ireland. I bet you all had a blast laughing at me behind my back and—"

"Bat, hush."

She sucked in a breath. How dare he? "You don't get to speak to me like that. Not anymore. You never should have in the first place."

Shar's eyes narrowed and his lips thinned. Bat held up a hand and twisted it, palm out, to stop him. It was a gesture she'd seen from some of the younger humans, though she wasn't sure she was using it right.

His lips relaxed then twitched up.

"The little goddess has grown."

The words didn't have quite the same endearing quality as they did when Shar spoke them. "I need to know what you know of Balor, and how he could use the vessel. And anything you could tell me about why he would be trying to come back. He was your right-hand man, I heard."

A snort came through the line. *"I haven't seen the bastard in over six thousand years. If I'd really known him, he'd have come back."*

Seth's voice was hard, but she couldn't help but imagine his expression. There'd be a hint of pinched eyes and turned down lips. Maybe slightly drawn brows, showing a pain he tried to hide.

"Beware his gaze," he finally said. *"He's single-minded, ruthless, and willing to make the tough decisions. It's why I sent him all those years ago."*

"Did you know...?"

"That he betrayed us? Yes. I also knew the moment he left this world, and that he wasn't truly gone. He is my creature, after all." A pause. *"The vessel is no longer ours, not really. We can't help you."*

"You mean you won't. There are still Fomoiri here. Ari and the other men of ba long to return home..."

"They may return when their duty is done."

Bat gritted her teeth. "That was cold, Seth." Then she sighed. "I know you don't mean it like that. But, you are also contradicting yourself."

Another silence, but it was somehow warmer than the others. Then he said, *"I've missed you. You're the only one who never looked at me differently, after..."* He trailed off.

"You were the one who walked away."

"I know. If—" A muffled noise. *"If I asked you to come back, would you?"*

"You were the one who walked away," she repeated. Every vision that came to her had a reason. Maybe that vision wasn't to show her Horus and Hathor only. Maybe she needed the reminder of the difference between Seth's

treatment of her, and her not-men. Shar stood before her, looking ready to face down armies—or at least one asshole god—for her.

And he wasn't walking away.

Wait. Seth *had* been the one to turn his back and walk away. And Seth did not change his mind, did not regret, ever. So why was he asking for her, now, after she'd just told him about Balor, and the vessel?

"What are you up to?" she asked.

"You have *grown."* Then he hung up.

She pulled the phone from her ear and looked at the red icon, just to be sure. "Asshole."

"What did he do?" Shar demanded.

"Hung up on me. And he gave me nothing. Not one thing. Just vague god-like ambiguity and no-answers. How do you guys put up with us?" She blew out a breath and stuck out her lower lip.

He shrugged. "We usually don't. The Fomoiri and solitary fae have never been ones to follow the gods."

"Huh. True." She pulled up Seth's number and dialed again. It went to the voicemail. "Seth, you wanker, you better call me back and tell me what I need to know." Then she scrolled through the contacts, calling and leaving messages for everyone, including Bastet. None of them answered. Also including Bastet.

She gripped the phone in tight fingers, wanting to throw it at something. But she needed it. It was her only current way of reaching anyone in Egypt except Bastet. *Who'd stopped answering her texts, come to think of it.*

Shar held out a hand and she handed him her phone,

glad to be rid of the thing. He grinned, slipped the phone in his back pocket, then held his hand out to her again. Ducking her head, Bat allowed him to pull her to her feet.

"We don't need them," he said. "Besides, I've found that the more cryptic the deity or oracle or seer, the less they know and smarter they are trying to sound."

That description didn't sit well with her. "Even me?"

"Nope. You're straight with us. You don't always make sense, and you have weird ideas sometimes, but you're upfront. Part of why so many of the pub's patrons like ya." Shar tucked her under his arm and steered her back toward the table.

She'd had more physical contact with the brothers, and Finn, in the last day than in the last two months. "You really mean it? What you said earlier?"

He stopped. "Yes. Every bit of it."

Including the parts about hitting his brothers and frustration and little jealousies, she added silently. "Give me a kiss."

He gave a little jerk and dropped his arm, twisting to look down on her. "What?"

"Give me a kiss. Dub keeps kissing me, and after I was shot, well, I did some comforting of Mell. Just a little kiss, and I'm not sure he remembers it. You're the only brother I haven't kissed. I'm not saying I know how well this will work. I mean, if I didn't fear it would ultimately hurt all of you, I would have done some propositioning much earlier. The Egyptians are not really very shy about these things, and as a goddess, I have had sacrifices of many kinds. But I know it is not really the same here, in Ireland, so—"

Shar slid a hand into the hair at the nape of her neck

and pulled her up, stooping to meet her halfway. His lips were firm, a little dry, and steady against her. He didn't devour like Dub, but coaxed. He nibbled at her lower lip then ran the tip of his tongue along it before teasing her mouth open.

Her hands gripped the thick muscles at his shoulders and she pressed against him. He was so tall his groin didn't hit the right spots, but that in itself was intriguing, different. Even with Dub, the height disparity was not so unmanageable. With Shar… he really was her giant.

He eased away but didn't go far. Leaning over her, his hand in her hair, he supported her weight, and she let him. He surrounded her, held her, tied her to him with that kiss, and she didn't mind. She looked into his lapis-eye, so similar to Dub's, but different. This close, she could see flecks of silver in the inner ring of the iris. "Do you really think we can make this work?" Despite her earlier resolution, if any of the brothers were unsure or doubted their ability to share her, it was better to know this now. "I will not get between the three of you. Though I want all of you, and I want to make this work, I will take Finn up on his offer if I need to." She wanted to make it clear her priority was still their happiness.

"Well now, where's the fun in that. Maybe you'd like to be between the three of us."

She slapped his shoulder. "Tease. Truth, please."

"Truth. The truth can be a tricky, tricky thing."

"So can you immortals."

He grinned, teeth flashing then disappearing again as he sobered. "Truth is, I will do everything in my power to make this work. Wait. What offer?" His brow quirked.

Heat filled her cheeks and she squirmed. "Well, he didn't come right out and say it, but…" She shrugged, the movement pressing her breasts to his upper abdomen. "I was getting lonely, and didn't want to unbalance things with you three. Plus, well, he's a good man."

"You're attracted to him."

"Yes."

"You care for him."

"Yes." She wasn't even sure when it had happened, but at some point over the last two months she had come to care for him very much. "Just as I do the three of you." Again, she felt the need to make that clear.

His head tipped back and he was silent. Then he straightened away from her. "He deserves some happiness as well."

She reached up, digging her hand into the hair at the nape of his neck, matching his hold on her and messing his braid. She wanted to see it unbound and flowing around him, as her visions had shown her. "We *can* make this work, right?" Some questions were worth repeating.

"We *will* make this work." This time the hesitation was gone from his voice.

Tension fell from her shoulders and the hollow sensation that had been haunting her filled with warmth, lifting her. She was still angry for the secrets, and for them keeping themselves from her for the last couple of months, but at that moment none of the anger mattered. She *knew* it would get resolved.

A howl sounded, muffled but drawing closer. It grew until the sound reverberated through the whole of the guardi's headquarters.

Bat jerked away from Shar as urgency filled her and sprinted through the shelves, toward the front of the library.

"Just get the damned med kit," a voice shouted from the hall. It sounded like Mell...

They were back. And at least one was injured. Her heart pounded. What had happened? Hadn't she told Dub to ensure everyone made it back in one piece?

Killer barreled through the library doors just as Shar caught up with her. Ailis and the others were on their feet. Oisin twisted to avoid her pup then made for the now open door.

Her pup sniffed at her, snorted, and spun to face the doors, taking up the guard position that had come to him so naturally.

"It's fine for now." That was Finn, his voice slightly muffled with distance. "Just get those bags and the rest to a warded room so we can ensure any spells or glamours are stripped. And take the sluagh to a holding room. We'll bring Bat to him." A pause. "Offer him water or something, and don't grab like that. He's not a prisoner."

A red-gold head of hair appeared in the doorway. "Bat, Shar, could you come with us for a moment?" His gaze cut to Oisin, who had paused a few feet from the doors. "We'll need you in the ward rooms. Did you have any luck tracking the cauldron?" He shifted and his injured shoulder came into view. Blood, mostly dried, smeared down his left arm and soaked into his t-shirt.

"No, but I have an idea." Oisin returned to his seat and his scribbles. "I'll be down in a few moments. Let me finish here."

Finn gave a curt nod then looked over his shoulder.

"What happened?" Bat asked, pushing at Killer, who refused to move. "Killer, you idiot, move. Finn is not going to hurt me."

Finn returned his attention to her. "Someone made their move. They didn't win." He stepped back into the hallway and out of her sight.

"Huh." She didn't like the look of that injury. Or, she didn't like that he was injured. Why wasn't it cleaned up? Why was he just walking around dripping blood? She placed the ball of her foot against her pup's hindquarter and shoved. Killer twisted around to give her an admonishing look.

Dub was the next to appear. He took in the tableau with a sharp glance then gave a piercing whistle. Killer bounded over to him, tail waving in a quick beat.

Bat frowned. "You are a fickle beast," she told her pup, who twisted, panted, and let out another resounding bark before returning his attention to Dub.

"Finally. What, you were going to let your captain bleed out?" Mell's voice floated into the room from somewhere.

"What is going on?" she asked again.

"As Finn said, we won."

Bat jabbed a finger toward him. "That is not an answer. And you are being deliberately cryptic. Cease."

"I am being cryptic, as you said, because we haven't yet figured out *exactly* who it is watching us, or how." Dub pushed the door open farther and gestured for her to come to him. "Now, there is someone who needs to see you."

Bat threw up her hands, much as she'd seen Ailis do, and stomped to her grumpy not-man, Shar right behind her.

"Don't worry about us! We'll just be here, doing… something until you return," Ailis called out.

Bat and Dub snorted in unison, which startled a laugh from the goddess. The raven let out a caw but stayed where she was with the men of ba, Ailis, and Oisin.

They were down the stairs and threading through a maze of hallways and rooms by the time she'd had enough of the silence. She understood wanting to ensure they were not being spied upon, but surely Dub could tell her something? She did not like being kept in the dark.

"What—"

"We're here." Dub halted before a plain white door, the same as all the others in this hall. There weren't even any markings to tell which room was which. How did he know they were where they needed to be?

Then she spied the thin panel of lights just above the door. These showed yellow. The door next to them indicated red, while the rest were green. Hmmmm…

"Is this like the traffic lights? Red is stop, green is go and orange is speed up?"

"Orange is not speed up. You've been talking to Ailis too much." Dub frowned, but there was no real ire behind it.

Bat shrugged. "She answers my questions."

"Stop pouting, *storeen*. I'll give you answers in just a moment."

"I wasn't pouting. I was poking. And it was not about this." Okay, maybe she was pouting a little. But not much.

She just didn't like that her life had been so disturbed. Though, it did break the ice in regards her relationships with the men. That was a silver lining to the cloud.

And where— "Where did Mell go? And Finn?"

Dub sighed, his hand hovering over the door. "Ya can't hold yer questions for a moment, can ya?" The words were exasperated, but the tone was teasing and his frown was now gone.

"I've been holding my questions very well, thank you very much."

Killer interjected a yipping growl of agreement.

"See, even Killer agrees."

Shar, wearing a wide grin, slipped his hand to the nape of her neck. "Give him a break, *a stor*."

Her eyes went wide. "I don't want to *break* him."

"That's not what—"

"Enough." Dub flicked his fingers around, the door clicked, and he pushed it open.

Killer sniffed, growled, sniffed again, then wagged his tail, nosing the door open all the way. Dub waved for her to enter.

Well, since I have his mightiness's permission…

"Keep pushing, goddess, and I am sure you will like what you get," Dub murmured as she slipped past him.

She stuck her tongue out and his eyes darkened.

"Stop teasing each other and get in here," Mell said.

Bat jumped away from Dub and focused on the room's other occupants. Finn, who had a clean bandage if not a clean shirt, Mell, and…

"Faolan? What are you doing here?" The sluagh—and

she still wasn't quite sure what those were except another type of fae—sat at the table beside Mell, head bowed.

He looked up at her voice. "Goddess. I saved it for ya."

Then his arms moved, shadows—where there should be none—shifted, and gnarled brown hands held her harp out to her. She took it, stroked her hand over the leather of the case. She slipped the instrument out and looked it over for any damage that may have been inflicted during the scuffle. It gave a soft strum of recognition as she ran a finger along one of the strings, and she sealed it up once more, satisfied it had survived well enough, and placed it carefully on the table.

"He was hanging around the pub, even after I kicked everyone out," Mell said.

"I was late, and I hadn't got my pint, now had I? Ya know I need my pint."

Bat nodded. It was true. Faolan was very good about coming in just as dusk fell, and having just the one pint. She tried to make a point of playing at least one song while he was there.

"Apparently, the intruders first came down the flue, and Faolan followed them—"

"Their shadows are not near as good as mine, goddess."

"—and got to the harp as they were arguing about who would be trying to pick it up, hiding it from them. They came back after we arrived and he showed himself to us. The pub is a little…"

"Did the bar break?" she asked.

Mell shook his head.

"Oh. Okay. I know how much Dub hates replacing that."

Dub's brows rose, and Finn grinned. "Though usually, he only hates replacing it because he's the one who breaks it," the guardi teased.

Bat beamed, happy that Finn had followed her lead in teasing Dub. It would be fun to gang up on the eldest brother. It was not nearly the same as when Mell joined in, Dub was nearly immune to his younger brother's jabs.

She returned her attention to the harp. "Why are we here, in this room? Do we think they managed to do something to it that I did not detect?"

"No," Finn answered her. "We already checked it over. There are no glamours, wards, spells or curses laid on it. We just haven't finished checking everything else Dub insisted we bring back. The attackers would have had much more time to work with the things left in the pub, and we need to be sure no traps were laid upon them."

"Who are they? Where are they? Did they get away? Oh, and I talked to Seth, but he really wasn't very helpful. Just warned me that Balor could be a ruthless bastard and to avoid his gaze, which I am sure you all knew already."

"They are in warded holding cells, the level below this. They are secure. So, no, they did not get away." Finn turned to Faolan. "We need to speak with the goddess alone now, but know that your assistance was greatly appreciated."

Faolan peeked at Bat then ducked his head again, much as Ari tended to do. "Will the pub be open again?"

"Not until we get the window fixed, and maybe

longer," Dub quickly answered, cutting off whatever explanation or reassurance Bat would have offered.

"You'll be one of the first to know, I am sure," she offered the sluagh with a smile.

Faolan flashed her a grin, revealing sharp teeth. They were not near as deadly as Ari's. "I will watch for ya, goddess."

She nodded and he rose, sweeping in his shadows toward the door.

"Faolan," she called out. She didn't care what Dub or Finn cautioned, what he had done deserved more than a nod. "Thank you."

The sluagh ducked his head and slid out the door. No doubt someone would ensure he was escorted out.

Bat, the brothers, and Finn sat in silence.

"Oisin mentioned he may have a way to track the cauldron using the shard. Neither you nor the ba men had any luck?" Finn finally started.

"No." Bat filled them all in on what had happened while they were gone, including the conversation with the Morrigan. In a split decision, she also told them what she knew of the blades, how they did not really kill but capture, and that the souls captured were used to keep something at bay. She ended with her frustration at not knowing exactly what that something was.

"Clever, really," Finn mused. "They gave us weapons that would 'kill' all while feeding the protections and keeping their secret. Too many would have balked on making sacrifices."

"You don't want to know what is guarded?"

Finn gazed at her, his green eyes both stark and soft. "I

155

really don't understand you." Then he shuddered. "No, I do not want to know. I have seen enough in my life that I wish I never knew, or could forget. Why add something else to it, and something that I may never have to deal with at that? The blades aren't in use anymore, so from that I can assume the protections are steady."

Bat braced herself for a vision that never came. Finn's words were just the kind that would trigger a flash. But since there wasn't one, she had to assume he was right, and she let it go.

"But this information does change things," Finn said. "If Nuada's blade works similarly, and was used to trap Balor, then it would explain how he would be able to resurrect himself. I had assumed he was attempting something similar to what happened with Oisin. But with Oisin, his wife sent him back from the Otherworld, and he accidentally locked himself out. He's been working for centuries to get back to her."

"Oh."

Finn waved a hand. "Whole other story, for a different day. It only has bearing here because we know that Balor is not trying to return from the otherworld, as he never went there."

"Seth did also mention he felt when Balor was gone, but he also felt that not all of him was gone." Bat supplied. "If... if the Fomoiri *are* from Egypt, what if their souls follow the rules of our land? What if a portion of his ba was not taken by the sword, but lingered in an effigy? If the body was preserved and prepared well enough, that could have worked. Or that fragment of soul could have hidden away in something that represented him. The old pharaohs used this method many times. The ba, especially, is drawn to likenesses."

"If there was a man of ba helping him at that time…"

Bat's stomach clenched. She didn't want to believe that one of the guardians of the vessel would have betrayed his fellows in such a way, but the possibility had to be considered, especially since someone—who had possession of Nuada's blade—had made it through the glamours and wards surrounding the wood. That person would either need to be extremely familiar with the pathways of the soul, or they would have needed to be brought through.

"We can't trust them, can we?" she whispered, her heart aching.

"I would say we can trust Ari, if only because we know he was with us when the attack occurred," Shar offered.

"Doesn't mean he was not involved somehow." Dub shook his head. "People so often assume there is only one betrayer."

"Chaos and evil *are* extremely sneaky," Bat agreed, though it pained her to do so. "I will need to look into their hearts." She sagged. It took so much from her to exercise that part of her power…

"It would be best, *storeen*." Dub leaned toward her. "But we need to take care of a few things before that, first of which is ensuring we have a safe place for us to work."

"Why can we not stay here?"

Finn and Mell exchanged a look. "I have no reason not to trust my fellow guardi," Finn started. "But as you said, evil is insidious. Plus, this is not really a place to sleep. I would offer my home, but it has one bedroom, and is only a little larger than the room we are currently in."

Flash. An old house, surrounded by green fields. Its paint was peeling, and the porch sagged. Two windows were boarded up. Beyond the house sat a stone building. Smoke billowed from a large chimney flue spearing up through the middle of the roof. The steady roar of fire and rhythmic clanging of metal on metal came from within.

Bat blinked and turned to Dub. "I think it's time you showed me your forge. You can't keep avoiding taking me to see it."

Dub frowned. "I wasn't avoiding it. I just haven't had a chance to go there. These last couple months have been busy. But you are correct, it's the best option right now." His eyes widened. "You said the second spear hadn't been made yet."

Mell thrust a fist in the air. "Yes! Time to take The Smith out of the closet and dust him off."

Dub flinched. "Watch yer words, Mell. You know he doesn't like anyone else using that title."

Mell rolled his eyes. "Just because ya studied under him doesn't mean he's better than ya. Besides, he's not been seen in a millennium or more."

"And you throwing around his moniker is bound to bring him out."

Bat leaned into Shar. "Who are they talking about?"

"Goibniu. He's not a god, but he's nearly as powerful as one. And best left alone. Dub studied smithing under him for a bit."

"Oh."

The other two brothers had stopped arguing and now stared at her. She tilted her head. "Are you done arguing? Would this forge really be a good place to go? The house did not look in very good repair…"

Dub grunted. "It will do. Won't take too much to make it livable."

"We have a plan then," Finn said.

They did? When had they made a plan? Her brows drew together.

"We need to stop being wankers and tell the goddess the plan, guys," Mell said.

"We finish questioning those captured and removing any spells or glamours placed on our belongings," Dub said.

"Then we investigate the invitation, attempt to track the spell back to its caster and see what else we can learn —" Finn continued.

"While Oisin and the men of ba continue their efforts to track the cauldron," Dub took back over.

"Then we get out to the forge, set up wards, blah, blah, blah," Mell added.

"And when Dub is working, you can do your thing and peer into the hearts of those around us. We will bring only Ailis and Oisin at first. We'll need him for the wards. After, you can check everyone as they come through them," Shar rumbled.

"And then—" Mell swallowed.

"We need to call Da," the three brothers said together.

"My team will continue to investigate any leads from the prisoners," Finn said. "And then we go from there. If we really do need to allow Balor to return in order to kill him fully, then our concentration must be on preparing for when he *is* back. Which means identifying the players and what his ultimate goal is, as well as prepping the spear. Locating the artifacts, while important, is secondary to those other steps. In fact, identifying the main players will most likely tell us where he is. And if we know where Balor is, that's half the work done right there."

"What about Tir Hudi?"

"A mythical island," Finn said.

"There has to be more to it than that. Why this place?"

"Puchi is the only one who has mentioned it, yes?" Shar asked, his tone musing.

Bat nodded.

"It could be he assumed it was Tir Hudi and not another lost island. Or he knew something about it we do not. Or Balor knows something, and Puchi picked up on that."

"Or the megalomaniac wanted to hang out on a magical island that is only rumored of, even among the immortals, and thought it would be a good hideout." Mell shrugged then shot her a grin. "I mean, if I were going to turn into a megalomaniac, I would want my hideout on a mystical island."

"And all of this is just more speculation." Finn stood. "We have our plan. When we've accomplished what we can, we'll reassess." He strode for the door, radiating an energy he'd been lacking up to this point.

Bat studied the other three men. They sat with easy poses, but that stillness was an act. Under it was the same energy and eagerness Finn held.

Mell must have noted her curiosity. "Despite what you may have seen of us, or our... reactions to some things, we *are* warriors. And this promises to be a very grand battle."

And just like that, the day caught up to her. She yawned and her stomach growled. "Do any of you realize that it is already the middle of the night? When did we plan to have this 'secure location' ready?"

Chapter Thirteen

Dearest Bastie,

I am going to keep sending these, and eventually you will answer me again.

I admit I am starting to worry. Are you in a pickle? (A new phrase!)

*I have decided to be selfish. I can imagine your response
—"It is about time!" you will say.*

Yes, it is.

- Bat, the goddess who is not going to let doubt slow her down anymore

BAT

inn's apartment was small, as he'd said, but it was well kept. The bed had those neat corner folds in the sheets and blanket, everything was put away, books and a few figurines lined the shelves of a bookcase in precise rows, and there wasn't a speck of dirt or grain of dust in sight.

The door shut behind her and Finn locked the door. "I've set the wards to recognize you. Take the bed. When we're done at headquarters, I'll come for you. Only me. And don't open the door." Then he contradicted himself. "If whoever is on the other side of the door says I sent for you, and they are not entering the apartment, they are lying. If I cannot come, it will be one of the brothers. Again, wait for them to come in, do not go to them, whatever they may say."

He looked around the apartment, much as she had. Was he trying to see it as she did? It was a little bare, but very nice all the same. "I like the painting over the bed," she offered.

It was a watercolor of gray cliffs falling into a blue ocean, waves crashing against a slim stretch of rocky beach.

Finn came to her side as Killer sniffed around the edges of the room. There really wasn't much for him to investigate.

"The Cliffs of Moher," Finn said, his tone stiff.

"Is there a story behind this one as well?"

"There is a story anywhere you step in Ireland."

She leaned into him, keeping the contact light. She was greedy for touch now that she'd begun to receive it, finally. "I am beginning to learn that."

"But, no, to answer your question." He shifted, accepting a bit more of her weight. "No story here for me. I simply liked it. An artist down in Ennis painted it."

"I like that. Sometimes there isn't a deep reason for

wanting something, other than 'I liked it'. I think having those things is just as important as the ones with some sort of sentimentality or history."

"I need to get back now." But he didn't move.

Bolstered by her success with Shar, and Dub's kisses, she plunged in. "I do want you, you know."

"Even with the idiot brothers beginning to come to their senses?"

"Yes."

They continued to stare at the painting. Then Finn sucked in a breath and released it in a controlled exhalation.

"Shar said you deserved some happiness," she continued. "I am thinking I do too. I am going to be selfish, as long as I can. I want *all* of you." *He* had been the one to come after her in the garden, after all.

"And if they don't agree?"

A new certainty settled over her. It was a decision not far off from her original conviction to not approach the brothers in a sexual way, but the difference was like that of a slavering cur and a well-trained hound.

"Then that is their loss, is it not?" she answered. If the brothers truly could not accept her forming a sexual attachment to more than one of them, and to Finn, she could pull back. And she would pull back from them all. She would not put one of them above the others. She would not leave them, this was her home now, but she would shut that portion of herself away. It wouldn't be gone, simply dormant. And if they ever changed their minds... She had already stated that she would give them as many chances as they needed, hadn't she? "And it would be your loss as well," she warned.

When you'd lived millennia starved for affection, two months or two years or two centuries, it didn't matter, it was a very long time to wait. It wouldn't come to that, though. Or, she hoped it didn't.

Some of the surety she'd gained in the library drained away, showing her the hollow place inside herself once more. It was a strange thing, that place. It didn't exist in the physical, but in her spirit. A place where something should have been, and now nothing existed. Had it always been there and she was only now noticing it? And why would it not stay filled?

"You would do that for me?" Finn asked, gaze still trained on the painting.

She shook her head. "I would do that for *me*." She didn't *think* they would balk, though. Or, not much. Mell had to have seen this coming, and Shar had already assured her they would make it work. Dub was the one she was unsure of.

Her hands trembled and she gripped the edge of her sweater, using it to hold herself steady. Finn reached down and pried her fingers from the lightly woven hem, folding them in his own warm hand.

She'd held off from the brothers for fear of upsetting not just their balance, but *them*. But wasn't she allowed to reach for what she wanted? Wasn't she allowed to at least *try*? She needed to stop assuming the weight of decisions that were not hers to make. And she needed to overcome her fear of losing them, once and for all.

They weren't Horus, and they weren't Seth. They

weren't any of the other Egyptian deities who'd left her on her own.

They weren't walking away. And she would repeat these truths until the last shadows of doubt were erased, and the hollow place filled.

The scene portrayed in the landscape really was beautiful. "Will you take me there?" she asked.

Finn brought her hand to his lips. "If we survive this."

"Well. Then I will have to make sure that you do." Bat turned to him. His profile was strong, the nose straight. A lock of red-gold hair flopped over his brow, and his lips had a slight curl to them. She'd thought, once, that he reminded her of Seth. He didn't, not in any way. There was too much... contentment in him. It wasn't quite the right word, but it was the closest she could find. Finn, though he maybe wanted more, was not dissatisfied with his life.

He turned his head to look down at her right at that moment. "I would like to kiss you now."

Her mouth went dry and she nodded. "Pl— please. I mean, maybe it will be horrible."

He bent a few inches closer to her. "And then we won't need to be worrying over nothing."

"Exactly," she whispered.

His lips hovered just over hers. Why didn't he close that distance? "I thought I'd simply offer you the physical. Sex, plain and simple. Goddess or not, you are a beautiful woman, Bat Sitru. And I've had a great, and true, love in my life already. It would be selfish to want another."

She pulled in a breath and her stomach dipped.

"I think," he continued, "like you, I will be selfish."

Then he closed that distance. He didn't dive as Dub had, but he also didn't linger. His good arm went around her and slid down to her butt, pulling her into him. He groaned, rocking a little, just enough to tease her. The muscles of his back bunched under her hands.

Then he was… gone.

A pinging sounded, and it took Bat a moment to come back to herself. She'd been getting far too many kisses, and not nearly enough satisfaction today.

The pinging continued until she found her phone in her pocket and answered. "'Lo?"

A soft chuckle. "I had to leave, or I wasn't going to. And as much as I am willing to embrace a bit of selfishness, things back here at headquarters still take precedence."

"Yes, of course. Yes." She blew out a breath as Killer jumped onto the bed, circled, and curled into himself. He was obviously ready to sleep.

"I'm sending over Aeden. He'll keep guard outside the wards. If anyone wants you to open the door—"

"Do not. I know."

"Good." He hung up.

Her phone rang again.

"Hello?"

"I… will see you soon."

Not a declaration of love, but his earlier words had been close enough. At least he had called back to give her a proper farewell. "I look forward to that time."

He hung up again.

Bat fell back onto the bed. She twisted her head to where Killer lay, not even stirring at the disturbance.

"Well, that either went beautifully, or we are both such awkward beings after all this time that it could not have gone worse?"

Killer let out a soft snore. She was sure the pup was faking.

"Fine. I'll get ready to sleep. Of course, no one bothered to give me anything to sleep *in*."

Bedtime preparations didn't take long. She found a shirt in one of Finn's drawers and donned that in lieu of sleepwear. She also used his toothbrush. That was the kind of thing people in a relationship did, right? And besides, his tongue had just been in her mouth. There was nothing unsanitary about it.

Bat lay on the bed, convinced it would be ages before she could sleep. Ailis had gone to her own home, refusing guards and assistance, and then slipped away. Sneaky fae... Ari and the other men of ba were still working with Oisin, and they'd been brought a pot of coffee, or four, before she'd left...

Her eyes slid closed. She'd have to make sure the brothers rested. Maybe they would need to take turns... Mell had insisted on helping with the interrogations... Dub and Shar were at the forge... Cuchi and his team were scanning the invitation.

She wasn't sure she trusted him...

But the Morrigan did say... and her instincts were to include him...

He was the one who hurt her giant...

Who looked like a pirate... Dashing...

She hadn't thought she would be able to sleep, but it came swiftly.

FINN

Finn settled into the chair across from the sluagh they'd captured at the pub, and licked his lips, attempting to banish the taste of cornflowers and pepper. Mell pulled out the chair beside him, making no comment on the teasing heat that Finn had yet to suppress.

Get your mind in this game. This is no time for distractions.

"What are you called?" he asked, pulling in a deep breath and analyzing the sluagh's scent. Was it one he had encountered before? Mugwort, musk, and the morning breeze over the bogs. Under that was a hint of... apples?

Shadows shifted, ebbing and flowing over the sluagh. It grinned, revealing teeth darkened with rot and old fluids. Its skin was pitted with scars and dabbed with dried blood.

"Why were you at the pub?" Mell asked, his tone a lazy contrast to Finn's.

Silence. But then, he had not expected the sluagh to answer. No, they would have to find their answers through what he didn't say. "It's curious." Finn leaned forward. "The sluagh are notorious for remaining neutral. You keep to your shadows, and the dark paths in the night. You hunt for the treacherous and lost. What were you offered, that you attacked the Dubros?" Finn tilted his head, peering through the veils of the creature's shadow. Nothing. He wasn't yet on the right track. "Or is it that you heard from Faolan about the goddess?"

The sluagh's thin red lips twitched.

Mell tapped the tabletop. "She really is good with the harp. You'd think it was hers all along, instead of the Dagda's."

Nothing.

"I'm wondering more about how he heard about that," Finn mused.

Mell crossed his legs and bobbed his foot. "Well, we all know how the rumors spread," he said. "I'm wondering how far they've spread, though. What bog did you say you came out of?" Mell tapped his chin. "It's got to be one of the ones in Connaught, the sluagh aren't allowed in the other areas of Ireland, now are they?"

The shadows pulled back then surged forward, masking the creature's face completely. That was fine, Mell didn't need to see the immortal's face to read him, and it was enough of a reaction for Finn to know they were onto something.

"That's right. I doubt it's Keelogyboy, or Faolan'd have known you. Maybe Slieveward?" Finn tapped his chin. "No, I've been there, I'd know your scent. In fact, we could rule out Carrane and Easkey for the same reasons." He turned to Mell. "Where else is there?"

"He could be from over in County Mayo. The damn place is half-bog, ya know."

"Hmmm... true. Wait. What was the name of that place your father's man liked? He was only half sluagh, but we once had a wonderful conversation about the play of the moon over the lake. He liked the quiet there. It was up north though, so I doubt that's it."

The shadows remained thick, but within them the sluagh jerked.

Mell tapped the tabletop, the signal to dig deeper.

There *was* something there, either with Scath, or with the area mentioned. Or both. So Finn dug. "Illies Hill bog. That was the name." Finned nodded to himself. "Yeah. That was it."

Mell nodded knowingly. "I know the place. Not far from Londonderry."

Finn suppressed a grin as the sluagh jerked. "That's where Alatrom sails from, right?"

"Yeah, Da says he prefers the port there to the one in Belfast. The customs agents are... well, easier to deal with is how he likes to put it." Mell shook his head and flashed an easy grin at the seething shadows across from them. "But that's not what we need to be discussing now. I'm sure this one here wouldn't go out of his bounds. What was the sentence for that again?"

"A century? Two?" Finn shrugged. "I can never remember. The Tribunal keeps changing it." The shadows eased. Looked like this particular sluagh wouldn't mind being locked away for a while.

"Never did understand why the restrictions were worse for the land-bound fae than for the Fomoiri," the sluagh muttered.

It was an opening, but a false one. At least the creature was beginning to speak.

Mell sighed. "It's because of mac Lir." He cocked his head at Finn. "Who made the deal again? I don't think it was the Crane clan. I would have remembered that. Was it the Bull clan?"

"Elatha? Doubtful. You know he married into the de Danann. Cichol? Of the Hounds?" Finn mused.

"No. They're too tied to the land. Practically farmers these days, you know."

"That's right. How they call themselves Fomoiri I don't know." Oh, he was starting to have too much fun with this. "Got to be Tethra then. The Lion clan, despite their names, have always had the deepest connection with the sea."

The shadows cleared around the sluagh, revealing its twisted figure. The wings were pulled back and bound in spelled ropes of leather, but that didn't stop the creature from baring its fangs.

Then, trembling, it opened its mouth wide, tongue flicking in agitated waves. Its head tipped back and it screamed.

"Well, farking bollix and shite." Finn didn't move. He knew this spell. They wouldn't be getting anything from the sluagh now. It was locked in the pain of its own mind. They'd have to call one of the druids from Dublin to untangle him. "Did you get anything before he went under?" he asked Mell.

Mell's gaze was glued to the shrieking sluagh, his face pale. "Strongest reactions were to the indirect mention of Scath, the north, and the Lion clan. Not Tethra, though, which was interesting. Nothing when my father was mentioned either." He pulled in a slow breath, held it for a moment, and exhaled. "Mostly fear, but there was also anticipation when mac Lir came into the conversation."

"The island?"

"Possibly. I suspect that particular god knows more of what's going on than any of us."

"Would he help?"

"Mac Lir?" Mell let out a scoffing laugh. "Only if he was bored and decided to play against himself." A pause. "Which is not out of the realm of possibility. But he won't answer to any of us land-bound Fomoiri."

There might be one person he would speak to. Finn hesitated, wary of even bringing up the possibility. But, it *was* a possibility, and as flippant as they all attempted to act, the return of Balor and gathering of the artifacts were heralds of death for many. *You've already admonished the others for attempting to protect her.* The self-admonishment did the trick and he forced his next words out. "He might take a call from Bat."

Mell opened his mouth, closed it, and bowed his head. "He might. But... let us see what we can glean from the other prisoners. And, later, my father. I can't be certain yet, but I'm not sure the clan leaders are involved. When their names were mentioned, there was no fear, but there *was* a slight hint of contempt."

"I'll keep that in mind." Finn rose and headed out the door, Mell a beat behind him. This information didn't change their current strategy, but it did put them a step closer to knowing the players.

At least I'm not hampered by "evidence" like the human guardi. While the Ceilte Guardi did follow many of the human procedures, it was mostly for the sake of organization, and allowing the fae clear rules to follow. And for their records, of course.

In this instance, Mell's impressions and Bat's visions were enough for them to work on.

He sighed. He'd have to write a report on this, wouldn't he?

They halted outside another of the interrogation rooms. "This one is the Fir Bolg, right?" Mell asked.

Nearly wiped out in the early battles, the Fir Bolg tended to stick to the bogs and forests, just as the sluagh did. Like the Fomoiri, their powers were closer to the elements. But where the Fomoiri stuck to the seas, the Fir Bolg preferred the land.

And they preferred blood.

Finn keyed open the door and stepped inside. The immortal, nearly the size of Shar, was limp in his chair, mouth twisted into a grimace and eyes rolled back in his head. Without a word, Finn stepped back, nudging Mell back, and closed the door. "We're not going to get anything more from them until the spell's unraveled."

Mell hit the wall beside the door with the flat of his hand and tipped his head back. "Can't Oisin do it?"

"Not this one." Finn wanted to hit the wall as well. But there was no use in that.

"Then what's next, oh Great Guardi Captain of mine?"

"Brat." Finn slapped the back of Mell's head. "Are you saying now you'll join up?"

The teasing light left the younger man's eyes. "Not a chance."

Finn sighed. He'd get Mell yet. The Fomoiri had too much passion inside him to remain hidden away for long. But the thing about immortals? They lived long, yes, but they also held onto things best left let go. He himself was no exception. He'd give Mell more time. "We get our not-so-secret hideout ready. Criedne will report to me once the scrying spell on the invitation is unraveled."

Mell bowed his head for a moment then lifted his gaze

to meet Finn's. There was an understanding there. This would not be so easy as they'd made it out to be in front of Bat. The sophistication and level of skill needed for the spells used surpassed the abilities of most in Connaught, and the fact the neutrals were being swayed...

"We can do this, right?"

Finn swallowed. "I have no doubts."

Mell nodded and set off down the corridor, no doubt in search of his brothers. Finn followed after, fully aware he'd just lied.

Chapter Fourteen

Bastet,
Oh! I just remembered. If you ever need to threaten an
immortal of Ireland, tell them you need ingredients to make
a koldala.
It is a dish I made up, and you need an eye and a little
finger to make it.
I was simply trying to make a point, but they believed me!
I think I have started new rumors of the savagery of the
Egyptian gods.
Bat, the goddess who apparently demands bloody sacrifices!

BAT

*B*at, a slash of sunlight lying warm across her cheek, curled into the striped chair she'd claimed as her own in the little cottage. It was set at an angle near the fireplace, one of those cushioned and upholstered monstrosities that you could sink into. Coupled with a fuzzy blanket, her fuzzy socks, and a roaring fire, if it weren't for the harp case propped against the hearth she could almost forget the reason they were camped out south of Sligo. That one object was enough of a reminder of the chaos she had found herself embroiled in. The shard was tucked away in a locked and warded box in a warded chest in Dub's room, but Bat had insisted the harp remain with her, where she could keep an eye on it.

The cottage wasn't really that small. There were four bedrooms, an attic room, a fair-sized living area, and a decent kitchen. It was just that they were currently trying to fit nine people—well, eight people and a very energetic dog—in that space.

Leaning her head back, her eyes slid closed, exhaustion overtaking her. What had she done that day? Not one thing except sit in this chair.

And delve into the souls of every person who now temporarily called the cottage home, looking for traces of chaos or the seeds of corruption. She'd even searched the brothers, Finn, and Ailis. They'd insisted.

It had taken a lot from her to do so many in so little time. Nearly all the power she'd accumulated over the last two months. Maybe she should go find one of the brothers and ask for an offering of some kind. Maybe a kiss. Or, she could find Finn. She was sure he would be accommodating. A sleepy smile pulled the corners of her lips up. It was certainly a good way to recharge. Maybe she *should* go find him...

There was a scratching at one of the windows opposite her. "Shh, don't wake her. Can't ya see she's bushed?"

"I'm no' making noise, ya are! And stop looking at her diddies. Tha's no' polite ta do wi' a goddess."

"Tha's no' polite ta do wi' anyone," a third voice hissed.

"Shh…"

Bat pried her lids up. Her gaze landed on three pixies standing on the windowsill, on the other side of the glass.

"Hush, ya, she's spotted us." A pink-haired and -winged pixie poked the one beside her, who was done all in shades of silver. The third, red from the tips of his hair to the toes on his feet, crossed his arms, huffed, and turned his back.

"Ummm, hi," Bat said. She really should work up some alarm, or at least startlement. But she was too tired… "How did you get in?"

The pink one placed her hand on the glass. "We're no' *in* the house. But the angry one and the scholar, they set the outer wards on the other side of our home, so it's more like we were always in. Ye're Bat, aren't ya? I'm Maire. I've heard of ya. Is it true ya found the cauldron but then it got nabbed? And ya have a piece of it? And the harp? Ye've played it? Will ya play for us? Is that it over by the hearth? Is Balor really trying ta come back? I never did like him. Made sport of hunting us, he did—"

The red pixie spun around. "Hush ya. Lookit, she can barely keep her eyes open."

Maire crossed her arms and pouted. "But Ciara knows her. Said we should help. So, here we are. Besides, ya just want ta look at her diddies some more."

The red one flared a bright orange. Blushing? And

what were diddies...? The pixie's gaze dropped to her chest.

Oh. She nearly snorted, and would have if she had more energy. "I do not mind you helping, but I won't be able to scan you today. Maybe you could come back tomorrow? The grumpy one has been very insistent that I not let in anyone who hasn't been scanned. Or maybe he needs some help in the forge? He was doing quite a bit of grumbling about how rundown he'd let it get."

"*Realta*, who are you—?" Mell came in from the kitchen, a sandwich and some crisps set up on a plate. "What the hell? Where did they come from? And you! Show the goddess some respect and stop looking at her breasts."

Bat snorted. It was just too much.

The red pixie *humphed*. "Why? *You* look at them. I've seen you. You sneak looks."

The silver one hit him. "Knock it off, Daire. And stop talking about them."

Daire spun on her. "Don't look, don't talk. Ye're taking all the fun."

Mell strode to the window and pulled the curtains.

"Hey!" three voices chorused.

"So, you're sneaking looks are you?" Bat teased Mell. They hadn't even been here a full day, how many times had he looked that the pixies noticed?

He waggled his eyebrows. "Of course. Who wouldn't?" He held out the plate. "Here. You've worn yourself out. I told Dub we should have given you another day to recharge."

She popped a crisp into her mouth and chewed. They were the good ones, with the "BBQ" flavor. Her favorites.

Speaking of, it had not been lost on her that almost every single one of her possessions had made it to her new room here, including her boots, her favorite scarves, and her fuzzy socks. Even the ones that had been in the laundry.

Mel squeezed in between her chair and the hearth and sat, elbows propped on his knees. "How are you doing?"

"You can't tell?"

His brows drew together and his gaze ran over her face. "Ye're tired."

She didn't bother answering that and bit into her sandwich. Mmmm… he'd put the salad cream on it…

"Good?"

She nodded and took another bite.

"So, how are you doing?"

She slowed in her chewing. How *was* she doing? Was there an easy answer? Did she have an answer? "I'm better," she said through her bite. Then swallowed. "I mean, it is a relief to know the things that were being kept from me. And," she peeked at him from the corner of her eye, "the kisses I am finally getting may be even more of a relief." She held the sandwich a few inches from her mouth, waiting for his reaction.

She was not disappointed. He didn't hesitate. Half rising, he guided the sandwich away from her mouth and leaned into her, pressing teasing little kisses to the corner of her lips and then drifting in to capture her lips fully. That last kiss was brief, but the ball of anxious anticipation—the one that had had her insides acting like a chittering monkey—eased. A different anticipation took its place.

She had her answer from him. He was willing to try, with her, with all of them.

Now she just had to wrangle Dub's attention...

"Are you sure?" she asked, suddenly needing to *hear* the words from him. "You know that Finn and I..."

"Yes. And yes." He pulled back and pointed to her sandwich, now partially smushed between her fingers. "Eat."

She took another bite, watching him all the while. Strands of dark hair flopped over his forehead and he brushed them back. *He really is very pretty.* Maybe she shouldn't think such a thing of the not-man. He wasn't delicate, not at all. But, while all three brothers were attractive enough that they no doubt had plenty of women seeking them out before she came, Mell was... the work of art. The one you wanted to just stare at, he was so... *pretty*.

His lips curled up. "What are you thinking?"

She swallowed. "That this is a very good sandwich, and I am regaining my strength nicely, with the offerings of food and kisses." Bat scooped up a couple crisps and shoved them in her mouth.

"What else?"

He could probably sense her lie. Or, her reluctance more like. "Ummm... you are very pretty."

"Pretty?"

A smile threatened, and she did her best to keep her expression serious. "Yes. Like one of those sculptures by the Greek man."

"Which Greek guy?"

She took another bite. Which Greek guy? There had been so many, and most of them sculpted pretty men, come to think of it. "All of them?" she finally said.

He chuckled and shook his head, watching her. Bat continued eating her sandwich. It was very much like their meals back at the pub, except now she got kisses and touches and, hopefully, more.

She liked this much better.

"I really am sorry," Mell finally said. He guided the sandwich from her lips to the plate, then claimed her hands in his. "We didn't mean to leave you alone like that. It was just... The same day Shar asked you to stay, Dub had an encounter with Scath and set up the meeting." He searched her face, gaze intent. "And we were only just coming to realize we *all* felt more for you than friendship. I..." He swallowed.

Bat kept her gaze level on his.

"Dub had wanted to send you away until we settled things with the clan. I'm not sure he would have actually done it, but he... he wanted to be able to start fresh. I'm not sure how much you know about the clan systems of Ireland, but a man's brooch is important. And a clan leader's brooch is even more so. Without that, he may as well have lost his identity.

"Our father lost his in the last battle between the Fomoiri and the sidhe. He had a replica made, and managed to glamour it sufficiently that the duplicity was hidden from everyone but Scath. Even mother never knew. Dub found out a few centuries ago, and latched onto the idea of finding it. At first I think he wanted to use it to take over the clan." Mell's gaze searched her face, his brows pinched. "Not now. We're using it to petition for secession, as leverage for permission to form our own clan. Or, that *was* the plan. Now, we may have to use it to gain the cooperation of the clan against Balor." He fell into silence, shadows flitting over his eyes.

"I knew some of this," she said. "I knew the brooch was important, and that there was a plan. Thank you for telling me the all of it."

Mell's lips quirked up into a not-quite-smile and gave her a small shake of his head. "Let me finish before you start throwing reassurances and forgiveness around as though you're a pixie with an abundance of happy-dust." He took a breath. "Back to two months ago. Dub was probably already plotting ways to kidnap you back to Ireland as soon as we'd broken free. I was the one who said you needed to stay. But I was also the one who insisted we not begin anything with you, not right away. I…"

Bat laid a hand against his cheek, the stubble pricking her fingers. "We can talk about this after, you know."

He shook his head. "No, we can't. Because we don't know how 'this' will go." The shadows were back in his eyes and his mouth pinched. His emotions were locked down tight, though, nothing leaking through. "I hurt you. We hurt you."

"That was never your intention." She ran her thumb once more over his cheek then pulled back.

"And now ye're trying to comfort me, who should be comforting you." Mell gave her a crooked grin. "But I'll take it. Now." He paused. "Are you really all right?"

"You can't tell?" she asked again.

He tapped her forehead. "Too much going on up here right now. And, as you said, ye're tired."

"Truth? I'm still angry, but it's… muffled. Or, not muffled, but not important right now. Not with everything we have to solve. I've come to a few decisions over the last couple of days. I'm not going anywhere, and I plan to fight for what I want—which is all four of you. And, I'll tell you something I probably shouldn't. It's something I said to Finn earlier, when he came to find me in the garden. It was about chances." She shoved a few crisps around on her plate. "I told him that I would give you all the chances you needed. All of you."

"That…"

"I heard another word recently. 'Pushover.' I am probably acting like one of those at the moment." She set the plate on a small side table then buried her hands in the fuzzy-blanket. "But I do not really care. As you said, we do not know how this will end. I am well aware of that. If, when this is over, my anger is not gone, I will find a curse to lay upon you three, or maybe I will take an eye here and a little finger there, and make koldala."

He jerked back. "That was real?"

She snorted. "No. But it would be an interesting recipe to try. How would you like to be my second pirate?"

His lips tightened in suppressed mirth and his shoulders shook.

"I mean, I would not want to take a finger, even the little one, it may affect your playing. And Shar has already lost one eye. I suppose I could take an eye and a finger from Dub, but is that really fair?" She snuggled into the back of the chair, her eyes drooping closed once more.

Mell half rose and pressed a kiss to her forehead. "No, it would not be fair. If it comes to that, you can have an eye, my blood-thirsty goddess."

She gave him a half-smile. "Okay."

"Rest. I'll check on Dub and those damned pixies." Clothing rustled as he passed behind her chair, heading for the back door.

"Wait."

The footsteps halted.

"When do the other men of ba arrive?" Ari had come with them to the cottage, but his companions had returned to the forest for reinforcements, so she had yet to scan them. She didn't want to fall asleep before then.

"Not until morning. *Rest*. I'll wake you for dinner."

She curled her toes in the fuzzy-socks, enjoying the softness. Whoever had invented them was truly brilliant. "All right."

DUB

The forge was a mess.

Dub, Finn and Cu Chulainn stood in the stone building, surveying the disaster.

"At least everything is still here," Finn said.

Dub grunted. Yes, everything was still here, but he must have not secured a window the last time he used the place to make Dano's tools, because there was debris everywhere. Something had nested in the kindling he liked to use to light the hearth, and coal, coke breeze and ash had been blown and flung around the space.

He poked at the hearth, digging around until he uncovered the tuyere—the blast pipe from the blower. A lump of cold clinker nearly blocked the hole and he fished it out as well, tossing it onto the workbench for now.

The bench and clamps were in order. All the tools were in their stands and slots. The anvil, floor mandrel, and swag block were also right where they should be. His supply of black iron and pre-smelted steel, and other metals, were in their storage racks and drawers. No, there had been no thief, he really had simply left a window open.

Damnit.

"We'll help you get cleaned up and then go for anything you need. You concentrate on figuring out how we're going to turn that shard into what we need," Finn said, plucking a broom from the far corner where the cleaning tools were kept.

Cu Chulainn grunted. "We need rest, and soon."

Dub's lip curled into a sneer before he could stop it. Finn rolled his eyes. Cu Chulainn had been harping on that same thing since mid-afternoon.

"Don't be rolling your eyes at me, Finn Cumhaill. You know I am correct. The only one of us to get any sleep in the last two days was the goddess, and the green-haired fairy. Even the bomen stayed up the night long to work on tracking the cauldron."

That was true. They hadn't been able to pinpoint an exact location, but they were certain of the direction.

Northwest, far enough away that it was no longer on land, and travelling farther through the night. The hope was that the cauldron was on its way to Tir Hudi, or Balor, and that when the time came to follow the connection would grow clearer the closer they drew.

Which meant they needed a ship. His stomach churned in protest at what kind of deal he would need to strike with his father...

Cuchi grabbed up a dusting brush and got started on the workbench and clamps. They'd need to be free of any contaminants and impurities. "We don't get some rest soon, we'll start making mistakes. There's no need to be going without, not yet."

Dub's fists curled and he took a step toward the other warrior. Then paused. Cuchi's eyes were bruised not just from Dub's hits, but from exhaustion. He, Finn and the rest of the guardi had spent the night and day not only checking each piece of clothing or personal item being brought from the pub, but also working on a way to track the spell that had been laid into the invitation back to its caster.

Whatever Dub thought of Cuchi, the man *was* skilled when it came to enchantments and rune-work. Of all the immortals in Connaught, he was probably second only to Oisin. He was also nothing if not clever, especially when it came to the manipulation of raw power. As he'd put it, "How do you think I got the reputation I have?"

There *had* been something attached to the invitation, a kind of scrying spell, just as they'd suspected, and as Bat's vision had shown. They hadn't succeeded in following it back just yet, but Cu Chulainn, Oisin and Sean from

Finn's unit had worked up a way to trail the connection to the original caster the next time that connection was opened. It all depended on when—and if—that happened.

"Go get some rest, then," Dub finally said, grudgingly. "And find Oisin. Take him with you. We do need you two sharp."

"He crashed as soon as the wards here were done," Finn offered.

Good. That was good. Dub sighed. The O'Loinsigh brothers were finally in over their heads, and there wasn't a damn thing he could do about it. This particular fight wasn't one he could walk away from, now that his goddess had become involved.

For a half-second, he contemplated drugging her and his brothers and shipping them off to Alaska. That should be far enough away, right? Let the gods and sidhe and other immortals battle it out once more, let them kill each other off.

What true warrior doesn't enjoy the kill? His father's words slid through his mind. His hand twitched and he itched to pick up his hammer, to beat his frustration out against iron and steel.

"Is that him?" The voice was light with music.

Damn pixies.

"Of course, it's him."

Great, there was a second one.

"How long have you lived here you don't know the smith when he shows up?"

Dub groaned. There were *three*. And where there were three, more were soon to follow.

"She told us to help, didn't she?" the first voice said. It

was slightly lower than the others. "But are we helping the frowning one or the bald one? Or is it the golden one?"

Dub's eyes closed as he grabbed at the ends of his frayed temper, and Finn coughed.

"I'm out," Cuchi said, heading for the door. "Wake me when there's food."

"I guess it's not the bald one," the third voice squeaked.

"It's the frowning one, I'm telling you. He's the smith. He was here only a couple months ago. Are you so blinded by the diddies you don't remember?"

"Shhhhhh."

Diddies? He could guess whose. Dub's eyes shot open as those frayed ends slipped from his grasp, and he spun toward the voices. One of the vent-opening shutters was ajar, and three pixies hovered there, fading sunlight flashing silver, red and pink through their wings.

The pink one chirped and they darted out of sight.

Finn let out a laugh. "Ah, so ferocious, the sight of him scares the pixies away."

"Don't mock me." What business did those pests have with talking about diddies?

"What mocking? I'd love to have the ability. Bad as mosquitoes most of the time. Even the ones at the office." Finn went to the far side of the room and began sweeping. Dust flew into the air. "But... they are useful."

Dub kicked the anvil. It screeched to the left, leaving tracks in the floor. With a sigh, he nudged it back into place then turned to the window. "Get in here."

The three figures zipped into view.

"Clean only. Everything stays were it is."

Heads and bodies bobbed in agreement. The red one zipped above the others in a jerk then settled, wings flying in a blur. "We can guard, too." Its little chest puffed forward. "I hear goddesses appreciate a good guarding."

The pink one fluttered to his side and slapped him. "Don't say dirty things about goddesses. It's a good way to give them an excuse to smite you."

He didn't need to listen to this. "Clean. *Quietly*."

The three froze, then zipped into action. They really were efficient. It took another hour, but he, Finn, and the pixies got the forge into working order.

Now, to finally get to work. The real work. "I need the shard."

Finn cast a warning look at the pixies.

"The one off the cauldron? I know where it is. Do you want me to go fetch it?" The silver one was out the window before Dub could say anything one way or the other. And that was the trouble with pixies. They knew far too much, and were far too able at getting into places they shouldn't be. If it really did come back with the shard, he, Finn and the entirety of the guardi would need to reevaluate their warding skills. Hells, he already needed to do just that, based on what happened at the pub.

It was a few minutes later that the silver pixie zipped back into the forge with a pouting face and crossed arms. "Stupid sidhe. Stupid druids. Stupid wards. Take the fun from things."

Dub suppressed a sigh of relief and scowled. "Don't be trying to go into places you shouldn't, and you won't have trouble with wards. Get out. Now. The rest is for me to do."

The pixies exchanged a look and Finn grinned.

"But the goddess told us to help you," the red one protested. "What if we just stay quiet? We can fetch, or play messenger. We don't mind."

Dub opened his mouth to deny them, and the pink one cut in. "Ciara also told us to help. And we know what you, and the goddess, did for Dano. Both the Littles and the Bigs are agreed. We will repay the Egyptian goddess's kindness. And yours."

His eyes slid closed. There was no arguing with the pixies once a decision like that had been made. While widespread, they were one of the most tightly knit communities amongst the fae. Once "the pixies" agreed, that was it. They were a little like demented bees with a collective consciousness. Some even had stingers.

"I'm out," Finn said, heading for the door. "I'll fetch the shard then check in on Shar."

"He's probably in the garden, or patrolling the borders of the land." Once Bat and her things had been settled in the cottage and the wards were set, Shar had disappeared into the small copse of trees near the rear of the property. There was also a small garden near there that Shar had begun a few centuries ago. It was not as well maintained as the one at the pub, but working on it would no doubt do much to restore Shar's equilibrium. Dub understood. A lot had happened, and it had ever been his youngest brother's habit to retreat to the land when he needed to sort his thoughts.

Finn gave a short nod then disappeared, leaving Dub

to his—almost—solitude. He sent one more admonishing glare at the pixies then pulled out the sketchpad.

The wisest course would be to create a cast of the shard, so he could forge the other pieces without damaging it. Doing that would take too long, though, and he didn't have all the necessary materials here in the forge. He'd have to work directly with the shard through the whole process.

The tricky part was going to be fusing the stone and metal—it was not something that could be done in the normal world. Oh, there were clever clasps and fastenings and inlays, but he needed the structural integrity of a true fuse if the shard was to be incorporated into a spearhead.

He needed to recreate whatever was done to the vessel that turned it into a cauldron. For a brief moment he contemplated calling upon Goibniu, but his old teacher would not appreciate it, and could just as likely do something to sabotage the spear as help Dub make it. The Smith was… cantankerous.

Finn returned a few minutes later and laid the shard on the workbench. Without a word he disappeared back out the door, leaving Dub to his work.

Dub examined the stone, not as an immortal this time, but as a craftsman. Three of the sides were smooth, nearly as slick as obsidian. Those wouldn't work. There was a notch on one end, and around the other side were three grooves. These he could use. They would help the metal find sturdy purchase with the stone.

Sketching a rough outline of the shard, he concentrated on those rough points. Then he began the creation of the runes. He'd need Strength, and Unity.

Earth, and metal. He was mixing Irish Ogham runes and the Anglo-Saxon Futhorc brought by the Druids, but this type of magic was less about the technicalities and more about the precision of intent and meaning. He needed to convince and direct the magic, and magic only ever did exactly what you told it to do. No more and no less.

He examined his construction. There was something missing. Strength, Unity, Earth, and Metal. *What* was missing...?

What was the shard? It wasn't only stone, or earth.

For Bat, it was... creation?

Life.

But that wasn't all. He needed this spear to not only give life, but to take it. It was a weapon, after all.

Death.

Once more he studied the runes. He sketched them again, Life and Death opposite each other, interlocking with the other four. A current started, a low pulse of energy.

But it still wasn't enough.

What *else* was missing...? Dub didn't sigh, and he didn't shift on the stool. He started again, sketching the runes in another pattern. This was what the Smith had taught him. Not just the working of metal, but the crafting of it. And to truly craft, you needed to be able to craft the magic. You needed to envision the end result of your creation, to... project it from your mind into the universe.

It was not something that could be done if you were impatient, or angry. In this place, in his forge, Dub could finally shed the frustrations and worries of the last couple months. Distantly aware that the pixies hovered in the rafters, he concentrated. Mell came with a plate of food and then left.

Still he sketched.

Night fell, and he lit the lamps. His eyes did not droop, and his fingers did not cramp. He was on the last page of the sketchpad when he found the missing piece. He placed it in the middle, between Life and Death, Metal and Earth, Strength and Unity. It tied them together, and created the bond he'd need to fuse the steel to the shard.

Love. A mother's love for her children, even those gone astray.

The tingle of power surged as he placed the last stroke of pencil to paper. He sat back, satisfied with the day's work. Tomorrow he would begin forging the spearhead. He'd lay the runes upon the floor of the forge, and upon the anvil. He'd sketch them over the steel and over the shard, and chant them as he worked.

As much as he hated to admit it, though, Cuchi was right. He needed to rest while he could. For now, for tonight, he was done. And he had a goddess to find.

He missed her.

Chapter Fifteen

Bastie,
I… have no words. But let me just tell you, the grumpy one
knows what he is doing…
- Bat, a satisfied goddess

BAT

She shifted, pressing herself into the soft mattress beneath her.

"I only need a drop. Just a drop and a tune."

The words were soft, seductive.

She opened her eyes to nothing, the dark pressing in on her. She tried to sit, tried to push herself up, but failed. Something bound her to the bed.

"Just a drop of blood, sweet goddess, and a tune on the harp. That's not too much to ask, now is it?"

She blinked. Nothing. There was nothing there, not

the bedroom, not the heavy wood rafters of the ceiling, not the posts of the bed frame, not the bedside lamp or the green-curtained windows.

"I'm not so bad, you know. All I've ever wanted was the best for my men, my people. The gods, they neglected us." The voice wove through her, seeking out the hollow places. It found a pinprick hole in her soul and slid in. *"I know they've neglected you as well. I wouldn't do that, sweet goddess. Not to someone like you, not to anyone. I've worked hard to return, to come back to those who need me. How could I turn from someone such as you, who needs so much?"*

She knew this voice now. It was Balor, somehow. He had penetrated their wards and come into her dreams. Or was this a vision? ...Then where was her sight?

"Oh, they taught you so little of the ways of the soul, and of life. How have you survived?" A hint of derision crept into Balor's tone and broke the spell he'd been weaving.

But he was still there, still in her somehow. She was weak, drained from the efforts of the deep scans she'd performed that day, and had yet to be able to replenish herself. Mell had brought her dinner and she'd gotten kisses from him, Shar and Finn before they sent her to bed. The small boosts might be enough...

She gripped the tendrils of seduction and deceit that Balor had sent seeking through her and tore them apart. They retreated then surged forward, invading through the weak points he'd found. Points she only now realized were not her imagination, but rips in her soul caused by the losses of her existence and past pain.

These were tears she could not afford to have. She

called upon Mother Sky for strength. *Please. Please, help me now.*

And she was answered. The response was distant, as though Mother Sky was farther away than a few thousand kilometers, but it did come. Power filtered through her, carrying a hint of dry air, warm sand, and clean lotus. Sending a pulse of thanks, Bat directed this power to the shadowed tendrils, forcing them from her and sealing the tears. It was a patch, not a true healing, but it would hold.

The only thing that would truly heal those tears was time, and trust. One she didn't have, but the other she was working on.

As Mother Sky withdrew, she sent a final pulse of power, just a spark really. *This is all I may give now, child. But it should be all you need from me.* A rush of tenderness came to Bat, echoing the feeling from the shard.

"*Storeen.*"

Bat stirred, freed from whatever it was that held her immobile. She blinked again, and Dub's face came into focus, bent over her. There were dark smudges under his bright blue eyes, and a dark stubble dusted his jaw. A lock of hair fell over his brow, and she reached up to push it aside.

It fell right back into a mocking curl that ended just above his left eye.

"Are ya all right then?" He frowned, one of the ones that showed concern.

"I am now," she reassured him. "What are you doing in here?"

He stood and stepped back from the bed, crossing his

arms. "I don't need to be Mell to know that you are lying to me."

Had she been lying? She pushed herself up and scooched back, propping her back against the pillows and tugging the blankets up with her. She wasn't naked —she wore an old t-shirt of Shar's. The fabric was worn to the perfect softness, but it *was* a bit thin. As much progress as she'd made with the brothers, and as much as she reveled in their touches, now didn't seem the appropriate time to flaunt her charms. Not when Dub was exhausted and beginning to interrogate her. She pulled her knees up to her chest and hugged them. "Where is Mell?"

He sat on the edge of the bed. "Sleeping. As is everyone else, and as you should have been." His eyes narrowed. "But you weren't. What happened? When I entered, your eyes were open, and they swirled with shadows I would normally associate with the sluagh."

There were the shadows again. She tilted her head. "Are there fae who deal in dreams?"

"Some. The Fir Dearg are known to cause nightmares for the fun of it, much as pookas enjoy a small spot of vandalism every now and then."

"Liam? Really?" The pooka had come in the other day, a tall and thin woman beside him, and they'd appeared alternately sinister and content. He'd found his love. She'd helped with that, and it warmed her to remember.

"Ye're avoiding this conversation. Why?"

She patted the bed next to her. "Because it is not an easy one for me to have, and I would prefer to do it once, when everyone is here. It is not urgent enough to wake them, not now. And because you are exhausted. If everyone else is sleeping, why aren't you?"

He searched her face. "Where is Killer? He should be here, with you."

Dub wasn't going to let this go. "He decided to stay with Mell tonight." It had been a bit strange, but she hadn't thought anything of it at the time, as her pup would occasionally sleep with one or another of the brothers.

She bolted upright as Dub stood and headed for the door. What if she wasn't the only one Balor had gone after tonight? Throwing aside the blankets, she headed after him and down the hall to the room he and Mell were supposed to be sharing.

Mell lay on the edge of the bed, one hand flung above his head and the other buried in the ruff of Killer's neck. He didn't stir as light from the hall slashed across his face. Killer lifted his head and let out a low *whoof*, as though to say *see, I got this*.

Dub backed out of the doorway, nudging Bat back into the hall, and shut the door. "He's fine." There was a wealth of emotion in his voice, but the only one Bat could pick out was frustration. He turned and pinned her in place with a glare to rival Bastet's when Anubis was toying with the cat. "You are *not* sleeping alone."

This was not a statement she wanted to argue with.

Grabbing her hand, Dub hauled her back to her room. "Get back in the bed."

She nodded and climbed up. Dub let out a low sound, and she twisted, suddenly aware of the position she was in—on her hands and knees, butt up and facing a healthy, if tired, male. The thin shirt she wore did nothing to disguise the roundness of her flesh. She *had* at least worn underwear.

"Ye're trying ta kill me, ya are." Dub took a step toward her, his hands curled into fists.

She stayed as she was, casting a teasing gaze at the not-man. She'd always thought he was attractive, from her first glimpse of those fierce eyes and the stubble along his jaw. She was finally ready to give in to that attraction. She wanted to explore the tattoos she had only been able to sneak glimpses of. She wanted to skim her hand along the column of his throat and lower, to feel the involuntary flexing of his muscles as she ran her nails over his skin.

"Come here," she said. Someone needed to take the next step forward in this relationship. And someone had to be first in her bed, or they were right back in the same predicament. In this, she would choose.

Dub crossed his arms. "What are ya doing?"

She wiggled her ass and watched as his lips parted. "Seducing you?"

His frown eased. "And this is seducing?"

Her gaze dropped to his trousers, and the growing erection at his groin. "It does seem to be working."

"You *breathing* works."

She smiled. Those were not the most romantic words she'd heard, especially uttered in that disgruntled tone, but they were his truth.

So they were beautiful to her.

The smile widened to a grin, and she laughed, dropping and rolling to her back. She held out her arms to this not-man who had a million different scowls and frowns and only a few smiles.

He gifted her with one and took a step toward her before stopping again. "Ye're sure? I'll no be going back to how we were after this, even if the others change their minds."

She raised a brow but didn't drop her arms. "I have already made a decision about that. If the others change their minds, then this stops. All of it. So you had best ensure they do *not* change."

He shrugged and gripped the bottom of his sweater, pulling it up a few inches.

Her breath caught.

He raised it to just above his navel, revealing a stretch of muscled abdomen and golden flesh. "I can't change yer mind about that one?"

She tore her gaze from that flesh and up to his lapis-gaze. "My arms are getting tired." She lowered the limbs in question and crossed them under her breasts, pressing the flesh together under the t-shirt. Dub's eyes dropped. "I am here, and ready, a goddess offering herself to you, and you would argue?"

He stripped off the sweater. "I am not quite such a fool as that."

Then he was over her, his head bent to capture her lips in a kiss that echoed the first one he'd ever given her. The sheer heat of it took her breath as his tongue slipped into her mouth and his lips devoured her. The shock and heat and need that he'd evoked the day of Dano's murder was back, but under it was something new. Something she had never experienced while lying with a man.

Trust.

She did trust him, she realized as she returned the kiss, her hands clutching at his shoulders and her nails digging into the muscles there. She didn't want him pulling back, not now that he was finally *here*.

This moment had been building for two-and-a-half months.

Finally. That was all she could think as he pulled his lips from her and pressed open kisses along her neck and down to her collarbone. Her heart pounded as blood rushed to her sex. The flesh there grew slick in anticipation.

Her hands skimmed down his back and around his waist, to find the fastener of his trousers. With a twist and a tug, she had the button undone and the zipper down. Slipping her hand inside, she found bare flesh.

"No underwear?" How would she get through her days, now, imagining him bare beneath one thin barrier of cloth?

He thrust into the warmth of her hand, the motion quickly stilled, as though he hadn't been able to help himself. "Forgot to pack any," he ground out. He pulled away and jumped from the bed, toeing off his shoes and stripping off his pants in motions so quick they were a blur to her eyes. Cloth ripped and he groaned, this time in a different frustration. "Fuck it," he muttered. "I'll make the pixies fix them."

Then he was back over her, his hands slipping under her shirt and pushing it up to reveal her breasts to his gaze. She arched her back, inviting his touch, and he did not disappoint.

Propping himself on one elbow, he gathered the flesh of her left breast in his other hand. "Do you know how long I've been longing to touch you like this?"

She let out a playful laugh as she pressed against his palm, seeking a friction he had yet to give her. She needed the sensation, craved it. "Probably as long as I have wanted you to touch me."

His hand slid down then back up and over her nipple, the calluses of his palm teasing the sensitive nub. "We were idiots, weren't we?" He continued this for a moment more, then gripped her breast in a hold just this side of too tight and bent his head to take her nipple in his mouth.

She sucked in a breath. What had he said? Idiots. Right. "Yes. Idiot. All idiots."

He chuckled, the deep sound vibrating through her. He pulled his mouth away.

"No," she said, her breath leaving her. "Go back." Was she begging? Just from this small touch? Goddesses should not beg.

When he didn't comply right away, she sought his gaze. His lapis-eyes were bright, burning with desire, the pupils wide. "I canna go slow, no this time." His brogue had deepened. "But I'll be careful of ya, *storeen*. So, so careful of ya. I'll no hurt ya, I promise."

"Do not," she said, pulling her arms from his shoulders. "Do not go slow." She gripped her shirt and tugged it up until it caught under her chin. "Bollix."

He let out a sound that may have been a groan, may have been a chuckle, and may have been something in between. "Are ya wanting this off then?" The hand at her breast disappeared, and then her shirt was gone.

"And these as well," she said, lifting her hips.

He hooked his fingers into her panties and pulled them down her legs in one swift move. "Now, where were we?"

She slipped her arm back around his shoulders, the heat of his skin radiating into her and filling that hollow place. "I was telling you to not go slow." She nipped his lower lip, putting a bit of bite into it. "I do not need gentle." Raising a brow, she sent him a slow, sly smile. "Goddess, remember?"

He captured her lips once more and grabbed her thigh, pulling her leg up and over his hip. She pulled up her other knee, letting her leg fall wide to allow him access to all of her. She could feel the slickness between her thighs.

She was more than ready for this.

He shifted up, finding her entrance. The tip of his shaft hovered at her opening for a few moments, teasing in slow circles. She dug her nails into his tattooed shoulders, and with a grunt he pushed home in one long stroke.

She lifted her other leg and locked her heels together, holding him to her just like that. He filled her. Not just with flesh, but with warmth. With acceptance, with longing, and joy and... and...

And love. She finally admitted it to herself. She did love them. And she'd been too much of a coward to face up to it fully.

Because if she loved first, and they changed their minds... where did that leave her?

His forehead dropped to hers. "I canna..."

Pulling herself up, she dropped a kiss on his shoulder.

Then she allowed his to pull away a few inches. He thrust, and she met his movement. Again he moved, and she met him each time. They set up a rhythm, and their words died away. The only sounds were flesh on flesh, and the rush of her breath mingling with the gust of his. Their skin grew slick with sweat, and her nails dug into his back once more, an anchor for the now pounding thrust of his cock into her.

It had been a long time for her, but she knew these sensations, this thrill. There were memories of flesh meeting flesh, of falling into a person so deep it was as though you were the same being.

But it had never been like this. Because she had never loved like this before. And this... *this* she wanted to never end.

So, she held him to her, gave of herself, as they lost themselves together. When his movement began to lose their steadiness, and she knew he was close, she angled her hips down, putting more pressure on the flash over her clit. She would come with him, and they would find their release together.

Yes, it had been a very long time for her, but she was no stranger to sacrifices of this kind. She smiled as the fluttering started in her womb. Almost there...

He thrust again.

Almost...

Sliding her hands up, she buried them in his hair and gripped, pulling his head back to that his throat was exposed to her. Locking her gaze with his, she whispered, "Now."

His eyes widened and went dark. He froze.

Then with one last thrust that sent them both into the headboard, he released inside her as her channel clenched around him, the wave of her climax spreading in a small explosion through her body.

They remained locked together, limbs wrapped around each other for one long minute. Then Dub sagged against her, his weight pressing her into the mattress. He laid a gentle kiss against her throat. "Thank you," he whispered.

Power surged into her. This had been a supplication, and a sacrifice. She had granted this not-man a part of herself, and in return, she had received so much more.

Her arms tightened around him once more. A few minutes. Just a few more minutes like this. Then they would rise, and clean themselves, and sleep.

But just a few more moments would harm none.

A pinprick hole in her soul closed as her eyes dipped shut. Dub rolled over, taking her with him, and she lay draped across his side. One of his hands skimmed down her side and settled on the flesh of her hip, lightly kneading it.

Bat lay her head on his shoulder, her leg draped over his, and nestled into his side. One of her hands rested on his chest, and she studied the tattoos there. The swirls and tangles and knots there were so intrinsic in the Celtic style fascinated her. She lifted her hand and traced a finger along one particular spiral that wound along his upper chest. Then she moved down to play with his nipple.

She loved the nipples on a man. They were so... purposeless. They were there simply to tease, as a pure delight.

"Stop that." Dub's voice rumbled through her.

"Why?"

"Because I am exhausted." His words slurred.

She lifted her head. His eyes were closed, but a small smile graced his lips. They were so rare, those smiles. Another of those pesky holes sealed.

The dark circles under his eyes had become near purple. She should let him rest. "I am going to shower."

His eyes shot open. "Not alone."

Her heart pounded and heat began to gather in her groin. "I thought you were tired?"

He raised a brow and grinned.

Eventually, they did sleep.

Chapter Sixteen

Dearest Bastet,

I really am worried for you now. I hinted at sex, and you did not reply.

Once I am done with the craziness of attempting to stop the return of an evil that should have been taken care of more than a millennium ago, I am packing up my immortals and my puppy, and we are tracking you down.

I am not used to this. You are not something I normally need to worry over. So cease.

- Bat, the goddess you are causing to worry

BAT

Similar to the first morning Bat had woken in her room at the pub, she stretched under the thick comforter that the brothers had made sure was in her room at the cottage. Or, she tried to. Something was different, though. An arm was wrapped around her middle, and her feet were trapped between two strong legs. And the legs were very warm. She scrunched her toes and enjoyed the sensation of being held as the night before came back to her.

Finally. The word echoed in her mind once more. *Finally.*

Then her stomach clenched, and not in the delicious way it had when Dub's fingers worked their magic. What would the others say?

It was a pointless worry, of course. They'd all agreed. But now that she'd moved forward with one of the men, would their reactions be different than when they'd only contemplated the idea? What about Shar? He'd already admitted that he'd have some trouble seeing her with others.

A swift knock sounded and the door swung open, revealing Mell with a breakfast tray piled high with eggs, bacon and... pancakes! Mell had only made them one other time, the morning after she'd agreed to stay, saying they were only for special occasions. They were different from others she'd tried, thin, sprinkled with powdered sugar and lemon. He also added a little orange in the middle, not too much, but the flavor was delightful paired with whiskey-tea. She pulled in a breath of tart sweetness and savory bacon.

Mell chuckled. "I knew the pancakes would distract you." He gave her a warm smile and a tendril of contentment reached her. Under it was a suppressed excitement. He bounced a little on his feet then stepped into the room.

She once again tried to sit up, and Dub tightened his hold, turning her into him. Her breasts pressed to his chest and only then did she realize she was naked. She'd slept the night through with no clothes on and wasn't cold. The damned not-man was better than a radiator. She snuggled into him, forgetting Mell for a moment. Dub let out a rumbling sigh and shifted, releasing her feet from between his calves and pressing his morning erection to the softness of her hip.

"Hey now, none of that with the kids in the room." Mell plopped onto the foot of the bed and grinned at them.

Dub groaned in frustration and half-pulled her under him. "Go away."

"No can do. The bomen are here, and we need the goddess up and fed and looking not quite so sexily disheveled."

Bat freed an arm and patted Dub on the shoulder. "As much as I am loving this moment, Mell is correct. And I should put on clothes before too many more people come looking for us."

"Well now, don't bother on my account." Finn's amused voice came from the doorway.

Shoving Dub's shoulder and craning her neck to the side, Bat could just make out a grinning Finn in the doorway. His smile matched Mell's, and she returned it with one of her own, knowing she probably looked like Bastet after a particularly satisfying hunt.

Shadows shifted just behind Finn, and Shar came into view. He frowned, but it was... thoughtful. When he caught her gaze, his lips quirked and he shrugged, as if to say *"well there you go."* It wasn't quite happiness, but he wasn't *upset*.

And he wasn't walking away.

She decided right then that he would be the next she took. There was much to do today, but tonight she would take her giant into her, make him fully hers. And she would belong to him. Her mind wandered to the morning after he'd been stabbed with the soul blade. To the hopes and... and *wants* he'd stirred in her with his words of staying. Even then she'd begun developing feelings for all three brothers, and known it would eventually become an issue. But she'd pushed it from her mind then, and again when they asked her to stay and gave her Killer.

Maybe she should have tackled it right then, instead of allowing the emotions their words had stirred in her to lead the way. It could have saved them two months of frustration and secrets. Shar's words of that afternoon came back to her. He'd said she was their beginning. She'd forgotten that, lost in her concerns about the growing distance between the four of them.

Then it occurred to her—the distance had *always* been there. And it wasn't only the brothers who created it.

In fact, it had been *her* doing all along, especially in the beginning. How had she not seen it until now?

Even after they asked her to stay, she held back from them. She avoided asking them questions of their past, and discussing her own. She didn't ask about the future beyond the next few days, didn't inquire about the Fomoiri clan gathering, or why they were living separated from the rest of their people. She didn't talk to Mell about his adventures, the painful and the joyous, only music, and his plans for the pub. She accompanied her gentle giant to the garden, but she couldn't bring herself to ask any more about the time he guarded the Rowan, though she knew it pained him. And Dub, her grumpy not-man, she had left to his own devices. Had she known he'd gained the title of the Smith? Or his plans for the brooch, and why he was so intent on ensuring the brothers broke free from their father? Or what exactly happened between him and Cu Chulainn?

They had taken on some of her pain, they knew some of what her past consisted of, but had she allowed them to really know *her*? Had she truly opened herself to them?

No. No to all of it. And that was something she needed to fix sooner rather than later. She needed to face what *she* had done, to truly heal from her past and move forward in the present, with this new life.

"One minute." She shoved Dub's shoulder again, and he rolled away, taking most of the comforter with him. She caught the edge and held it to her chest, part of her thigh and hip exposed. "Everyone come in."

Mell flashed a wicked grin, similar to the one he sported when she first met him.

"Not for that," she admonished him. "No, come in, and shut the door. I need to say something, and I want to say it with just the five of us, and I want to be sure I am understood." Her words were possibly a little foreboding, because Mell's grin faded and Finn sobered. Dub groaned, rubbed his face, and twisted his head to stare at her. Shar stepped into the room, shoving Finn before him, and closed the door behind him.

Despite her earlier fears, she focused on her giant, the only one whose demeanor remained calm. "I will say this, and then we will get to work. I..." She swallowed, struggling for words. "I want to apologize."

Dub growled, Mell shook his head and Finn frowned. Again, Shar was who she remained focused on. The brother who had first asked her to stay, and who had called her their *beginning*. Even if he'd had doubts about his own reactions to seeing her intimate with others, he'd been the most *sincere* with her, the most honest of the brothers.

"Let me say this, please. It is not easy for me, but I need it to be said, and I need you to hear it." Her eyes slid closed.

The mattress dipped as a weight settled beside her, opposite Dub. "Tell us, goddess. We will listen." Finn laid a callused hand on her shoulder, then skimmed down her arm to link his fingers with her.

One of the holes, the pinpricks of doubt and fear and pain that Balor's tendrils had found the night before, closed at those words and his touch. She gripped his hand and opened her eyes. Power filled her, but it wasn't that of a goddess. It was the power of a woman who finally faced her *own* shortcomings and pain, and fought to overcome them.

"I need to apologize," she said again. "Because I came here damaged. Until last night, I did not realize just how extensive that damage was, only that I needed more than my current existence. Before my visions led me to this green land, I managed my days by clinging to the idea that I was perfectly fine on my own, even when I did not believe it. I lived in the *now* of my existence, and concentrated only on that." She finally moved her gaze from Shar's and focused on Finn's fingers intertwined with hers. "I came into existence with one purpose, though it was not fulfilled until two millennia after my birth—I was supposed to unite the Upper and Lower Kingdoms.

"At my birth, I was faced with a choice. Because while I did have this purpose, I was different somehow. Most deities… well, their nature is their nature. They are who they are. Seth is thunder and storms and just a bit of savagery, never quite content, though still an honorable man. Isis is beauty and grace. Horus seeks truth and healing and has remained young at heart. Hathor is… femininity, the mother, the nurturer. Bastet is full of mischief and loyalty. Apep is chaos. I could go on, but the point is they were all born with their natures. I was not, I only had a purpose."

"*Realta*, you don—" Mell started, his brows pinched.

"I do. *Please*."

"Shut up." Dub sat up, his glare directed at his brother. "We listened to you about respecting her pain, letting her heal. Well, pull your head out of your ass and let her fucking heal." His expression softened to something close to pity. "She is not you. Let her *speak* her pain."

Mell's face froze into a blank mask.

This was not what she had intended. She was telling them this in order to, yes, begin her healing, but to also to bring them closer to her, and each other. "I would like *all* of you to remain silent until I am done." She directed this at Dub, along with a small frown and a light slap on his shoulder. He did deserve it for starting with Mell.

Mell snorted, his expression easing, as Dub turned his glare on her.

When neither spoke again, she continued. "I had a choice to make. The light or the dark. Chaos or order and justice. Both sides whispered to me, called me to them. But I chose justice, and became who I am. I... existed. Though I was different from the other deities, and they knew it, I still had my worshippers, and I loved and guided them. For two millennia I was a guide and mother and caregiver for those I loved. I sought justice for them, and I helped their souls to the Land of Reeds when the time came. It was a good life, and existence. I had sacrifices and offerings of many kinds, including, yes, male companionship.

"When Narmer was born, I had a vision, and I knew it was time. I travelled to Thebes, then on to Nekhen and after that to Sep, looking for Seth. I'd known for some time that I would one day join with him and Horus. We all knew, and I considered them friends, and my fate."

She paused, her gaze on the lumpy folds of the comforter. This was the part she didn't know how to explain, because she didn't understand it herself. Mell shifted at the edge of her vision, and she ignored him. Shar stepped up to the foot of the bed and sat beside his brother, one leg propped on the edge of the bed so he could twist to watch her.

"I will not tell you everything of that time. Many things happened, and maybe when our current... situation is done we can have a night where we talk of times long past, the good and the bad." She waited until they nodded, all of them being careful to abide by her order to be quiet.

That small sign of respect warmed her. Horus would have kept his silence for a while, but eventually would have become distracted and tried to cajole her out of her worry. Or have wandered off. Seth would have listened for a bit, then told her to get over it or order him to hurt someone in vengeance.

"There was a war, yes," she said, continuing her tale. "Many say Narmer was a bloodthirsty man, and he could be. But he knew Egypt needed to be whole, to not fight amongst itself, if it was to survive much longer. For that peace to be possible, Horus and Seth needed to be willing to get along. That was where I came in. I kept the peace, mediated, and yes, took them into myself.

"But we were never... *true* lovers, as I had always thought we would become. We did not love each other, not as Horus loves Hathor, or Oisin loves his wife though she is lost to him. We were companions, and friends. And we managed for centuries in this way. In the beginning, I stayed with them at the palace in Memphis. But after not too long—a few decades only—I grew to miss my home and left for a visit. The next visit was longer, and even longer ones came after that, until I resided in my small temple permanently once more, only leaving for a few months every decade or so to mediate troubles. They did not seek me out." She met Mell's shadowed gaze then shrugged, a rueful smile tugging up her lips. "They abandoned me, yes, but I left them first, in a way." Mell's lips parted and a cross between anger, resentment and melancholy pushed at her before it was withdrawn. "We can certainly argue that they wronged me first, by not loving me in the way I had expected," she said in acknowledgement of Mell's reaction. "But we can also say that I allowed the situation."

She waved a hand. "I am not stating that everything after was my fault, but I can see how I allowed it to come to pass. How it set a precedent with the other gods and goddesses. I was Bat, who'd come into existence for one thing, and one thing only. And when that was done... well, it is hard to be without a reason for existing. Man has been trying to figure out his own reasons for longer than I have." It was an amusing thought, that man had been in existence longer than she had, and that her troubles so well matched theirs. She really was different from other deities.

"*Storeen*," Dub said, and the single word held amused exasperation.

"Right, back to my point. There was a single moment when it truly ended, between the three of us, and the purpose for which I was born was finally over. It came to me as a vision two days ago, the day the invitation arrived, and Ari came to us, and secrets were revealed. I had come for a visit to Memphis, and Horus informed me he would be formally joining with Hathor. Seth was there, in the back of the courtyard, when they told me, and he...

walked away, never saying a word. They said I longed to be free of my duties, and I could not correct them. It was not really that I longed to be *free* of my work, I only wanted to choose it. How selfish is that? When most gods never get to choose so much as their nature, I wanted to be able to choose not only my nature but my duties and my freedom." She paused and let out a short laugh, though she was not amused.

Finn's thumb ran over the back of her hand, silently encouraging her.

"When it came to pass that I no longer stood between Seth and Horus, it... ripped something from me." The words were coming easier now. "I felt betrayed that they walked away. That they left me alone, as did the other gods except Bastet. I clung to that pain, and used it to get through my days, the idea that they had left first. I tried to be content in my temple. But... if I look at it, I was the one who left first." She let out a soft laugh, no longer seeing the bedroom or the four men around her, but a young Horus and more carefree Seth, as she'd known them at the beginning of her existence. "And I have to wonder if that hurt them," she whispered as she shook her head and focused on the present once more. "There is a point to my telling you this. This morning I realized I had been doing the same to the four of you. The only difference? You— you did not walk away."

She had to collect herself as tears pricked her eyes and her throat closed. Relief at finally saying aloud something she had known to be the real truth for millennia, but had been too weak to admit, welled in her, healing a few more of those treacherous holes in her spirit.

"And while I feel I do deserve to be angry about the secrets you were all keeping, I was keeping just as many of my own. I did not reach out to insist you tell me those secrets, or try to learn more of you, or your past or motivations. I was so focused on my own pain, I missed yours." She turned her head and met Finn's hazel gaze, more green than golden-brown. "This time *I* was the coward."

"Are you done?" Mell set aside the tray and leaned toward her, propping himself on one hand. There were no tendrils of emotion escaping from him, but she could see it in his clear eyes, in the small smile that tugged at the corners of his mouth, and the easy set of his shoulders.

"Not quite." Her words were teasing. She *wanted* to be done, and to be able to lean into the playful brother and steal a kiss, but she needed to finish what she'd started with her confession.

"Finish then," Shar said, steady as ever. Was it her imagination, or had the anger and frustration he'd shown since she talked to Seth in the library disappeared?

"Yes, I will finish." She took a breath and bent her head. "I would like to start over between us. Not fully, because I have come to know and care about all of you, but I would like to start over with no secrets. Not for us to —what is the word—*spill* everything now, but with the promise that we will spend time learning both the hard things and the easy things. And—" Here was the part she had really been dreading to say. "And I need you all to know that I—" the words wouldn't come out.

Mell leaned forward another couple of inches and

caught her attention. "I know. I know what you are trying to say. And it is okay if you can't say it yet."

Another of those holes closed. It was a slow process, but now that she'd spotted them, now that she was truly confronting her pain, they *were* healing. Finn squeezed her hand, Shar nodded, and Dub settled a hand over her thigh under the covers. All four of them were there, *with* her.

"I love you." Her words were soft, barely audible, but all four of them stilled, as though a paralyzing curse had been triggered. A new wave of relief filled her at finally saying it. At saying it *first*, at having the courage to open up that part of herself.

A warm breeze brushed past her, and along with it a loving touch. Nut—Mother Sky—was with her in that moment, and Bat remembered the moment of her birth, and the decision she had made.

For I am she of the two faces, who has been saved, and I have saved myself from all things evil.

She waited, but none of the men returned the words. Expecting the hurt to come pouring in, she braced herself.

It did not come.

She had done her best, she realized. She had done what she needed to do, and she was satisfied with that. They would say the words, eventually.

"You are amazing," Dub said. Head tilted back, he gazed blankly at the ceiling.

Of all the men, she expected to hear those words from him the least.

Mell gave a little bounce then launched himself at her, landing with a soft *oof* against her chest and nearly sending Finn off the bed. Shar barely caught the tray of breakfast. Wrapping his arms around her, Mell didn't speak, but he opened himself to her. For a brief shining moment, she saw all of him—the lockbox of pain, the joy, the longing for a home that matched hers, the doubts and fears. And at the center was something so pure, so simple, it brought tears to her eyes once more.

It was his love for her. He may never say the words, but he'd shown her. He had allowed her a glimpse of this place in himself two months ago, but this was *more*. This was his promise to her, and it was from someone who, in his own way, was the most guarded of the four men.

"Get off." Dub shoved at his brother, and Mell's arms tightened around her.

"No. She's mine now. All of you can bollix off."

Bat laughed at Mell's words, for she could tell he was joking. Joy danced in his voice and played through the connection he'd formed between the two of them.

"Ye're pulling the blanket down, and if you don't stop, no breakfast will be had, and the men of ba will continue to wait," Shar said evenly. There was a suppressed heat there that Bat would definitely explore tonight. "Plus, world-destroying entity trying to return to the living, blah, blah."

A new wave of laughter hit Bat.

"Great, and now she's hysterical," Finn said, standing from the bed. "What are you doing to the goddess, Mell?"

"Mine, mine, mine." Mell buried his face in the soft spot where her shoulder met her neck. "Mine," he whispered.

Dub shoved his brother again, putting some of his *strength* behind it, and Mell rolled off her and over the edge of the bed. The eldest O'Loinsigh pulled the covers over her once more, rose from the bed, collected the breakfast tray from Shar and placed it in her lap. "Eat. Shower. We'll keep everyone busy. Come down when you're ready." He slid a hand into the hair at the nape of her neck and tilted her head back for a kiss. Then he whispered in her ear, "You are right, we are not walking away. I've already told you this. It is good you are finally realizing it." Then he was gone, scooping his clothes up from the floor and striding out the door naked. She admired the view, the sleek muscles she'd explored with her hands the night before, the bunch of his buttocks as he walked, the way his tattoos rolled over his skin.

Oh, yes, he was a worthy sacrifice to a goddess.

When he disappeared into the hall, she turned her attention to the other three men. Mell picked himself up off the floor, gave her a small salute with his right hand and a grin, then vanished after his brother.

Shar stood and gave her a soft smile. The juxtaposition of it against the eye-patch and his huge stature thrilled her. "I will have tea ready for you when you come down." Then he was gone as well.

Finn resumed his seat beside her on the bed. "They may never say the words aloud." The words echoed her own ideas.

She eyed him. He and Mell both claimed they had no power to read thoughts, but sometimes she did wonder. "I know. But, in their own way, they are saying it, aren't they?" Every time Shar made her tea, or coaxed the best strawberries from his garden, wasn't he saying it? And for Dub, hadn't allowing her to stay been a declaration of its own? For Mell, well, even revealing a part of his true self... what she'd just seen in him told her how hard it had been for him to give her the glimpses he *had*.

And Finn... "What about you?"

He ran a finger over her shoulder then down her upper arm before drawing it back up to her neck. "I'll be able to say the words once the true feeling is there. But while this has been growing in me, it is still new. Would you be saddened if I could not, in the end, love you in return? Fully love you, even if I do give myself to you?"

She twisted her head to hold his gaze with hers. "Yes."

He leaned in to gift her with a light kiss. "Then I will try. I am willing, more than willing, goddess. You are one of the few truly beautiful people in this world. It is an honor to be loved by you, and it would be an honor to love you. But I will not give you the words until I am sure. It may be tomorrow, or it may be years. Are you willing to wait?"

"Yes," she said again. For now, knowing that there was something there on his part, and that he wanted to try, was enough. And his honesty was a gift in itself, one of respect and courage. He told her the truth, and did not flinch from saying it. He gave her just what she had given all of them with her confession.

"Good." He rose. "Eat. I will see you downstairs." He hesitated at the door. "And I do not want you to worry about what the other fae or immortals may say when it becomes known that you are involved with all of us. Despite what you may have seen with Grainne, the fae have always been... free with their favors. It is only considered a violation of trust if you have committed yourself to someone and then betray that commitment. In this case, you have committed yourself to the four of us. There is no violation, no betrayal."

A small knot of worry loosened. She had already made her decision on this point, but it was welcome knowledge that she was not violating a major taboo for the immortals. "Thank you."

He gave her a nod and then, like the O'Loinsighs, was gone. She turned her attention to her now cold breakfast. She ate it all, even the eggs.

It was one of the most delicious meals of her existence.

As she set aside the tray and rose, she realized she had not told them of Balor's tricks the night before, so caught up she was in confessing what she'd realized.

When she'd dealt with the men of ba, she would tell everyone. They would all need to be vigilant for his tricks, especially if he could break through the wards. And she might need to start scanning everyone each day. It would be a serious drain on her powers, but she'd received a boost from Dub last night, and a bit more from the breakfast.

Actually, the breakfast had given her more than she expected. She examined the well of her power. It was... steadier. Had she been losing a bit of herself every day due to the holes in her being?

Interesting.

Her mind turned to what still needed to be accomplished. As with finding justice for Dano, she would do whatever she needed to in order to send Balor truly on from this existence, and to his judgment at the hands of Anubis, Ma'at, and Ammit.

And as with Dano, she had the O'Loinsighs, Finn, and Ailis to help her. There were others as well: the men of ba, Cuchi, the Morrigan, the raven, Faolan. Each had helped.

She was not alone in this fight.

Another hole sealed itself as she laid out her clothes for the day and headed for the shower.

Chapter Seventeen

SEARBHAN

*H*e studied the men of ba who were waiting on the other side of the wards, about ten yards from the cottage. When Oisin and Dub had reset them, they'd concentrated on the area in the back and around the forge. Only so much power had been available by the time they had made their way to the front of the property. Shar didn't like how close the boundary was, but he understood the priorities.

Seven ba men stood there, including Ari. He'd expected more, and while it was hard to read his visage, Ari was not pleased.

"Where is the goddess? And why must we wait?" A ba man, slightly taller than the rest, crossed his arms and leaned forward, as though he were going to press through the wards.

Ari held up a hand. "Cease. I have explained why this is important. We will wait."

The taller one stilled then nodded. "I am anxious. I do not appreciate the violation of our home or the slaughter of my friends."

Shar could understand. He himself was not happy with the fact there were so many unknowns, that he didn't know who exactly he could trust. He'd never been like Dub, skeptical of everyone except his brothers, nor was he Mell, using his powers to constantly monitor the reactions of those around him. Despite some very memorable moments, he preferred to trust.

But there was also something off. The trees whispered and reached out to him, as they had not when he and the others had first arrived at the cottage. He extended his senses and asked.

The one on the far left. There are shadows on his heart. We... do not like him here. It was a younger ash, maybe only a few decades along. The thoughts were unformed, more a general feeling.

The one to the right of the leader. He led shadows to the Rowans. This was from a centuries-old oak.

If this was true, why did the rowans not tell him when he was there, right beside them?

They do not trust anymore. Not just you, man of the green, but any. They do not trust any but the ancient ash and the oaks. A tangle of ivy along the path murmured.

Shar suppressed the sorrow those words brought to him, swallowing his guilt. His was not the only failure, but his had been the last. When he'd allowed Grainne and Diarmuid to overcome him, he'd betrayed the trust laid in him by the earth itself. Since then, though he'd always take comfort in the plants and the wood, he did not deserve that comfort.

And if he did not deserve the forgiveness of the wood, did he deserve a goddess, or her love?

He wasn't sure, but he would do his best.

Studying the two men of ba in question, he didn't see anything off about them. The one on the left stood a few inches behind the others, and the one to the right of Ari stood easily, feet spread and arms loose at its sides. Nothing about their demeanor would have caught his attention, as the taller one had with his belligerence.

Finn exited the front door and stepped down onto the path to stand beside Dub. Mell leaned against the cottage wall behind them, idly plucking at the air as though playing his guitar. Ailis was near Cuchi on the other side of the cottage's front stoop, arms crossed and eyes narrowed at the men of ba.

Did she sense something as well?

Killer bounded around the corner, three pixies clinging to the fur of his back, and charged the men of ba. He stopped just short of the wards and lowered his head, letting out a menacing growl.

Shar stepped forward. There *was* something off. "Ari," he called out. "Cross over for a moment. The goddess will be out soon to see the rest of your men, but we need to speak with you in the meantime."

Mell straightened from the wall and strolled over to stand between Shar and Dub. None of the others changed their stance, but the immortals were now positioned in such a way that they could effectively cover the goddess when she did arrive.

Ari tilted his head and opened his mouth then shut it. Without a word he nodded, stepped forward across the wards and around Killer—who didn't budge from his warning crouch.

Tension hung in the air, the situation a delicate balance. While Shar knew who the trees were suspicious of, and that the others suspected something was off, he didn't have a way to convey this, or to coordinate a strategy for dealing with them. Despite the slaughter he'd seen of their home, the men of ba were known as fierce warriors, and were feared and avoided for good reason. If the wards did fail, he had no doubt those gathered before the cottage could subdue the traitors, but there was no guarantee they could do it without injury.

And time lost to injury was not something they could afford at the moment.

He also didn't want to give them the opportunity to run, to report back once more to the enemy.

Ari stopped in front of him. "What did you need to speak to me about, Protector?"

The word rang with the weight of a title, and Shar pulled his shoulders back. Once, he'd been unworthy of the designation. This was his chance to earn it back. "The men with you. Who did not accompany us back to the guardi office?" He was relatively certain the guardi wards would have reacted to anyone entering with evil intentions, so matter how well disguised.

Ari's red eyes narrowed. "Can you not tell the men of ba apart from each other, Fomoiri?"

This was new, this antagonism. What had happened when Ari went to retrieve additional men? Shar's heart sped. Had *Ari* been corrupted somehow?

Razor claws clicked together, the man of ba's many-jointed fingers twitching in agitation.

"Shar..." Mell's voice carried on the breeze in a low warning.

Shar braced himself as Ari planted a foot behind him and half turned to Dub, who had taken his attention from the ba men still on the other side of the wards and slipped up to position himself near Mell. He was close enough that, with a little strength applied to his speed, it would take him a fraction of a second to close the remaining distance to Ari.

Killer started up a low growl as the pixies' glow intensified. Shar reached out with his power to the ivy, the closest vegetation. It stirred, a couple vines snaking across the grass toward Ari's back foot.

Then he paused. Killer still focused on the men of ba *outside* the wards, not on Ari. And though Ari's fingers flicked and his shoulders were pulled back in readiness, his teeth—those razor weapons—were not exposed.

Wood creaked behind them all. "Wait." Bat's voice rang through the yard. Shar didn't turn to face her. In fact, none but Ailis even so much as turned their head to the goddess, and the tension rose, like a bow pulled taught. The slightest change would release the potential of the moment.

Soft steps padded behind him as Bat descended the stairs and crossed the yard to stand beside Shar. Her hand landed on his back, over the tensed muscles, and she rubbed in small circles. "My friend," she said, focused on Ari. "My friend, we have a problem." Her tone was gentle, but there was steel in her words. "And I believe you know what, and who, that problem is." Her voice was low enough it would not carry to those beyond the wards.

The man of ba closed his eyes and inclined his head. "Yes, goddess." His fingers twitched then curled into fists, hiding those deadly talons.

"Would you like me to have them taken care of?" she asked, again in that tender voice.

Shar's chest grew heavy as the weight of those words settled over him. His goddess was too generous sometimes. She worried for the feelings of this man of ba while traitors waited yards away. *Would you love her this much if she was any other way?*

No. He answered his own heart. *No, I would not.*

"No, goddess. I will take care of it." Ari's head tilted back and he looked up with shining red eyes. "I had hoped..."

"You hoped that you were wrong. And it is why you chose who you did to come with you here. If there is time, and I have the strength, I would offer to examine the hearts of each of the remaining men of ba. But..." Here she paused to kneel beside the man of ba and lay a hand on his arm. "I think you have maybe learned the trick of it? Of seeing into the core of another?"

Shar wanted to back away. This seemed like too private of a moment to be witnessing. He turned his attention to the remaining men of ba—Ari was *not* the threat here. They shifted restlessly. The pixies had pulled away from Killer to hover in the air above him, just on the edge of the wards. Their wings gleamed and the sunlight flashed off something in the red one's hands.

"I have, goddess," Ari was saying. "I have." There was such sorrow in those words.

But Shar couldn't pay attention to that now. Something was coming through the trees.

The shadows, an ancient oak whispered. *They are far, but they come this way. Help also comes.*

At that moment, the ba man who'd stood to the right of Ari twisted, swiping his claws through the one who stood to his left, and the other traitor pulled a blade, this one gleaming with a dull light similar to that of the lann de anam—or the cauldron.

Killer leapt, his jaws closing around the arm holding the blade. The pixies darted in, the red one darting past the ba men and growing. He twisted and landed on feet now large enough to belong to a young adolescent. His blade had grown with him.

Shar's muscles tensed, but his goddess was still beside him. He would not leave her side, not for Killer, not the men of ba, and certainly not for the pixies. He glanced down.

A single tear welled in Ari's bright red eyes and spilled over. Then he was gone, sprinting back toward the wards. Dub, his strength in full display, also headed for the men of ba. Finn and Cuchi were a beat behind, as Mell and Ailis headed for Bat. Shar pulled her behind him until she was surrounded, immortals on all sides.

She spoke not a word. What was she thinking? How did she remain so calm? Was it because she claimed she couldn't die? If she was different from the other deities, was she different in this way as well?

The men of ba fought, needle teeth and razor claws sparking in the morning light. Killer whined as claws slashed into his side, but he didn't release the arm in his jaws. Bat pressed to Shar's back at the sound and his belly twisted, but he didn't move.

Dub reached them first. Shar knew it was only a fraction of a second, but time seemed to have slowed as he waited for the end of a battle he would not enter—not unless it crossed the wards somehow.

The eldest brother had pulled his sword from the pocket of space he kept it in, and slashed down across the arm of the ba man with the blade, sending Killer rolling away, the limb still between his teeth.

Then Ari was there, hand outstretched and fingers pressed together, forming a spike with his claws. These he drove into the chest of the other traitor, whose jaw hinged wide in a silent scream. Behind Shar, Mell, and Bat both let out small groans.

What was *this?* Shar watched as the red of the traitor's eyes faded and darkened to dried blood, his rough skin, so like bark, cracking and shrinking like a tree being eaten by rot from the inside out. It took only a second or two, then Ari pulled his hand away to reveal a fist clenched in blood. He held it up, twisting it in the air as the second traitor— now minus an arm—dropped to his knees. The other for ba men flanked him.

Dub stepped away, Finn and Cuchi following his example. Again, this didn't seem like something to be witnessed, but no one was willing to turn away. Killer, three slashes cutting through the fur at his ribs, stood and, with only a slight limp, trotted over to Shar and dropped the arm—and blade—at his feet. Then the hound turned once more to face out, toward the danger.

The pixies—including the red one who was back to its original size—zipped back to hover around Killer. "We do no' want to be witnessing this part, giant," the silver one said. He really did need to learn their names. "The immediate crisis is over, but if ye're talking to the wood again, ye'll be knowing there's more trouble on the way. Ye'd best not linger."

"We'll help." This from the red one. "But ye've got two days, mayhap three, before the shadows arrive. They're gathering and hunting, but they'll be here soon enough. The trees whisper to us as well. And we listen better than you."

Shar nodded and they were gone, flitting around the corner of the cottage and no doubt off to spread gossip.

Ari, one hand still clenched in a bloody fist, stepped up to the kneeling man of ba.

"I did not know they could do this," Bat whispered. She wrapped her arms around Shar's waist in a hug. Mell made a low and soothing sound. Ailis remained silent.

Shar laid a hand over one of his goddess's and gave it a light squeeze. He wanted to close his eyes, to go back to the time just this morning when Bat confessed her love. To the stars that had shone in her eyes in soft swirls. To the glimpses of flesh, and the promise he'd seen in her face as she gazed at him as though he was the rock she wanted to cling to. When he'd first glimpsed her that morning, and seen her apprehension at his reaction to her having slept with Dub, his hesitation had melted away. No, he did not like seeing her with others, but he liked even less that expression on her face. And could he begrudge his brothers the happiness she was bringing to them? Or Finn?

Could he be the cause of her pain, for the sake of a few bruised feelings?

No.

Also, he still had to make her tea.

Ari thrust his non-bloodied hand into the second man of ba. Shar watched as the life was ripped from this immortal. Then Ari stood with two red fists held to the sky, and he flung his hands open. Cries filled the air, so faint it could have been his imagination, or simply the breeze on a bright Irish morning.

Bat took a breath, her chest pressing to his back, and let out a soft sigh. "It is over." The words were more a vibration against him than audible sounds. "The souls will be on their way for judgement."

Shar loosened his grip on her and turned. "Have you checked the other men of ba?"

"Yes." Her eyes were clear, though her mouth pulled down in sadness. "It was just those two." Then her expression hardened. "And they will receive judgement, I have no doubt of that."

"Good." He picked her up, one arm under her butt. "We are going to finish getting you your tea while everyone gets cleaned up, and see to Killer's wound."

"It is better now," she said.

Sure enough, Killer, the wounds now neatly scabbed

over, had picked up the arm once more and stood beside them, looking up.

"Good dog," Shar said, and Killer wagged his tail.

Bat let out a soft laugh. "Sometimes I think he likes you brothers more than he likes me."

"We share an understanding."

"Oh?"

He set off for the cottage. "There is something precious we *all* guard."

Chapter Eighteen

Bastet,

I am assuming you are alive and simply being stubborn,
worrying me for some mischievous reason. Otherwise…
Well, something happened that I believe you would have
enjoyed. I have told you of the pixies, yes? Well, one of the
ones at the cottage just propositioned a guardi captain, and
it was wonderful. You should have seen his expression.
- Bat, the goddess who is relearning to find humor in even
the darkest situations

BAT

She wrapped her arms around Shar's shoulders and held tight. She'd been trying to make light of it, but what Ari had just done had shaken her.

He'd… ripped the souls from his men. That was something she'd only heard of Anubis being able to do.

Even here in Ireland, the only way to kill an immortal was with the soul blades or for them to choose to move on… at least, that's what she'd been told.

Shar finally set her down once they reached the kitchen. She took a chair at the small table as Ailis and Mell entered. Her gaze caught Mell's, and the shock she felt was mirrored there. He'd sensed at least some of what had occurred, the… agony the men of ba had experienced as the part that gave them life was torn away.

She couldn't blame Ari. They were traitors, and at least one was responsible for allowing in the creatures that had used Nuada's sword to slaughter his people.

Killer lay at her feet as Shar set a cup of tea before her. Ailis took the seat beside her.

"Well," the fae said. "That happened."

Killer whined in agreement. Bat nodded. Though he'd healed remarkably fast, she needed to get her pup cleaned up. And she still needed to tell everyone about Balor's infiltration.

They really had been corrupted. She'd been thinking of the soul-searching she'd been doing as a mere formality. Important, yes, but despite the suspicions that there were traitors among them, she hadn't expected to find any.

The voice last night had been insidious. It was sweet, and coaxing, and knew how to find the weak points. It was four steps and about six millennia ahead of all of them.

"We need to stop reacting, and find a strategy that will get us ahead of this," she said, picking up the steaming cup of tea.

"You are correct," Finn said from behind her.

Cuchi stomped in as well. "Dub is taking the bomen to get cleaned up. You send the dog as well." He pulled out the chair at the head of the table and sat.

There was a tapping at the rear door. *Tap tap tap.* Pause. *Tap. Caw.*

Cuchi opened the door and a raven hopped in. Einin was back from... wherever she'd gone. Though the Morrigan said the raven was there as a messenger and to help, in reality the thing did whatever it wanted to, and disappeared at the most inconvenient times.

"I also need to fill everyone in on something that happened last night," she informed them.

"Well, now, no need to be telling everyone about that." Mell gave her one of his wicked smiles.

"Not that, you rogue. Something I forgot to say this morning, and it was very foolish of me." She set her teacup down. "It is time to cease being foolish."

"Agreed." Ailis cast her a wide smile. "I hate it when people are foolish. It's so pointless."

That was the wonderful thing about Ailis. She always seemed to know exactly what to say to diffuse a situation, or rile it up—depending on what needed to happen. And she was always just... there.

Other than glamour, and a small amount of the empathy Mell possessed, Ailis also seemed to have a sense of being in the right place at the right time. Bat had decided it was another power of the fae's, even if no one had outright stated it as a power. Maybe it was luck. A small gift bestowed by Fate herself.

"Yes, there are things I need to fill everyone in on as well," Shar said, taking a seat on Bat's left.

Reaching out, she linked her fingers with his. "We will wait for everyone."

"I'll go check on 'em!" Maire, the pink pixie, popped up from behind a small potted plant in the corner by the back door and hovered until Cuchi once more opened it.

It wasn't but a few minutes before everyone had gathered in the kitchen. The space was small, and Bat thought briefly of moving the meeting to the living room, but decided against it. Kitchens seemed to be meant for things like this—family meetings.

She contemplated everyone there: the O'Loinsigh brothers, Finn, Ailis, Cuchi, Ari, the four other men of ba, Killer, Maire and the other pixies, and Einin. A random conglomeration of beings and immortals, and yes, in a way, family. Even Cuchi. For they shared a common purpose.

Dub took the remaining seat at the table as the ba men stationed themselves against the wall. Bat didn't hesitate a moment longer. "You all need to know of something that happened last night."

She filled them in on the voice, and how it had reached out through dreams, how it used a soul's points of weakness. It was hard for her to admit, there in front of everyone, that she did have those weaknesses, but she said it, for she wanted to emphasize that *all* needed to be on their guard.

When she finished, there was silence for a moment, then Shar spoke. "The trees are whispering. They say the shadows are gathering, and hunting. Maybe this is what they meant. They also say the shadows are on their way here and will be here in two days, maybe three."

"Then we need to conclude our business today, and move on to the next step tomorrow." Finn crossed his arms and leaned against the counter.

"Won't be easy," Dub said. "I've got the pattern worked out, but I still need to make the damned thing. And anyone who thinks a magical weapon can be forged in a day has their head up their ass."

This was a fair assessment. "What do you need?" Bat asked.

"I need to be undisturbed, by hounds, pixies, goddesses, and damned sidhe. I need the shard fully restored, which, if I'm correct, means Finn and Cu Chulainn have to give up a bit of blood. And I need the shaft."

"I'll do the shaft." Shar let go of her hand and pushed his chair back. "There's a length of ash I spotted yesterday that will probably work. And if not… "

"We'll help you look, Protector." Daire zipped up to hover next to Shar's shoulder.

"And that leaves me to call Da." Mell stole Shar's seat and laid his hands on the table, palm down, calm and oh so careful.

"No." Dub shook his head. "We're changin' the strategy there. We're surprising them." He looked to Finn. "You can get us to Londonderry, right?"

He frowned. "It will be a stretch, but if I can't get us all the way, Cu Chulainn can get us the rest of the way?" Finn raised a brow at the other guardi captain.

"I can." He paused. "Are we bringing the other guardi in on this? It would be smart to have the additional backup, especially walking into that viper's nest of savages."

Dub's mouth tightened, then he sighed. "I wish I could argue with you. But, yes, most of them are venomous in one way or another. I'm not sure it's a good idea to go marching in with a contingent of guardi. Have them ready, though."

Flash. An Island, sheer cliffs on one side falling into the ocean, green hills and beaches on the other. Five ships were anchored in a small bay, and boats full of men rowed to those beaches. A seal's head popped above the water's surface and winked at her.

"We will need a guide. An ocean guide. A seal." She'd just seen Tir Hudi, and been given the clue as to how to find it. And maybe, just maybe, they'd get there not too long after the others who sought it.

"One of the selkie, or maybe mac Lir's many children. But they won't help without the permission of the god." Finn sighed. "And if we are going up against the Fomoiri, I don't think we will gain his permission."

"But it is not all of the Fomoiri," Cuchi cut in. "You reported yourself that you doubt the clan leaders are involved."

"True."

Silence settled.

"I will talk to him, and explain," Bat said. "How do I reach this mac Lir?"

Dub shook his head. "Not on a cell phone."

Mell slid a glance at Finn. "What about Oisin?"

Finn shook his head. "Won't do it. Hasn't talked to

dear old father-in-law since he got himself locked out of Tir na nOg. Too embarrassed."

"I may have a way," Ailis said, her mouth pulled into a thoughtful frown. "There's a gremlin comes into the store sometimes, and she lives out by the selkie preserve off Enniscrone. She's had dealings with them, and may be able to get us an audience, at the least of the bull of the pod."

Finn and Cuchi groaned in unison. "I'm not sure we want to involve that pod," Cuchi said. "Do you know how many times I've already had to go out there due to the reports of malicious mischief?"

Finn crossed his arms and bent his head.

Bat waited. She knew what a selkie was. It would fit her vision, but she would also trust Finn's judgment on this particular group of the water-dwelling immortals.

The sea had never been part of her domain.

He lifted his head and met her gaze. "It's worth a shot. If nothing else, we'll be able to get a better idea of where the sea god stands on this conflict. And an idea of where any of the gods stand, honestly." He eyed the raven. "It still seems suspicious to me that they are not stepping in."

Caw.

You have corrupted my Finn, goddess of Egypt.

Bat held her silence. This was not a discussion she was willing to have in front of the others. It was not a discussion she was willing to have at all, in fact.

But she would not want to get Finn in trouble with his boss either.

He never used to question me.

Maybe not aloud. Bat kept the thought to herself. Or thought she did.

No, he never used to question me. You truly are different from other deities. Real enough to my immortals that they can't help but feel comfortable around you, and mysterious enough they can't help but love you. It's a deadly combination.

I am not trying to kill anyone, or take away your followers.

Well, you better be trying to kill at least one *person.*

The raven flew to the tabletop and hop-stepped toward Bat. It cocked its head one way, then another. A glint of gold, clutched in the claws on one of the raven's feet, caught her eye. Einin extended the foot and dropped a golden ring onto the surface of the table. It fell with a soft ping.

If you cannot reach mac Lir, use this to summon his wife, Fand. Toss it into the seas, she'll find you. A mental snort. *Just make sure Cuchi isn't around for that, or you'll find yourself in a whole other heap of mess.*

Bat picked up the ring and slid it over the middle finger on her left hand. *Thank you.*

I told you, I would do what I could to help. I do not agree with the Tribunal's decision to stay out of this, even if I must abide by it on the surface.

Should Bat ask? She did understand following the visions as they were laid out for you, but it was also strange to her that they were not involving themselves in such a large affair.

This hasn't yet touched more than a few sluagh and other solitary fae. Anger stirred behind the Morrigan's words, reminding Bat that there were at least a couple of things she had in common with this war goddess—a hate of injustice. *Even with the Treasures resurfacing and going missing, they sit in their complacency. Even the Dagda washed his hands of this affair when he left the harp for you to find. Maybe if more of the sidhe were being hurt, or showing up in the seer's visions it would be different.*

Balor is sneaky. Could he have…?

A sigh. The raven hopped back. *Corrupted them? I doubt it, not the gods. But others? Possibly. And thus I do not want to push it, not without knowing the extent of his reach. The wisest thing we could do is to stop him before he can implement whatever plans he has brewing, which means you being in the right place at the right time, without him knowing about it. The less people involved, the better. Call Fand if you need to, and tell her I am calling in the favor owed. But try not to, I've been holding onto that favor for a very long time now.*

The raven turned, waddled to the edge of the table, and flapped down to the floor to cuddle in next to Killer. The hound gave her a sniff, a small lick—causing the raven to ruffle its feathers—and settled his head back on his paws.

Bat looked at her gathered allies. "A way to reach Fand if mac Lir is uncooperative."

"Fuck. I can't be there for that. In fact, I shouldn't be anywhere near mac Lir." Cuchi stepped back and began pacing.

"Steal someone else's girl?" Dub asked.

Cuchi threw up his hands. "If a beautiful woman was asking you to rescue them, what would you do? You'd say yes! I think I have a curse on me, to always be accused of running off with other men's women."

Bat narrowed her gaze and searched the energy around

him. There was no curse but hers. "No," she said. "I think it is simply your nature. You could change it."

Ailis let out a peal of laughter, tipping her head and then the chair back. It brought a chuckle from a few of the others.

"And now we get to work," Bat said. "There will be no… cavalry sweeping in to save the day."

Ailis nodded. "We are the cavalry."

Ari tilted his head. "There are no horses."

Bat smiled at him. She knew this phrase. "I will explain after we have gotten everyone to work."

Dub rose. "I'm off to the forge then. Come fetch the shard and put your damned blood on the thing, then bring it back," he said to Finn. "Also, figure out a way to keep those dreams out. He's probably got a Fir Dearg swayed to his side, or another of the ba men, if he's able to creep into people's dreams in such a way." He didn't even spare a glance at Ari as he said it, but Bat did.

Ari nodded. "There is one other missing and unaccounted for. I will handle him the same way I handled the other betrayers."

"I'll get Oisin working on it and back out here." Finn headed after Dub. "He can't stay in his library for this one. I'll be back in a moment, and then we need to check with the teams on what they've found of the Fomoiri's movements over the last months," he shot back at Cuchi.

Shar bent and pressed a quick kiss to Bat's forehead, then headed after his brother and Finn, leaving Cuchi, Ailis, Mell, the men of ba and the pixies.

Killer whined then nudged her foot. "Right, my pup. I'm going to get Killer cleaned up." She turned to Cuchi.

"Make sure you allow the shard to taste you. I should be back soon." She pushed back her chair and a leg caught on something. Glancing down, she saw the severed arm still clutching the dagger that resembled the soul blades. A small pool of blood sat under it.

"And no one thought to remember that this was here?" she muttered.

Ari knelt. "Allow me. This should not be in your presence any longer."

It was true that severed limbs were never pretty to look at, but this particular one did not bother her any longer, except as a reminder that Ari had been betrayed. Regardless of the power struggles, the wants and desires of an immortal long thought to be dead, or what he was promising to others, that was what she abhorred—the betrayal. Balor was coaxing people into duplicity and treachery. He was… coaxing them into embracing chaos.

"What is that dagger? It looks like a soul blade, but… not." Mell had risen when Bat did, and now peered down at the dagger.

Ari pried it from stiff and clutching fingers and handed it to one of his men. "It is a *des*, one of the original ceremonial blades gifted from the vessel upon our creation. They will not kill, not as the weapon we are seeking to forge could kill, but it could maim the spirit if wielded by someone knowledgeable in its use. It is not a pleasant sensation."

She needed to ask. Would he want to say, in front of so many witnesses? "Ari? What you did out there…"

Large red eyes met her gaze and held steady. "Is something only the head of the clan may accomplish.

When Puchi passed on, the power came to me. And, no, I may only do this with other men of ba. It is the ultimate punishment, and it saddens me that I was forced to use it at all."

She opened her senses and used a bit of her hoarded power to search Ari. There was the loss and grief he spoke of, but she sensed no regret or resentment as she had earlier in the front yard. She sensed no areas where chaos could dig its claws.

Ari would be well.

Bat nodded. "I do understand this."

"Would have been a nifty weapon, though, if it worked on others," Ailis said, her tone thoughtful.

"I agree," Cuchi said.

Mell made a low sound of protest in the back of his throat and Bat caught a glimpse of that desolate field of blood and pain he kept locked away. "I have to admit, I do not agree with the use of a weapon that can't be fought against."

Ailis's eyes narrowed. "What do you think we're makin', oh great and wise Fomoiri who hates weapons? Do ya know how ridiculous ya sound right now?"

The rear door opened and Finn stepped into the kitchen carrying the shard, wrapped once more in his sweater.

"Stop." Bat nodded to Ari then gestured for Ailis to stand. "Ailis, will you help me get Killer cleaned up? The wounds have closed, but I don't want him to get an infection."

Ailis sighed. "Yeah, I don't want to be arguing with stubborn men about their hypocritical ways. I'll get yer Cu

Sidhe all sparkling clean for ya." The fae stood and patted her thigh. "Come on, Killer darlin'. Let's let Auntie Ailis take care of ya while yer ma attempts to talk sense into the foolish." She paused at the back door, beside Finn. "And when I'm back, we need to talk about other resources. I think ye're all underestimating the use of us fae, the solitary and the trooping, and how much we do give a shit, unlike the sidhe and the gods." She shoved open the door, allowing Killer to slip outside, then slammed it behind her.

Bat grinned. Damn, she did love Ailis. And she still wanted her and Bastet to meet. The entire male population—gods, immortals and humans alike—would need to run for cover.

Turning her attention to the next task before her, she held out her hand for the shard. "I am not sure if I need to be present when this is done, but it would be best not to risk anything going wrong. I would also like to give Ari and his men some time with it once it has been restored, so we may see if the connection to the vessel is any stronger. Not too long," she hastily interjected the last as Finn's mouth opened in protest.

"Fine." Her sidhe held out his right hand, palm up.

Carefully, oh so carefully, she pressed the edge to the meat of his palm until a line of red blood appeared. Copper filled the air as that blood was absorbed and the wound sealed.

Finn let out a heavy breath. "That…"

"Is not what you expected, was it?"

"No." He rubbed at the vestiges of remaining blood, the thin line smearing across his palm. "No, that is not what I was expecting at all." Taking a step back, he gestured for Cuchi to step forward.

The bald man wore a frown very similar to Dub's, but approached her. Without a word and only a little hesitation, he held his right hand out to her. Then he curled it into a fist, and pulled back. "I do have one thing to ask of you, goddess."

She tilted her head. "And what is that, guardi?"

"If we survive this, I would have you remove my curse." There was no resentment in his voice, no mocking arrogance, none of the entitlement he'd sported only days ago. "I am a warrior. I always have been, I have no other way to be. If I cannot use my sword arm…"

Bat considered it. She had been angry when she'd laid it on him, lashing out at an easy target. Had the punishment been deserved, or had she been deflecting? She lowered the hand holding the shard and studied Cuchi. Not for seeds of chaos, but simply to see what she could.

His beard was longer, yes, but well kept. A short line of stubble had begun to form on his head, thinner on top. Faded blue eyes met hers, and in them, beyond the assurance and traces of arrogance and entitlement, was…

Loss.

She still did not like him, this not-man who had injured her giant, but she could understand him a little. To have your purpose taken away on a whim… Well, it was something she recognized in him, something she could empathize with. Reaching out with her power, she adjusted the parameters of the curse for a second time.

"Done. When we have survived this, the use of your

arm will be restored. Until that time, though, the curse remains. You may not use your sword except in defense of the O'Loinsighs." She held her chin high. He *had* deserved a bit of punishment after all.

He inclined his head in acknowledgment and held his hand out to her once more. "Then do your worst, goddess of Egypt. Do your worst." He flashed a grin. "Just try to avoid taking the pinky."

Bat blushed at his teasing. Of course, that little joke would come back to haunt her.

Finn slapped Cuchi's head. "And this is why so many men, and gods, don't want ya around. Ye can't help but flirt. And this time, I'll be the one after ya if ya take it farther. Just be glad Dub or Shar didn't hear that."

"*I* heard it," Mell muttered, then grinned. "But I can also tell ya didn't mean it, Cuchi. Just keep yer tongue in yer mouth."

"Or," Ari added, his eyes lightening to a brilliant crimson, "I will use that tongue for another recipe I know of."

A high giggle came from the same plant Daire had appeared from behind. The silver pixie zipped into view. "Ya need to do something with that tongue, sidhe, I can show you something. I like to take on a Big every now and then."

Bat snorted as Cuchi's face turned red. "Get away from me, ye pest."

"Eh, eh. Ye'll regret that, I'm thinking. But, ya change ye're mind, just call out for Taire. I'll be there in two shakes of a… tongue."

Oh holy foreign gods, I need to remember this to tell Bastie.

And three pixies, named Daire, Maire and Taire? Bat laughed. Some things, no matter the direness of the situation, deserved to be laughed at.

Sobering, she held up the shard. "Hand please, and then there is much to do."

Cuchi, his face still red, held his palm out for a third time. "Just do this so I can be done with this. I need to contact my team and get to work." He shook his head. "Joking as though the end of the world wasn't about to bite our arses," he muttered.

Bat grabbed his hand and pressed the shard to it, and she was not careful. The edge sliced into him, and blood welled and pooled in the cup of his palm. The shard drank, pulling in all that was offered.

"Dammit." Cuchi jerked his hand away. "Bloodthirsty, the lot of ya." He stared down at his hand, then eyed the shard. "It's female, isn't it? Never satisfied."

A pulse of amusement came from the shard in Bat's hand. Yes, this little piece of creation was feminine, and she didn't mind teaching an arrogant male a lesson or two.

Bat waved her free hand. "You may go. Do not forget to inquire about a way to keep Balor from our dreams. It seems the wards do not affect that."

"We will be able to help with that as well." Ari gestured to the taller man of ba. "This is Femi, he has some skill with the soul's aspect of dreams."

Femi stepped forward and bowed. The earlier agitation he'd been showing was gone, in its place a blank face and veiled teeth. There was no corruption in him, but he was… more hollow than the others, more easy to excite to anger. "Who should I go with?"

Finn raised his brows. "Do you know anything about runes?"

"The druids' way?" Femi shrugged. "Some. Not matter, though. I show what need to do to guard the paths of dreams." His accent was thick, but understandable. Then he fell into a babble of Irish, and Finn's eyes widened.

"I thought that was a myth," Cuchi said.

Femi shrugged. "No myth. I make. I show. Need place to work."

Mell headed for the rear door. "If you don't mind small spaces, you can use the little room next to the forge. Dub uses it to sleep in sometimes, but he won't be needing it."

Femi headed after Mell.

"Can you really make dream guardians?" Mell's voice held suppressed excitement. "I heard stories of them, from my ma, but I've never seen one. How do they work?" He pulled open the door and stepped out.

"You… coax part of soul…" Femi descended into Irish once more and Bat caught Mell's answering nod as the door swung closed.

Well then. Abandoned for a promise of a dream guardian. Whatever that was.

Finn must have caught her puzzlement. "They are like dragons, but in spirit."

The winged serpents. Interesting. Bat had encountered a dragon once. It travelled from China during the Shang dynasty, looking for similar civilizations. They'd had many a conversation through the night on political philosophy. "I do like dragons."

Cuchi coughed, Ari and the men of ba grinned at her, and Finn laughed.

"Only you would like a dragon," Finn said.

"Oh, no, they are quite pleasant to converse with. I met one from China. His name was Wu, and he was well versed in the concept of the gods appointing the ruler." She paused. "I would like one of these when they are finished. Now," she continued, waving a hand, "please go check in with your men. We still need a better idea of the extent of Balor's forces. Whether he has an army backing him, or a few key players. The handlings will be quite different."

Her time with Seth, Horus and Narmer was coming back to her. Late night strategy meetings, and whispered plots. Missions of stealth were vastly different from battles of brawn. If Balor held the advantage in numbers, they'd need to solve that with gaining numbers of their own. And if it was simply that he had gained key allies, well, they still needed to know who those were.

Cuchi gave her a mocking bow, and Finn inclined his head in a much more sincere gesture. "The Druid from Dublin should have arrived by now, and has hopefully untangled the pain spells laid on the prisoners," Finn said. "Though they are not the main players, they should be able to lead us to others that will contain more information. And at least one of them knows who among the Fomoiri are involved with Balor's plots. I will also collect Oisin."

"Let's go. Wasted enough time talking." Cuchi strode

for the front door, then paused just on the other side of the doorway leading to the living room. "This may seem frustrating now, goddess, and as though there are only a few working to solve this. But the Morrigan is backing the effort, and the resources of the guardi are at our disposal. When the time comes, and despite what you may have heard of the sidhe and seen of their gods, they will be there to fight. There are nearly a hundred guardi spread over Ireland, and every one of those would welcome a fight against Balor of the Evil Eye. The pixies have already decided to support you, and where the pixies go, the rest of the smaller fae soon follow. You have made friends of sluagh, pookas and a Far Gorta. The leprechauns think rainbows follow in your wake, and wisps would probably fight to dance in your shadow."

Bat stared at the bald man—at *Cuchi*, who she could not quite bring herself to like. She was finally seeing a side of him that she could have some trust in, some faith.

"It is true, none of those misfit fae have much power on their own," he continued. "But I would rather face down a horde of rampaging Vikings than a nest of angry pixies. I would rather charge into the flames of a dragon than tangle with wailing banshees. And leprechauns out for vengeance are nothing to laugh at. So, while it may seem overwhelming, the resources to win this *are* there. You just need to call upon them. And it will need to be *you*. They will not answer the call for anyone else at this point." Cu Chulainn turned away and headed for the front door, his steps heavy against the wood of the floor.

She continued to stare after him, shaken. These were all things she had told herself, that had already occurred to her. But, she *had* been feeling a little overwhelmed, she realized. And to hear such words from someone she did not consider a friend, but who *was* an ally, eased her. Cu Chulainn would not have said those things if he did not mean them.

Finn laid a hand on her shoulder. "I will leave you with Ari. No doubt Ailis and Mell will be back soon enough. In the meantime, see if there is now anything further you can get from the shard on the cauldron's location."

Nodding absently, Bat turned to face Finn, pulling her attention from Cuchi.

Flash. Finn, blood dripping into his right eye from a slash across his forehead. His mouth was stretched wide in a savage grin. He held a sword in one hand and an axe in the other, and faced a man twice again his size, a true giant. Spaced out behind Finn in a loose formation were others she knew: Meera, Neall, Faolin. Old Mike, Ciara and her hound, Liam. And others, whose faces she did not yet know, but was certain she would.

Cuchi was correct. She needed to call upon the forgotten and abandoned fae—and the friends she'd made. "When Ailis returns, I am going to have her begin contacting those she knows," Bat told Finn. "We will spread the word to meet here. I will not be able to check them all, but Ari can help with that now."

The man of ba nodded. "Yes, I will do that. I am not sure if it is being connected to you as the goddess, or a power I have gained now that I am the head of the clan— much as Puchi had his visions—but it does not exhaust me as it did you."

Finn nodded. "I am not sure I can transport everyone."

Her lips tightened into a thin line. "Then we do as Cu Chulainn suggested, and call upon the guardi for help as well. I assume most know the trick?"

He gave her a bow. "Yes, goddess, they do."

She did not like that tone. "Am I being too imperious?"

He snorted, then leaned in to press an all-to-brief kiss to her lips. "No, goddess. *My* goddess. I..."

She waited.

"I am simply adjusting to having a goddess that I not only am willing to follow, but that I *want* to. The Morrigan... well, if I am truthful, she is one of the best of the lot. Maybe it is because there are always wars to be fought, but she is not as... removed as many of the others. And she is a good leader. But even she has her capricious moments, callous and uncaring." There was a pause as he gave her another quick kiss. "I have never seen you be such, even when frustrated." He stepped away from her. "I will arrange to have extra men here to help transport those who show up. Please do be discreet."

Bat snorted. It was a very satisfying sound to make. "Who do you think does *not* know what we are doing and why?" She had no doubts the enemy knew of the shard, and what they were trying to create in the forge. The treacherous men of ba would have been able to tell them at least that much. Their current advantage was not secrecy, but that Balor remained preoccupied with getting to Tir Hudi and gathering up the remaining pieces he needed for his return, whatever those may be. It was to the enemy's advantage that Bat find *him*. She just had to make sure the circumstances of that finding were to *her* advantage.

They had the shard.

They had the harp.

They had her visions.

Warmth filled her, the gentle touch of a mother, and the fiercer embrace of a lover. The surety of a job well done, and the satisfaction of justice delivered. *Ma'at?*

I am here, Bat. You know my influence must be subtle, but know that I am here. You are not *alone in this.*

And now they had Ma'at, the goddess of Order and Balance, who was usually thought of more as an idea than a being. Which meant they had any person, immortal or otherwise, who believed in the right of order and in overcoming the atrocities of life.

They had all these things, and they had *her*. And she was coming to know herself well enough that she had no doubts she would do everything in her—admittedly limited—power to see Balor sent to Judgement and his heart devoured by Ammit.

She laid her hand over where Finn's still rested on her shoulder. "Go. Coordinate and gather information."

With another short bow, he withdrew.

She turned to Ari. "Let us see what we may discover now."

Chapter Nineteen

FINN

*P*ausing at the entrance to the guardi headquarters barely long enough to be considered respectful to the pixies that guarded it, he headed inside and straight to his desk. Criedne, his lieutenant, had been instructed to leave whatever findings they'd come up with on his desk.

It was frustrating to not be directly in on the investigation. He didn't doubt his team's skills, but reading the information second hand was different from being there when it was found. When he was there he was able to pick up the little things that could sometimes make all the difference.

And the damned report isn't here. What had his team been *doing*?

"Cumhaill." Sean, another of his team, ran up from the

direction of the research rooms and labs. "The Druid just finished with the prisoners."

Not hesitating, he headed for the interrogation rooms, Sean just behind him. "Have they started the questioning?"

"No. And this was no ordinary spell. Whatever was done tied not just their senses up in knots, but their minds as well. Took nearly eight hours to unravel."

It must have been the ba man. The one they had yet to catch. If the natural skill they possessed over the soul was combined with the dark spells used to twist and inflict pain... Finn shuddered. The sidhe and other fae had grown complacent through these centuries of peace. Oh, there had been wars fought, but they were fought with human weapons. The major conflicts of the immortals had ended with the fall of Balor. Even when the Milesians had come to Ireland, that conflict ended quickly, and with minimal bloodshed.

It took only moments to descend to the warded rooms. Sean indicated a room halfway down the hall on the left and Finn laid his hand over the ward-lock.

The sight that greeted him was not one he'd been expecting. The sluagh that he and Mell had managed to get a few impressions from sat at the plain wood tabled they used in these rooms, crying.

"I don't know. Don't know, don't know. I don't, I don't."

A smaller woman, wearing the light gray robes of a Druid master, stood in the far corner, her eyes wide. She turned to Finn. "He has been as you see him from the time I unraveled the pain spell. I scanned him for any other enchantments, and he is clean. It seems the pain was connected to any knowledge he may have had of Balor and his plans. Unfortunately, that connection was only evident once I lifted the spell."

"Why is he crying?"

The sluagh flinched.

"I had to be sure. Some things can still be hidden from a scrying spell, but few are able to both hide from a scrying spell and pain applied in certain areas." The Druid's expression did not change, but a new note, one of dark satisfaction, had entered her voice. "And any who would dare seek to steal from the gods, well, you must be doubly sure of them, mustn't you?"

Sean coughed. Finn held his reaction in, but he knew what the bloodthirsty woman was saying.

"Did you get anything useful at all?" he asked. That was all that really mattered.

"I know where he was from, and when his memories become spotty."

"Let me guess, he's from near Londonderry, and he made a visit to the port about six months ago."

The Druid nodded. "Yes. He intended to ask one of the Fomoiri clans for help in relocating back to Connaught without getting caught out. Who he talked to, and what deals he may have struck, though, are beyond us."

"Did you at least find out who else he knows? Who he may have talked to?"

"It is from before the memory loss, but of course." The Druid bent an admonishing glare on Finn. "I am not a child, and I am not inexperienced in gathering information."

Finn held his retort. They didn't have time for him to begin arguing with an aging Druid about respect. "And the Fir Bolg?"

The Druid sighed. "I have not even begun on him. Just as with the pain spells, once the memory wipe was triggered with the sluagh, so was it set off with the other prisoner. However, since it was not a direct wipe, I may be able to uncover some of the memories." She held up a small hand. "And no, I do not know how long it will take me. I will be doing this as carefully as I can, and careful, when dealing with the unknown, takes time. Best to assume you will not be getting any information from this quarter."

"Well, that's shit on a monkey's arse," Sean muttered.

Finn did not disagree. He'd been counting on finding out what the sluagh knew to begin getting an idea of Balor's forces. "Where in Londonderry did he go?" If he knew where on the docks, he could narrow it down. There were only two Fomoiri clans who sailed out of that harbor.

And one of them was the O'Loinsighs.

The Druid shook her head. "All he remembers is that he was headed there."

"And why was he trying to go back to Connaught?"

To woman's eyes tightened. "Family. Said he had family he was trying to see." She shrugged. "Or that's what he now believes. But to imagine the sluagh concerned about family..."

Finn held in a sigh. And there was the arrogance that made it impossible for most of the solitary fae to have any faith in the guardi or the gods of their own land. Fear, yes, but not faith. It was no wonder Balor had no trouble in finding allies, if the kinds of whisperings Bat had reported from her dream were anything to go by.

He glanced at the sluagh. His shadows and glamours had been stripped, and his wings were half-wrapped around his shoulders. He clutched at his belly, fangs flashing as it muttered.

It looked as though justice had already been served in this instance. "When his sentence is served, ensure he makes it back to that family he'd been trying to find," Finn instructed Sean.

The Druid opened her mouth, no doubt to protest, and Finn jerked his hand up, cutting her off. "Please see what you can get from the Fir Bolg. Report it directly to Criedne, and I will take it from there." He inclined his head. "Thank you for your service."

Then he was gone. He had no time to waste on useless pursuits.

"I didn't see a report on my desk," he said to Sean as they headed back toward the main room.

"Criedne got a lead from one of the woodland fae on unusual goblin activity," Sean said. "The goblins are usually neutral in these kinds of conflicts, but because so many of the neutrals seem to be choosing sides, she wanted to follow up on it. Everything from the pub is sorted and catalogued. We closed it up tight. No one, human or fae, is getting into the place until the O'Loinsighs are ready to open again."

Sean kept close on his heels as Finn changed direction once they hit the main floor and headed up the stairs to the library. He'd give his lieutenant another two hours to complete that portion of the investigation. "Keep talking. What else do you have?"

"Cu Chulainn's team has been compiling the Fomoiri's movements, as they have better information sources from their time up north and work in Galway. You know Sligo's not a big port town."

Finn nodded. He did know, it was why the brothers had settled here all those centuries ago. Close enough to the water that they could still feel connected to their heritage, but far enough away to avoid the rest of the Fomoiri—and their father.

"Okay then. Let's go see if Oisin has made any progress on the invitation. And then I need him with me. Someone's been corrupting through dreams, and we need guardians. I have Mell and a boman working on it, but I want Oisin's input."

Finn pushed open the library door only to find it empty. "Well, shit then." He turned to Sean. "Any idea where our wayward librarian would be?"

Chapter Twenty

OISIN

*O*isin crouched over the pocked and worn wooden research table. He liked to do most of his fiddling here, in this hidden room. The library was his home, but this was his haven. A lab at the back of a small network of rooms off the library, he retreated here when he needed absolute silence.

He studied the cream and gold invitation spread before him. A stretch of fresh black leather—treated to repel the residual magics of any enchantments—lay underneath. He wanted to isolate the exact elements that went into the scrying spell. There was something off about the spell. He hadn't caught it in his first examination, but he could sense it now—a second spell just below the first.

He'd been looking in the wrong place for the connections he should be tracking.

Tracing one of the more advanced Sight runes, he closed his eyes. Sometimes his mortal vision interfered with his ability to trace the weavings of a magical working.

There. Just under the main spell was an additional rune. One of Sight, but tacked onto the main scrying connection. It spun a second connecting thread off of the main one, and sent it off to...

The main scrying spell activated, setting off the trace he'd laid. Shit. That wasn't the one he'd needed, but it would at least give him a clue as to who could have laid in the secondary spell.

He scrambled for a recorder–stones they modified to hold the images from scrying spells—and activated it just as the trace connected with the other end.

A darker room, a round porthole behind a shadowed figure. "Let's see what these whelps of mine are up to." A bright blue eye in a weathered and bearded face moved closer. "Think they can split from the clan. You don't leave the clan." The eye squinted. "Scath! Get in here."

The figure moved away as another, this one half-shrouded in shadow, moved into view.

"Something's blocking the scry. Would that Egyptian bitch have been able to do this?"

"Doubtful. There's not much to her." The darker figure leaned over, eyes narrowed.

Oisin tracked the direction of the connection in live time. North. North and a little east. Then the tracker split...

The second caster must be in the room. That meant...

His tracing spell hit the end of the connection. One

piece attached itself to the bearded and blue-eyed man, the other to the shadowed man, and then anchored itself back into the invitation.

He knew who had cast both spells.

And he could now find them.

Sealing the recording stone, he tucked it away in his pocket. Then he plucked up the invitation. Time to find Finn and the others.

Chapter Twenty-One

AILIS

"*C*iara. It's Ailis. Ready to get to work?"

After returning a clean Killer to Bat, the Egyptian goddess had told Ailis what she wanted—as many of the misfit fae as they could get ready to do what they could to stop Balor. Those who were willing to fight should be at the cottage by morning and ready to roll. Everyone else, well, they just needed to be ready. They needed to know to be on the lookout for seductive whispers, and misleading hope.

It wouldn't be easy. Those who had already met the strange Egyptian goddess would be the easiest. Word had been spreading, and it helped that the pixies had already made a decision on the point. But there were plenty of the forgotten and forsaken among the immortals, those the sidhe called "neutral" that had probably already been tricked over to the dark side.

"Tell me."

"Those who remember the truth of Balor, and are willing to fight, need to be at the cottage by dawn. And everyone needs to be on the lookout, there's shadows in the woods that don't belong there." Ailis herself could sense them, drawing closer, and they were running out of time.

It happened sometimes, these little flashes of intuition, as she liked to call them. For the most part, she was a normal fae. A touch of emotional manipulation, a dash of nature-speaking, and a whole heaping handful of glamour. And then sometimes, at the crucial moments, she knew what needed to happen.

Like her little outburst in the guardi library. Though, she hadn't needed timely intuition to tell her that Bat had made a mess of her feelings for the O'Loinsigh brothers, or that the brothers would need more than a kick in the ass to straighten things out. Throw Finn into the mix and… well, she'd been tempted to run out and fetch some popcorn.

"I'll call the leprechauns, and spread the word to the other Bigs," Ciara said, referring to the pixies who lived their lives in their larger forms. *"And—"* a pause and a drawn breath. *"I'll be there, with Fina and two other pups who still haven't found homes. I remember Balor."*

Those last three words held a wealth of meaning, and Ailis knew Ciara wouldn't rest until she'd reached—and convinced—as many as she could.

"Good."

The line went dead. Ciara was on it.

Who to call next? Con. The old coot had his fingers in everything, even more so than Ailis—it's what the trooping fae did, after all.

The line rang for a solid minute before being picked up. *"If ya need to speak, speak."*

"Ya' old coot, spread the word. We're fightin' in this one."

"Ailis. Well, now, I don't know about that. Not too keen to be losing me head for the sake of deities I haven't seen in ages."

"What about for one Egyptian goddess who likes to play a tune at night?"

"If ye're after thinking that'll sway me, ye'd be wrong, even as sweet as she is."

"What about if I told ya the cauldron's back, and Nuada's sword and Lugh's spear are missing?"

"Well, if ye're talking like that, I may have to reevaluate."

It must have been information Con didn't have yet. And it also must have told him just how serious the situation was. "I'm after thinking you should."

"And the pub, I saw it was boarded up."

"Sluagh and at least one Fir Bolg."

"So they're stirring the ancients, are they?" A cluck of the tongue. *"Can't be having that, now can we?"* A sigh. *"I'll put it out there, but don't be expecting too many to trouble themselves. Ye know the fae ain't what they once were, too set in our new human ways, we are."*

"Ye're a good man, Con. A good man."

"Well, I wouldn't be going that far." A heavy breath sounded over the line. *"Don't be getting yerself killed, Ailis. I like ya, and I don't want ta have ta mourn ya."*

"Don't fash yerself about that, old man," Ailis said with a grin. She had no intentions of dying any time soon. Her intuition tugged at her, telling her she still had one more grand adventure after this.

This time she was the one to hang up first.

Who next?

Ah, the banshees...

Chapter Twenty-Two

BAT

They would need to get the shard back to Dub soon, but she wanted to make one more attempt to contact the main piece of the vessel of creation via the shard.

What was the saying? Third time is the charm?

There had been the attempt back in the library at the guardi headquarters, and then again right after Finn and Cuchi had given their blood.

Dub had insisted on getting the shard back, and she *had* given it, but Daire had just zipped in and informed her that the Smith was working on the socket, and would not need the shard for an hour or so.

Ari had sent Nour, one of the other ba men, to fetch it, and here they were, trying one more time.

"Now," she said, wanting to make things clear. "I am

not trying to find the exact current location of the vessel, but I want to have an... assurance that we will be able to locate it precisely once it *is* time. Finding the island is fine, and the first step, of course, but we must be able to locate the vessel on the island." If Balor decided to hide it in a cave somewhere, she wanted to know where that cave was, how deep into the hills or under the ground.

"Yes, this would be good." Ari nodded.

"And we will need to break through glamours," Adom said. Smaller in stature than the others, he sat to her right, his legs swinging back and forth. Odiom, the last man of ba, remained silent, staring at the shard on the table. Then he sighed.

Bat reached out, with both her power and her hands. "Join me?" The invitation was a formality, but she noticed the men of ba did better when there were clear directions from her.

Ari laid two fingers along the length of the shard, careful to avoid her flesh with his claws. The other three men of ba matched him, their razor claws crossing in a careful tapestry. A shaft of sunlight filtered through the thin curtain over the kitchen window and flashed off the edge of the shard. Static and ozone, the scent of restrained power—and of Seth holding his temper—filled the room as each of them funneled power into the small piece of creation.

Please, she sent to the shard.

?

Where is the larger part of you?

Vague impression reached her, of a dark place filled with damp and salt.

Mother, where are you? The thought had the flavor of Ari.

A consciousness stirred in that dark place.

Mother, we are looking for you. It was another of the men of ba.

The shard pulsed under her fingers. This piece of the vessel, restored, had become its own small consciousness. It knew there was a new purpose for it, and had assured itself it was among its children. The greater part of the vessel had no such surety. Someone had taken it, and while some were familiar, they were not giving it what it needed.

She was… scared.

But the voices of the men of ba had provided some comfort.

Bat could understand this.

"Continue to call to her, she is listening," she told Ari. "I will lend you what power I can."

Ari nodded and closed his eyes. Bat followed suit, allowing the call of the vessel to guide her. She thought of comfort, and home, and love—all the things she had found since coming to Ireland, since coming across Dub, Mell, Shar, and Finn. Since finding a friend in Ailis, since being given Killer. She filtered out the lingering traces of frustration and anger, concentrating on now and the future she wanted. Bundling those feelings together, she channeled it to Ari, Nour, Adom, and Odion, asking all four of them to use it in their calls to the vessel.

Gathering the last of what she had built up the night before, scraping the power from the corners of her soul, she sent one last push, and felt the men of ba do the same.

Just when she thought they'd failed, there was an almost audible click, and the vessel reached out. Bypassing the shard completely, it wrapped tendrils of mixed need and assurance around each of the men of ba. It touched upon Bat, skimming over her with a faint recognition, then passed on.

That was fine. They had accomplished what needed to be done.

Bat opened her eyes to find the shard glowing faintly, and the four men of ba staring in wonder, their eyes shedding a red cast upon the table.

She laughed, relief and hope pouring through her. "We did it," she breathed out.

They had done it. They really had.

"Yes," Ari whispered as he slid his fingers from the shard. "Yes, we did it." He focused on her. "Thank you."

Bat shook her head. "No. This is not something that required thanks."

"Nevertheless," Ari said, falling into ancient Egyptian. "I must thank you, goddess. You remind me of Nut in the early days, you have the same warmth. I am glad to have known you."

Why did that sound like a farewell? "Ari?"

He smiled, careful not to reveal his needle teeth, but didn't say anything else. The other men of ba remained silent.

Chapter Twenty-Three

MELL

*M*ell swept a hand over the seat of a dust-covered chair, and joined Femi at the low table they'd set in the middle of the small staging room connected to the forge. Sharp pings sounded through the walls as Dub worked.

"Need more hawthorn," Femi said.

The man of ba had been working steadily for the last hour, twining leather scraps to hawthorn and iron nails. He had twenty small bundles prepared.

The weaving was done in a precise pattern. Occasionally, Mell could just make out the impression of a rune in that pattern, but it was none that he knew.

He rose, going to the small pile of twigs and leaves the pixies had helped him gather. It had dwindled to a handful of scraps. He gathered what was left and placed it next to the pile of nails in front of Femi. "How many more will you make?"

"As many as I can until the guardi magician arrives. Then I will show him the way of the casting, and he will help me finish them."

Femi must have meant Oisin. Impatience built in Mell. He wanted to be doing something, not babysitting a man of ba while it wove amulets. "Can you show me?"

A bright red gaze met his through the haze of old dust that hung in the air. "Do you recognize the runes?"

Mell's lips tightened. "No."

Femi shook his head. "It would take too long to show you. Better to show once. The magician can then teach you later, after the Evil Eye is once more defeated." He returned to his weaving, using his claws to twist the leather and hawthorn around the nails.

Mell sat once more, watching as Femi's fingers flew in an intricate dance. If he could just learn those movements, he could help instead of being an errand boy...

"I'll need more hawthorn, Fomoiri."

Tamping down on his frustration, Mell rose and went in search of the pixies.

Relegated to an errand boy...

Chapter Twenty-Four

DUB

*H*e took the shard from Ari and gave the ba man a short nod. The timing was perfect. Turning back to his forge, he didn't bother to see the other immortal out.

He'd prepared the socket and the casing of metal that he would need to coax into enveloping the shard. He'd practiced the runes, the order he would need to speak them in, and the pattern he would need to beat into the metal. Smithing with runes was tricky, unless you were etching them directly into the metal.

In this case, he wasn't. He had to hammer the pattern into the metal—first the socket, then the spearhead itself. And he needed to do it with a precise striking pressure: hard enough to shape the metal, soft enough to not shatter the stone of the shard.

He placed the prepared spearhead casing on the anvil and went to the bellows, pumping them until he had the necessary blast going. Like the force of his strikes, the heat needed to be exact. Enough to heat the iron, but not so much it would cause the shard to expand too quickly and crack.

Concentrating, he didn't see Mell cross through the forge on his way to gather more hawthorn, nor did he notice when Finn returned with Oisin.

He kept the bellows going and he coaxed the metal. He lost himself in this world of fire and heat that Goibniu had given him the keys to.

Chapter Twenty-Five

SHAR

*H*e'd been correct. The ash was perfect. It had a strong grain, and wouldn't need too much shaping.

He didn't have his usual tools, but he'd found a knife in the forge that would do, one that Dub had intended for Dano.

Work like this was better done with minimal blade work anyway. The best woodwork was not done with carving, but with coaxing. A true carpenter shaped, he did not force.

Looking up from where he sat in a shaded spot under one of the old oaks at the edge of the property, he cocked his head.

Hurry, protector. They come. The trees had continued to whisper to him. They could not tell him the exact numbers of the enemy, but he'd begun to get an idea of where they were. The majority were to the north. Gathering and coming from the north. There were others to the east, closer, but they were not headed in this direction.

He bent back over the ash wood, funneling power into his fingers as he smoothed out the knots and bends. He'd gathered it living from the tree, and with the tree's permission. Living wood was best, and would only enhance whatever other enchantments Dub had prepared for the spearhead.

Three more hours, maybe two if he pushed himself. They needed to be gone by morning.

A warm breeze stirred the branches over him.

When this fuss was over, he was going to come back to this spot, and bring Bat with him. He'd lay beside his goddess on a soft blanket and ply her with strawberries. They'd laugh, and he'd tell the old tales as the trees knew them.

His fingers worked. They would fight this battle, and they would return home.

He would not fail this time.

Chapter Twenty-Six

FAOLAN

*H*e stood amongst his fellows, on the edge of the bog, hidden in the shade of an old ash tree. "I'm telling ya, the goddess thanked me."

Carrig fluttered his wings and bared his fangs in a dry laugh. "Well then, that just means she owes ya. Not that ya owe her."

Faolan shook his head. They didn't understand, because they hadn't been to the pub with him. "She's different, I'm *telling* ya. She…"

"Don't you dare say a goddess cares, Fao." Dalaigh crossed his arms as he sent shadows to snapping at Carrig's feet. "Ya know better'n tha'."

Faolan pulled himself up to his full height. "Ya still don't understand." He gestured for them to come closer. "There was this one time with the Morrigan…"

The gathered sluagh leaned in, always willing to hear a good tale, even if it was of a strange Egyptian goddess.

Chapter Twenty-Seven

MEERA

*T*hree banshees gathered in front of the boarded-up windows of the Dubros, streetlights glinting off shards of broken glass and slick cobblestones.

"Are we really going to do this?" Teagan asked. "When we accompanied the Fomoiri on their departure from Egypt, I never did intend to return. I won't use my voice for people who never deserved it, in mourning or otherwise."

Meera bent her head. She'd once thought just as Teagan still did. Then Bat had walked into the pub one night, and played a song that spoke of home. And the home Meera envisioned had not been the green fields and stone walls of Ireland, but the sands of Egypt. Not the pale skin she now wore, but burnished gold flesh.

What was it like now, her once home? And had her life changed all that much once she'd come to Ireland? Gods and goddesses who were too preoccupied with their own business to bother with a mere banshee. She still wailed for the dead, in warning and in mourning.

The only difference? She chose who she would wail for.

And she had never once had to use her voice as a weapon since leaving that land of reeds and lotus and sand. Never once had to watch as ears bled and eyes burst with the power of the sounds she made. She'd been created as a weapon, then condemned to cry for all eternity in penance for those she'd killed.

"What if they do deserve our help?" she asked. An image came to her, of Bat, her dark hair down around her shoulders and blue-embroidered boots on her feet, calling out a teasing remark to a frowning Dub as she set a plate of food in front of Old Mike. A goddess, teasing a Fomoiri and serving a wisp.

And it wasn't just Bat. The O'Loinsigh brothers had run that pub in one fashion or another for nearly eight hundred years. Rumors had it that they'd located the Crane Clan brooch, and had been planning to bargain for their freedom.

They were good men, as men went.

Neasa caught her gaze. "I could do with a good fight. See if I've still got the old magic."

Teagan's brows rose. "Your aim was always shit. You'll probably start taking out the friendlies."

"Does that mean you're coming along as well?" Meera asked, a thrill of anticipation coursing through her limbs.

Teagan hung her head then tipped it back and shrugged. "Someone has to make sure the two of you don't end up slaughtering entire populations by accident."

With a last glance at the temporarily abandoned pub, and her home away from home, Meera turned on her heel and headed out.

The word had been spread. Meet at the O'Loinsigh brothers' cottage at dawn.

Chapter Twenty-Eight

SAOIRSE

*T*he selkie rose from the waters and used her flippers to propel herself across a slick stretch of rock. With a roll of her body, she shed her skin and rose onto two legs, wrapping the fur around her hips.

A goblin stood at the edge of the preserve, beside the rail that separated the tourists and the road from the rocks below. She was familiar. Saoirse cocked her head. This one visited sometimes, and lived in the area.

The sea whispered to her, of small ships carrying even smaller men. One of those ships carried a precious cargo, and the sea wanted it for itself. But that would violate the Treaty, so the sea held herself under control.

"Dechtire," Saoirse greeted the stooped woman.

"Ailis sent me," the goblin said.

Ailis. The name, too, was familiar…

"She's the shopkeeper who sent over that sauce from the states you guys like too much. The B-B-Q stuff."

Ah! That was right. Drizzled over a fresh-caught cod, it was quite delicious. Saoirse nodded. "I remember now."

"Ye've probably heard about the Egyptian goddess who came to Sligo a couple months back." The goblin looked down and bit her lip, her pointed teeth making small indents in the flesh.

Saoirse blinked her eyes. She had heard, but she had disregarded the news. It would have been the height of foolishness for one from that land to travel here. All kinds of trouble would be stirred...

"It was true?" she asked.

Dechtire nodded hard enough to send tendrils of gray hair flying. "It was. I saw her once. Popped into the Dubros for a quick pint, and she was playing the Uaithne."

Saoirse's head went back. Again, she had heard the rumors, but could not believe them. This was news indeed. "What is it that Ailis needs?" For no one would send a goblin to talk to a selkie if they did not want something.

The goblin's brows drew together. "Well now, she didn't say exactly, but apparently this goddess is after wanting to talk to mac Lir, and they're wondering if any of you can help with that."

A sly grin spread over the selkie's face. Oh, pa was going to love this. "It seems you're talking to the right selkie. Tell me where to go to find this goddess."

She sent out a call, to the ancient entity that tended to

lurk in the deepest trenches these days, playing with his monstrous creations.

Da?

?

Ye're going to need to be coming to the surface, just for a bit. There's a goddess wants to talk to ya.

No.

She's Egyptian.

There was a sigh, accompanied by vague exasperation, and the waves crashed just a bit harder against the rocks. *Is this about those Fomoiri? They haven't violated the Treaty, and that's been in place for near six thousand years. There's no reason for me to concern myself.*

This was true. Her da did not concern himself with much these days. *Well, then, do ya mind if I play with them for a bit?*

The waters smoothed. *Just don't go getting yer skin stolen. That's a mess I don't want to have to clean up again.* A pause as the sea surged back and then forward once more, sending up a warning spray. *And no violating the Treaty. I don't want to have ta be dealing with Apep again. Best to let that sleeping god lie. Ya can help, but ya can't kill, that was the deal.*

Saoirse pouted. *Like with the fishermen?*

Like with the fishermen. Only so many tributes can be taken in a year, you hear me?

How many for the Fomoiri?

They offer tribute of a different kind, and it has already been paid, child.

Fine. She paused. *What if they break it first?*

The only way they would break it is if they killed one of my children. Are you going to be sacrificing yerself?

No. No, she would not be doing that. But she would go and play for a bit.

Saoirse returned her attention to the goblin. "You may tell Ailis that a conversation with mac Lir is unnecessary. Now, tell me how to find this goddess, I have messages to relay."

Chapter Twenty-Nine

OLD MIKE

Old Mike paused, then ducked behind a twisted oak, pulling the panting tourist behind him.

They'd been on the run for two days now.

It had started the very same evening Old Mike had met the man at the pub. A tourist, out to hear the old stories. It was the perfect bit of mischief. Mike was just going to show him a bit of the bogs, then flit away.

The man 'd find his way back by morning latest.

But there had been shadows prowling in the crannies of peat, and hiding amongst the dwarf shrubs and birch. Shadows that didn't belong sneaking in his bog, or going after a wisp and human who were minding their own business. Old Mike may have had no problem leaving a human to get lost here and there, but to leave them at the mercy of the shadows?

He shuddered. It didn't matter how many times the sluagh were called "neutral," their nature was to hunt, and to torment what they hunted.

He'd taken the tourist back to town, but the shadows followed. He'd gone to the pub, but it was boarded up. They'd gone to the man's hotel, but the shadows had been there as well.

"Mike," the small voice caught his attention. "Old Mike, look up."

It was a pixie, no more than an inch high, and cast all in shades of deep purple, helping it blend with the Ling heather.

"Get to the brother's cabin. Get there, the wards are strong. The goddess is there."

The human shuddered, his skin both graying and sporting a feverish red across his cheeks. He'd been unwell since he came into the pub, but the two days with minimal food and rest had nearly taken him down. For the last half-day he'd been following Old Mike in a daze, no longer questioning what they were running from, what the shapes that chased them were, or talking about the voices that haunted him.

There was a welt across one cheek from when the shadows had closed in the night before. They'd only escaped because Old Mike liked to keep a bit of salt and iron in his pockets. It confused the tracking magic, and helped with the wandering.

In this case, it had saved their lives.

Why were the shadows after a wisp who'd done naught but follow his nature? And why were they after a tourist from the Americas? It made no sense.

"What's going on?" He scanned the rolling hills of the bog. The light was fading, but there were no shadows where there should not be. The sluagh that chased them had been lost for now.

"Get to the cottage, they'll explain. But guard yer dreams, old man. Balor's begun to whisper his poison."

The wisp's eyes slid closed as the weight of the name settled over him. Balor. He shuddered. Those were times he did not want to live through again.

The tourist groaned and shuddered. "Cold. So cold. And the voices." He reached for Mike's shoulder. "Please make them stop. Stop them. Please."

Mike took his hand. "Ye're gonna be okay. We'll get ya ta the goddess. She'll know what ta do. She'll help ya, okay?" He looked back to the pixie. "Can ya show me the way? Never been to the brothers' cottage."

The pixie nodded. "We have to hurry. Unless ya know the runes for *blinking* us there?"

Old Mike shook his head. He was a wisp, he'd never needed to learn the ways of the Druids and sidhe.

The pixie bobbed. "All right then. Ya hold that one tight, and don't lose me or yer way."

Pulling himself and the tourist up, Old Mike's lips pulled up into a thin smile. The irony of the pixie's words was not lost on the will-o-the-wisp.

Chapter Thirty

Bastie,
Oh, I have so much more to tell you.
Have you ever made love to a one-eyed pirate?
Wait, who am I asking. You must have.
We should compare notes.
- Bat, the goddess who is going to tease you with hints of
exploits until you respond

BAT

*I*t was the end of the day, and everyone had gathered once more in the kitchen, including Oisin, who had arrived in the early afternoon to help with the dream-guardian amulets. Bat, Ailis, Mell, and Oisin sat at the table, while the others had ranged themselves through the small room.

It was a bit crowded.

"I'm near done," Dub said from where he stood beside the rear door. As soon as the meeting was done he was headed back to the forge. "I'll want a pixie, just the one, to be on standby to run possible messages."

The three resident Littles—as she'd learned they preferred to be called—popped up from behind the potted plant they'd claimed as their own. "I'll do it!" Maire zipped over to Dub's shoulder and stuck her tongue out at the other two. Bat suspected the pink pixie had a bit of a crush on her grumpy not-man.

It was cute.

"No noise," Dub warned.

The pixie nodded hard enough to send herself bobbing in the air.

"Right then." Finn, who stood near the head of the table, gestured to Cuchi.

"My team is still compiling the data coming in on the Fomoiri's movements. Two days aren't truly long enough for a comprehensive analysis, but I'll tell you what we have so far." He paced in the small space between the kitchen counters. "Of the four clans, only one has been travelling outside their usual routes—the Hounds. There were some rumors of new contracts a few months ago, and the change in pattern was put down to that."

"New contracts," Mell said, his voice flat. "Taken in a different light—"

"It could mean an alliance with Balor," Finn finished. "Or, it could simply be new contracts. That's the trouble with half-researched information."

Cuchi nodded, taking no offense at his fellow guardi's words. "Exactly. It is still only a supposition, but a fairly safe one to make. As for the other clans, there have been rumors of a few desertions, but again they are not confirmed."

Dub shook his head. "If you are hearing rumors of that, then they are most likely true. A Fomoiri does not leave the clan lightly." His lips lifted in a wry smile.

"Most center around the Lion clan, but there were a few of the Crane clan."

Mell snorted. "Da's got ta be boiling."

Dub shrugged.

All of this was not really new news. "Anything else?" she asked.

"We know who set the scrying spell on the invitation." Oisin pulled the cream-colored cardstock from a pouch at his belt and set it on the table. "The spell is neutralized for now, so we need not fear anyone listening in. There were actually two spells, one attached to the first, set to bypass the original." He met Dub's gaze. "The first was laid by your father, the second by Scath. You can track both now, you just need the invitation."

Mell reached for the card. "This is good news. If nothing else we can keep tabs on Scath. And won't *that* curl *his* toes?" Mell's grin was more than a little wicked. He held the card up and cocked his head at Dub, who nodded. Mell tucked it away in a fold of space.

"Next," Finn said, pointing at Ailis.

The fae gave him a mocking salute and shook back her green hair. "The word's being spread. I told them dawn. In fact, there's a few out there now need ta be checked and crossed over the wards. They're okay for now, but I'd no be wanting them twiddling their thumbs the night through, not if there're enemies headed for us even now."

"I'll check them, goddess," Ari offered from his position against the wall behind the breakfast table.

Finn nodded then looked to her.

"Right. My turn." She straightened in her chair. This was very much like the war councils she had been an observer of, where Seth, Horus, and Narmer strategized the consolidation of Egypt. "The men of ba were able to establish a connection to the main body of the vessel. The shard, unfortunately, cannot be used as a guide, but as long as we have Ari or one of his men with us, they will be able to give us direction, and not just in a general sense. We will be able to find it amidst a labyrinth of caves if need be."

"Except for me." Femi frowned, his wide lips pulling down to reveal a snip of needle teeth. "But the amulets are completed." He passed a wicker basket to Shar, who placed it on the table. "The librarian now knows the way of making them as well. Each of you should take one to wear. Best to keep against skin." The taller man of ba nodded and folded his arms.

The amulets were simple: a piece of iron and a cutting of hawthorn, twined together with leather. Bat picked one up and raised it to the light.

Oh. Magic glimmered along the leather, soft patterns swirling together and binding the strength of the iron to the protective properties of the wood. Interesting. She slipped it over her head. Would she get to meet the dragon-guardian? Eagerness and curiosity had her swinging her legs and bouncing lightly in her seat.

Mell leaned toward her. "They're just a construct, *realta*."

She stilled as heat rushed to her cheeks. Mell chuckled.

"The shaft is complete," Shar said. I laid some basic protective runes into the grain." Shar nodded to his brother. "They won't interfere with what you have worked up."

That means he does not need to work further tonight. Bat bit her bottom lip. Despite everything, she still intended to join with her giant tonight. The urgency, more than distracting her, had solidified her earlier decision. They really did not know what would happen after this, despite their plans and strategies. *She* did not know, despite her visions. And because of that she was done hesitating.

Mell and Finn both looked at her, heat in their eyes. Mell, she knew, could probably sense her desire. Could Finn? His nostrils flared and his eyes narrowed. She tilted her head and her hand crept up to clutch at her necklace.

Then she stopped. There was no reason to be nervous about that. In fact, if they could sense it, all the better. Bat allowed a sly grin to cross her face, and Mell echoed it. Finn's and Dub's eyes narrowed. The others in the room had gone silent, sensing the anticipation in the air.

She rose. "Well, if there is nothing else that needs to be discussed for the next few hours, you will need to excuse me."

Shar stood a step behind her chair, her ever-present and steady guardian. She took his hand and headed for the doorway. With only a gentle tug of encouragement, he followed after her. Just as she turned into the hall, she shot a look over her shoulder. Mell's grin was still firmly in place, Finn was shaking his head, and Dub stared at them with darkened eyes. He gave her a slight nod.

Bat continued, Shar following along silently in her wake. He did not speak as they climbed the stairs, or even when Bat paused outside her bedroom. He did not say a word as she pushed open the door, and brought him inside, nor did he make a sound as she led him to the bed. When they stood beside it, she turned to look up at him.

His single eye had darkened, just as Dub's did. His expression was tight, his lips a thin line. Had she made a mistake in not asking him first? She did not think of that, just assumed they would want to be with her now that the hesitations on both sides were handled.

"Are you—?"

"Do you remember the night after I'd been stabbed by the soul blade? You stayed with me."

Her chest tightened. She remembered it very well. She'd been unwilling to leave his side for even a moment, afraid that the patch she'd made on his soul would not hold and somehow break open.

It was also the day he asked her to stay with them, setting into motion a journey and adventure of a different kind—one where she felt she was finally becoming the goddess she was always meant to be.

"Do you remember," he continued, taking a step forward to mere inches separated them, "that I also said I could warm ya very well?" He brought up his hand and rested it on her shoulder, then skimmed it up to cup the back of her head, his fingers threading through her hair.

He left heat in his wake, and it travelled lower, over

her breasts where is swirled around her nipples, then farther, dipping into her navel, before settling at the juncture of her thighs.

Oh. Oh, that is brilliant. The heat teased, bringing her need up another notch.

"I remember," she whispered, all her attention on what he was doing between her legs with just a hint of his power. "What is this?"

He tugged her to him, so her breasts pressed to his chest. There was more heat, enough to penetrate both of their clothes. "This is… healing, in a way. It is a little bit of life. My life."

She laid her head against his chest, listening to the beat of his heart. It was steady, if a little fast.

"And I offer it to you, *a stor*. My little goddess. It is yours, to do with as you will." He pulled in a breath, pushing his chest against her. "My heart, my power, my life."

She wrapped her arms around him. These were the words she had longed for, the ones she told herself she did not need to hear.

Another of the pinpricks in her soul closed, and the hollow place filled with the gift of his declaration. His other hand settled in the small of her back, and they stayed like that, wrapped together.

How had she managed without these touches the last two months? A kernel of anger stirred, but this was directed at herself. When she first arrived at the pub, she had been attracted to them, and while she had not wanted to cause them any grief, she had acted upon her impulses. Why, oh why, had she not continued to do so?

"Cease." Shar's voice rumbled through her. "Cease thinking upon it. What is done is done. As you said this morning, you did not allow us to know you. Maybe this is true. But we also did nothing to change that. We can continue to blame ourselves, to regret, or we can move on with what we now have."

Her arms tightened around him and her fingers curled into the light sweater he wore. "You are correct. I know you are. But if I had continued to act as I did when I first came... Dub had kissed me, I was being held by you and Mell, and I thought nothing of responding to the three of you, not at first. I should have continued thinking nothing of it."

"No. No, that would have been the worst thing you could do. Because while you may have thought nothing of those actions of affection in the beginning, the 'touches' as ya call them, *we* were not ready to accept that all of us wanted to give them to you. A few flirting glances and a kiss or two are much different from a solid relationship. And..." His hands went to her shoulders and pushed her back enough that he could meet her gaze. "And whether it is what you intended, you allowed us the space we needed—that *I* needed—to come to terms with things. This I can admit."

"You are saying we all erred. This is true." She thought for a moment. What was the saying? "It takes two to tango?"

He grinned. "That one would work." The smile fell away. "We have not had much of a chance to talk, just the two of us, have we?"

"There was the library."

"Which was a few minutes of reassurance before you called someone who should have known better than to walk away from you." Oh, there was anger in her giant's voice.

She let it go. "If we had tried to talk then, I am not sure how it would have gone," she admitted. "I seem to have changed my mind a thousand times in these last few days. First, I was determined to keep my distance, then to wait for you three. Then I decided I would not leave you, but I would gain my physical pleasures and needs from another. At one point I was sure I would be willing to accept whatever you three would give me, and a few hours later I resolved to be selfish—I wanted all of you or nothing. If one of you were unwilling, then everyone—including Finn who had become my back-up plan—would be off limits. Now here I am, once more willing to take whatever you can give and waiting for the rest." She let out a soft laugh and laid a hand against Shar's cheek. "I am a fickle goddess, am I not?"

"Or, you were simply coming to terms with what you truly wanted, for yourself and for us?"

"Or, I was simply doing that." She ran her thumb over his lips. Her gentle giant had such a way about him. "Are you sure you are not the one with the power of emotions?"

Shar shook his head. "I don't envy Mell his powers. You were right, that time you accused him of hiding behind a mask of conjured emotions. It is not always easy for him to tell what is real, and what is something he has constructed. And his younger years..."

Her earlier vision came back to her, of a younger and bruised Mell.

"Well, those are for him to tell you, *a stor*. Not that he would mind me sharing, but I think he needs to do the telling of it."

Shar was correct. And they were now far from the reason she had brought him to her bedroom. She slipped her hand from his cheek into the hair at the nape of his neck and tugged, bringing his face down to her. She placed a firm kiss upon his lips. "Enough talking for now. It is not what I wanted to do this night."

"Yes, goddess," he said. Then he took control of the kiss.

She pushed into him, needing to be closer. Clothing. They needed to remove their clothing. Her free hand dove under his sweater and flattened against his back and the shifting muscles there. Their tongues tangled as Shar picked her up and kneeled upon the mattress.

He laid her down then straightened, stripping off his sweater and loosening the button on his trousers. In seconds he'd removed the last of his clothing.

She took him in. He was thicker than his brother, but not quite as long. He would stretch her to the point of near pain.

But sometimes a bit of pain only enhanced the experience. And she was more than ready to take whatever he gave her. He climbed over her, his braid falling over one shoulder. Her hands studied him, just as her eyes had done, skimming over the muscles of his shoulders, and down his sides only to return to his front and the mounds of muscle there.

He reached for her sweater and she sat up quickly. She didn't have enough clothes with her for something to be ruined each night by one of her men.

One of her men. They were *hers*.

Heat surged in her, tightening the flesh of her breasts and causing her hips to rise in invitation.

"Eager, are ya?" Shar stripped her of her sweater in one smooth move, and Bat shrugged out of her bra. He pressed her back down, alternating between kisses and teasing nibbles as his mouth made its way to her breasts. "These, now. These deserve to be worshipped."

His palm cupped her breast, and she sucked in a breath. His hand tightened, kneading her, then moved to the other, then back to the first. He plucked at her nipple, then pinched so carefully before rolling it between two fingers.

He did it again, over and over, switching breasts until Bat wanted to cry out in frustration. Then he laid his mouth over the taut point of her right breast, and she moaned. As he had with his fingers, he switched to the other breast, over and over. Bat's hips moved, pressing up and into his thigh in silent invitation and demand.

"Almost, little goddess. Almost." There was dark satisfaction in her protector's voice. He loved that he drove her just a little mad with want, simply from his lips being laid upon her.

She reached between them, determined to get rid of her jeans. There was definitely no reason to have these on. It was a struggle, as he continued to distract her, but she eventually got the buttons undone, and the pants pulled halfway down her thighs.

"You will need to help me with this," she finally ordered.

With a grin, he began tugging on the cloth, teasing pulls that did nothing to remove her pants. With a growl of frustration, she pushed wiggled up the mattress and evaded his hands, finally pulling the pants off herself.

"I would think you'd want to help with this," she groused.

Grinning, he reached for her, and for a moment she contemplated avoiding his hands.

But, that would not only punish him, it would punish her as well.

She allowed herself to be captured, and Shar grabbed her by the waist, pulling her to him for another kiss. They lay together, facing each other, one of his hands spanning her back, the other sliding lower to grab the flesh of her ass and pull her into his groin, grinding his erection against her lower belly.

"Yer so soft," he murmured, his voice hoarse.

She rubbed her still sensitive nipples against his chest, then pressed her hands against him, rolling him onto his back. She followed, straddling him. Placing her hands over his pecs, and those wonderfully useless man-nipples, she braced herself.

He reached out, steadying her with a hand on her hip, and then grabbed his erection, holding it in readiness for her—offering himself to her.

Power surged into her. This was a position she had been in many times over her existence. And as with Dub, it meant so much more.

She paused, taking in the moment. Shar, her one-eyed

pirate-giant, tattoos swirling across his broad chest and over his shoulders, his skin damp with a light sheen of sweat, looking up at her as though she were his entire world.

She was positive she looked at him in the exact same way, for right then, he really was her world. It was the two of them, loving each other, understanding each other—protecting each other.

She positioned herself and slid onto him, working to take him herself, just as she had promised. She was slick, but his girth stretched her wide, and she rocked her hips, inching down onto him.

He held himself still, allowing her to take control. When she was fully seated, he gripped both her hips, his fingers digging into the flesh there. "I love these," he said, squeezing her. "I love how much of you there is, how I don't feel as though I have ta be oh so careful of you, no' in this."

She smiled. His words were such a contrast to Dub's concerns. "And I love *you*." The words were easier to say the second time. In fact, she would probably begin saying them all the time—she felt… free. Free to simply be herself, to love who she would love, however she chose to love them.

Another pin-prick closed.

Leaning forward, she partially pulled off of him, and gave his collarbone a light kiss. Then she leaned back, finding the angle she wanted, and moved.

She rode him, his hands on her hips, his body laid out for her use. She rode him, her thighs and hips working. She rode him, claiming him as her own, finally.

Their gazes locked. This was the part she loved. She enjoyed the heat, yes, and the burst of sensation, but it was the intimacy she loved, that she craved. And that was exactly what Shar gave her.

She sped up, the tightening and light spasms in her channel telling her she was close.

Shar's expression tightened, as did his fingers.

She would have bruises.

Bat didn't care.

And then he was no longer still. She wasn't sure how he had held out so long, but suddenly her giant not-man was moving. His hips thrust into her, matching her strokes, and he moved her.

Her breath coming in short pants, she strained. Close. She was so close. The sensations and friction gathered at the juncture of her thighs then burst, and she threw back her head, breaking their eye contact.

Shar sat up, still hard inside her, and wrapped his arms around her. Then he rolled, taking her with him, until she lay on her back and he was heavy between her legs. He buried one hand in her hair and propped himself on his other elbow, keeping a majority of his weight off her.

"My turn," he whispered, then pulled out until only the tip of his shaft was still inside her. He plunged in. She was both swollen and slick from her orgasm, and it was delicious. He pulled out again, then thrust once more. "Mine." Another thrust. "For right now, you are mine."

She wrapped her legs around him and held on. This time was for him, now. In fact, she didn't even want another release, not as long as he found his.

"No," he growled. "You come with me."

Did he have some mind-reading ability that he kept from her?

"You." Another thrust. "Come." Thrust. "Too." One more.

The heat began to build once more, rising in a rapid wave. Shar's braid draped over one shoulder, swinging with each of his movements, and she reached for it, twisting it around one hand.

The hand in her hair flexed, the taut pulling pressure shooting down to her core. She angled her hips so that his thrusts hit closer to her clitoris—if he was going to insist she find her release with him, then she had better comply, had she not? She met each of his movement with her own.

When he lost the rhythm of his movements, and she knew he was close, she slid her free hand down her body and to the juncture of her thighs, scissoring her fingers around the hood of her clit and his penis, increasing the pressure for them both.

His expression tight, he drove into, seating himself fully, and shuddered. Warmth filled her as he came. He jerked, hitting against her hand, pressing to the nub of sensitive flesh at the apex of her vagina, and the pleasure coalesced in a rush, sending her over the edge once more. The tingles she associated with sexual pleasure swept from her core and through her body, down her limbs and back, settling into a low throb between her legs.

Shar sagged over her. She ran her hand up and down his back as he caught his breath.

"You do know that this means you are now mine," she said, keeping her voice teasingly light. "No other may have you."

He sucked in a breath and his shoulders shook. "I'd no' want another, *a stor*. Ye're damned near killing me, how could I handle a second one of ya?"

She gave a mock frown and pinched his butt. Then grinned.

Bat had her giant, and her grumpy not-man. Now she simply needed to claim the laughing immortal, and her guardi.

Chapter Thirty-One

BAT

*D*ub lay the completed spear across the kitchen table. The sun had yet to rise, but the sky was lighting to a dull silver in the window over the sink. The eldest brother had dark circles under his eyes, just as he had the night before, and soot streaked across his forearms and knuckles.

"It's done," he said, then stepped back. Mell, Shar, Finn, and Cuchi crowded in next to her around the table to study the weapon.

Bat took a last sip of her tea and set the cup in its saucer. One more thing done. In another hour the sun would be up and it would be time to head for Londonderry and the Crane clan of the Fomoiri—and the brothers' father.

The spear matched her earlier vision perfectly—a

simple wooden shaft and leather bindings, while steel had been carefully molded around the restored shard. A faint glow played along the length, lending it a quiet air of near divinity.

Flash. The spear, a gray hand clutching it as blood ran down the shaft. Soft lights played under the skin of that hand.

Flash. A pair of large brown eyes widened in pain.

Flash. Mell, the spear held before him in a two-handed grip, sparring with a silver-haired man wielding the golden spear.

Bat looked to the middle brother. "You will be the spear's keeper, at least at first." She wasn't sure yet what the other visions were seeking to tell her, but they would come clear soon enough. And she had received another clue. The man in her first vision of the golden spear had been dark haired. She focused on the pale porcelain of the teacup. Had she missed any other details? Or was this a newcomer? "Is there a fae with silver hair? He is the one who wields the golden spear."

Silence greeted her words and she worked up the courage to look up. Cuchi looked at the ceiling, his lips pressed together. Finn and Dub wore matching frowns, their brows lowered and eyes narrowed on her. Shar stared at her with lips parted and eyes wide.

Mell pulled out the seat to her left and dropped into it. "Well, now, that would have been good to know. Could have saved us a bit of trouble." He paused. "I thought the one who held it had dark hair."

She bit her lip. "He did."

Surprisingly, it was Cuchi who finally answered her and put her mind at ease. "It's probably Quinn, from the Hound clan. But, there is more than one silver-haired immortal running around Ireland."

"True," Dub said, his tone brusque. "It still would have only cast suspicion on the Hound clan, not confirmed anything."

Finn sighed. "It does at least confirm some of the reports of their activity. But, we already knew at least some of the Fomoiri were involved, if not the clan leaders. Quinn is Cichol's second in command, much as Scath is for Alatrom of the Crane clan. If Balor has swayed two of such high rank, then we can expect his forces to be formidable."

Bat nodded. She had already assumed as much. It would only make sense, after all. Balor had been their leader for millennia.

"It would've only been surprising if the Fomoiri *didn't* follow him," Shar said, echoing her thoughts.

Dub snorted. "Da's grown to love his wealth too much. We're not the only Fomoiri to settle into a less barbaric existence."

From his tone, Bat suspected these were words that had once been thrown in his face. Perhaps by the woman who abandoned him? Bat still wanted to know what happened to this woman, and maybe lay a curse of spotted skin or thinning hair upon her.

"Regardless, we know Scath is up to more than a bit of spying for da," Mell interjected. "No reason not to be smart in our assumptions."

"And none of this changes anything about what we must now do," Finn said, bringing the conversation back to the point. "The sun will be fully risen in an hour, and we have to set out."

"I'm off to shower." Dub paused long enough to drop a kiss on her head and then he was gone.

"You have everything packed up?" Shar asked her, taking the seat to her right. His hand landed on her thigh.

Remembered heat of just a few hours ago swept up her chest and into her cheeks. "Just a small bag, but yes." She sent a confirming glance at the bundle sitting beside the front door. A duffle and the harp case. She'd not pulled out the instrument except the once since it had been recovered from the pub.

Killer slipped into the kitchen, his nails clicking on the wood floor. He squeezed between her and Shar's chairs, and pressed his head to her thigh, dislodging Shar's hand. She dug her fingers into the fur of his ruff, then up to scratch just behind his ears, in the spot he liked.

"I'm going to go check on the fairy and the rabble," Cuchi said, striding for the front door.

More fae had arrived during the night. First, there were a few more pixies. Then a leprechaun, an old friend of Dano's, had shown up around midnight. An hour later it was three of the trooping fae, dripping with pointed laughter to match their sharp looks and swimming in glamour. And more continued to trickle in as the moon rose and the night passed.

Camped just inside the wards, they had remained the night through, putting up only a token protest when informed that the men of ba would be "peering into their souls to see if they were going to be wankers," as Ailis put it.

Bat wanted to spend the remainder of the time before their departure out there, speaking with those who had gathered to help. But something nagged at her. Something she felt she should have figured out by now. A connection she should have drawn...

Flash. Isis waded in the reed-covered banks of the Nile, her gown gathered up and tucked between her legs. Her slender limbs glimmered with the light of the stars above. Behind her, straddling the line between the fertile black lands and the red lands of the desert, stood Seth, blood dripping from the curved blade of his sword.

Isis bent, her hand disappearing into the waters. A moment later she straightened, a carved and decorated puzzle box held in her hand. In it was the final piece of Osiris, the key to his resurrection as the Lord of the Dead, and the ruler of the Land of Reeds.

The air stirred until a storm rose, disturbing the sands of the desert beyond. Seth nodded, his duty done, and turned away, disappearing alone into those sands.

Moisture welled in Bat's eyes and she blinked, freeing a lone tear. Though it had not been the purpose of the vision, it had reminded her of how lonely Seth had always been, just as she was, and for a moment she wished she could have been the one to relieve that loneliness.

But she was certain now—that had never been her fate. And despite her earlier confessions of how she'd been the one to leave him first, she suspected that in some ways Seth was destined to always be the one forced to walk away.

I hope he finds someone who will follow after him.

Shaking off the thoughts, she focused on the vision once more. This one had been of the past, not the future. What did she need to know from it? She'd just witnessed the final piece of Osiris's resurrection, yes, but what did that have to do with Balor?

She stood. "I need to call someone. It will be fast." A new urgency stirred in her. They were running out of time. "And we may need to leave sooner than an hour."

That urgency clarified into an uneasiness she had sensed before, just over two months ago. Evil was approaching, a point of chaotic malevolence. Stronger than what she'd sensed within the treacherous men of ba, this was truly wicked.

"*A stor?*" Shar rose with her, his arm brushing her shoulder as Killer paced a small path just behind her.

Mell stood as well, and Finn was staring at her intently. She locked her gaze on his. "Get them ready. Get them all ready to depart as soon as I'm done with this call. Something is coming, and it is worse than Grainne."

Finn's hazel eyes darkened and he nodded. Without a word, he strode out of the kitchen and through the living room, following Cuchi's path to the front door and beyond.

"I'll tell Dub," Mell offered. "And make sure everything else is gathered."

"If it is not prepared by the time I am done, it will be left behind," she warned.

Mell dashed away.

"I'm staying with you." Shar crossed his arms.

Already her mind was turning to the vision and the upcoming conversation. Pulling out her phone, she scrolled through the contacts until she found the name she needed.

Osiris. And the likelihood of reaching him was as slim as Bastet giving up coffee.

She hit the green dial button.

"Hello."

She nearly dropped the phone. "You answered."

"Is it so shocking?"

"Well, yes." In all of her existence, she had seen Osiris a handful of times, and talked to him even less.

"Our paths have not had much of a reason to cross before this."

Her lips trembled. His voice was smooth, low, and comforting. He sounded like... Urgency warred with the need to keep hearing that voice.

She grabbed Shar's hand with her free one, and warmth filled her, steadying her. "No, I suppose there has not been much of a reason." Suddenly she was grateful for that fact. While Osiris was not a deity aligned with chaos, there was nevertheless something eerie about him. "I am going to ask you a question, and I need you to answer me, please." She was not going to bother explaining about Balor. No doubt Osiris had already heard. "What was in the puzzle-box that Isis found on the banks of the Nile?"

He sucked in a breath. *"And why would you need to know that, young one?"*

Her heart pounded in anger and her eyes narrowed. "Answer me."

Silence, so long she suspected he hung up.

She did not have time for this. She opened her mouth to say just that, and he finally spoke. *"The heart of a god. The final piece to bring me back. Not many know this, but I was truly gone."*

She sucked in a shocked breath. This was not the story as she had heard it.

"And this is information you would do well to keep to yourself, Bat of the two faces. Some things are not meant to be told. It is not simply a matter of trust, or an issue of information falling into the wrong hands. It is both those things, yes, but some things... well, they corrupt simply by the hearing of them."

"And you will tell me this thing?"

"Have you not already chosen your nature, she who has been saved not once, but twice now?"

Bat's heart gave one last pound then settled. "Yes."

"Then you need not fear this. The box contained a seed. A seed of creation that was birthed from the vessel at the same time Atum came into being. And that seed was hidden and locked away, saved for the time it would be needed for my resurrection. My fate was decided from the moment of creation. As you know already, the vessel holds much more creation in her than simply one being, as great as Atum was."

"Then..."

"If you were a being corrupted by chaos, and you knew the vessel was capable of creating the seeds of godhood—not just life—what would you do?"

The fingers holding her phone went numb, and her lips would not move. She swayed.

Balor did not simply seek new life. He sought something so much bigger than that.

He sought true eternity.

And if he attained it, he could tip the balance in Chaos's favor.

The world would descend into ruin. It wouldn't happen overnight, but it was a real possibility.

"I will destroy the vessel before I allow such a thing to happen," she heard herself say.

"*And you may have to. But conceive of this for a moment. You would be destroying what remains of the original creation.*" The words were rote, as though he lectured on a not-too-original topic. "*Remember, you may not tell any of this, not even to the other deities. I know of no weapon but Seth's sword that has ever brought down a god, and it was designed wholly for me. We… tested it once. It did not work on the other. Again, it may have simply been my own fate to have died at Seth's hand, but what would happen if other deities began to fear they were vulnerable to true death?*"

They would strike at their enemies first. The tenuous treaties and stalemates that had been struck around the world would crumble, as those who had never had to face death were confronted with the possibility.

And, again, the world would descend into ruin.

The weight of the information she had just received settled over her.

"I understand," she said, and hit the disconnect button. She bent her head, shutting out Killer and Shar, whose eye had narrowed in concern and whose hand gripped hers in a hold just short of pain. She studied her feet, and the boots encasing them. The blue embroidery was as vibrant as the day she'd received them, a bit of kindness from a small red-haired man who played the fiddle.

She focused on the smooth brown leather, and the care that had gone into the stitches. They were the first gift she'd received in this new land.

Faced with the enormity of the consequences should they fail in stopping Balor, she concentrated on this one small thing—on the offering that had given her a new purpose in this land of green and damp. She'd decided the day she received them that she would fight for the balance inherent in her small slice of life, and for order and justice.

That small slice had now grown from a pub in a town in County Sligo, to something much, much larger.

"What happened?" Mell asked, standing in the kitchen doorway. Dub stood behind him, his hair damp and ever-present scowl firmly in place.

"I—" She couldn't tell them. She wanted to. She wanted to tell her not-men exactly what Osiris had told her, but the warning was fresh in her mind.

"*Storeen.*"

She tried again. "I cannot tell you."

Shar's grip tightened on her hand, and she met his lapis-eye. She shook her head. The words were there, waiting to be spilled. She knew she could trust them, but as Osiris had said, it was not only a matter of trust. This would not corrupt her not-men, but there was also the matter of the information making it to ears it should not, and she had already seen first hand how quickly information traveled amongst the fae.

"Goddess." Dub shoved Mell aside and took a stance in front of her. "Tell me." His tone was hard as the steel he forged.

"Dub." Mell laid a hand on his brother's arm. "Let this one go."

She nearly broke then, nearly told them. Shar's pleading wouldn't have done it, nor would Dub's stubbornness. But Mell's understanding would have been her undoing—except Cuchi chose that moment to burst back into the house, pixies swirling about his head.

"Ye'd best get out here. Trouble's arrived."

"The shadows're close, goddess," Daire said, zipping up next to her.

A dark purple pixie she had not yet met, drooping between Maire and Taire, nodded. "We barely got 'em to ya. And the human's no in good shape."

Human? Why would a human have been brought to us?

"Let's move." Dub gestured to Shar, who scooped her into his arms. Mell double checked the locks on the back door as they all headed for the front door. Grabbing her pack and the harp from near the front door, Dub waited for the middle brother to finish his check and snatch up the spear. With a few flicks of his fingers, Mell had the spear hidden away in the between-space the brothers used to stash their weapons, and had caught up, Killer at his heels.

Seconds after Cuchi interrupted them, Bat, Dub, Shar, and Mell were on the front porch.

Chapter Thirty-Two

Bastie,

Help.

Please.

Though I now know you cannot answer for some reason, or you would have already. If you are able to, please send help.

- Bat, the goddess who is officially in over her head

BAT

The fae and other immortals were up and waiting, their packs and weapons—which ranged from slingshots to daggers to staffs to bows—shouldered and strapped on. In addition to the pixies, leprechauns and trooping fae, there were banshees, sluagh, wisps and a half dozen others she couldn't identify. There was Meera, and Neall the Far Gorta—the hungry man. Faolan was there as well, and the sluagh waved to her. She lifted a hand, hampered by Shar's hold, and waved back.

Ari, standing on the edge of the wards, caught her attention. He gazed at a figure half-hidden by a brown-haired and curvy woman. The woman looked up from where she talked with a squat gray-haired lady and grinned, the expression reminding Bat of the seal's wink from her vision. Then the woman stepped forward, and Bat had a clear view of just what hovered on the edge of the wards.

Old Mike, his pants tattered at the hems and mud-splattered, stood with thin shoulders sagging under the bulk of another figure. Her sense of chaos—that inner radar that told her when true evil was near—increased in volume as she stared at the blond-haired man being supported by the wisp.

"They can't cross," Ailis said, ascending the steps to stand beside Shar on the front porch. "It's the human, and Old Mike refuses to leave him. Says the shadows are after the man, been after them since leaving the pub that day."

That would have been... three days? Nearly four. Had it really only been three days since she'd learned of Balor and the vessel had been taken?

"He's the point of chaos," she whispered. "The human. It is the tourist, I think. But... he was not like this at the pub. He did look ill, but I had thought it was because of his travels. I did not peer *into* him, though." She should have. Looking back on it, she had wondered if this particular human deserved a closer look.

She would not be second-guessing her instincts from now on.

Flash. A small stone figurine in a glass case upon a marble pedestal. It was squat and broad, bearing three eyes, one larger and in the center of the forehead. People passed it on all sides, some pausing briefly before moving on. One man paused, took a step, then went back to the figurine. It was Daniel. His eyes flared with a deep green light, then faded to their normal gray.

"We need him," she said. "Put me down."

Shar's arms tightened around her and he made a sound of protest.

"Now is not the time," Dub said from behind them.

Shar allowed her to slide to her feet.

"Are there any more of the dream-guardian amulets left?" she asked, heading down the steps and toward the edge of the wards. What she was sensing was not the human himself, but a lost and buried piece of Balor's soul. As she had suspected, it must have attached itself to an effigy and thus escaped being captured in the sword.

This was not a new concept. The pharaohs had used this method for centuries to ensure the different aspects of their souls did not depart before they were united in the journey to the Land of Reeds. Bastet had even told her of a book she'd read where the villain utilized this very technique to hide away as he attempted a resurrection.

Excitement filled her. This was the key, the advantage they needed. She stopped just on the edge of the wards—Shar right behind her—and bounced on her toes. The air was cool and fresh this early in the morning, and damp mist hung in the sky, waiting either to turn to rain or for the sun to burn it away. She offered Old Mike a smile, and a nod of gratitude. He'd done well, so well, in keeping this man alive and from the hands of Balor's minions. "Thank you," she told the wisp. "You may not know this yet, but what you have done... it may mean the difference between defeat and victory over Balor. So, thank you, Old Mike, wisp of County Sligo."

Dull lights flushed under his skin for a brief second and the wisp ducked his head.

She turned her attention to the tourist. What had he said in their oh so brief conversation? That he was planning to do a tour of the country, and look for old tales.

Was Balor one of those tales he had intended to find?

"Daniel?" Her voice was sharp, but she needed this man's attention.

He groaned and his head swayed, but he did not lift it.

"Here." Mell approached from her right, one of the hawthorn-and-iron dream-guardian amulets held out in one hand.

Taking it from Mell, she stepped over the wards and placed the amulet over the human's head. "This may help," she told him. She hoped it would. Having a shard of evil thrust inside you was extremely different from opening yourself to it in the first place. Much would depend on Daniel himself. Did he listen to the whispers, or did he fight them? That he was still with Old Mike was a good indication that he was fighting, at least for now.

After a few seconds, Daniel's shoulders drew up, jerked, then sagged. His head lifted and he blinked, his grey eyes sunken and bloodshot. He blinked again. "What?"

This man was Balor's key, what he needed to pry open the enchantments on the sword and break free. The pieces of a soul would always fight to be reunited. He needed the cauldron for life—and godhood—but he needed this little piece of spirit that had burrowed into Daniel Corous's mind and attached itself.

"Do you remember me?" She kept her voice even, steady. It would be no use to cause him to panic.

He blinked again, then glanced over at Old Mike. "From the pub? And... we've been running. There were voices." He shuddered. "There are still voices. What is happening to me?" The last was whispered in a desperate attempt at answers the man knew weren't coming.

Shar's arms wrapped around her and he pressed his chest to her back. "*A stor*, we do not have time. Something is coming through the trees."

Daniel hunched in on himself with those words. "Yes, they are coming closer. I... feel them. Please..." He met her gaze with wide eyes, the panic clear. He did not want to be taken. Balor may have been using him as a vessel for this fragment of soul, but he did not have a full hold on the human.

Reaching out and laying her hand on his shoulder, she ignored her instinctive need to recoil from the coating of malicious intent that seemed to lay on the very surface of his skin, and gave Daniel a reassuring squeeze. "We will sort this out later, after we are away from this place."

She'd barely finished the words when Shar stepped back, taking her with him, and deposited her between Finn and Mell. The guardi captain had his phone pressed to his ear. "Get here now. We're leaving in a few minutes." A pause. "I don't care. Finish it later. Just *get here*." Finn disconnected and shook his head. "They'd planned to be here an hour from now. Won't be long. Minutes."

Killer pressed against her leg. The other fae and immortals were gathered behind Ailis and Cuchi. Dub stood beside the brown-haired woman a few yards away, listening intently to whatever she conveyed. They exchanged a look, he handed her Bat's pack and the harp, then gestured toward Bat before turning his attention to the tree line.

Faolan stepped from the huddle of fae. "I will help guard," he said as he passed her and took a position next to Dub.

Shar looked between her and his brother. "I need to be up there, to hear the trees. Whatever is coming is *close*." He leaned in, his lapis eye darkening to sapphire. Knowledge glittered there, something he seemed to know that she did not yet grasp. "Whatever happens, you need to get to Tir Hudi." He pressed a firm kiss to her forehead, then stepped away and turned on his heel, joining his brother. Ari and Femi also ranged themselves along the line of the wards, on either side of Old Mike and Daniel.

The brown-haired woman stopped before her and handed over the harp. The duffel she kept, slinging it over her own shoulder beside a second, smaller, bag. "I'm Saoirse. We'll do longer introductions later, but let's just say I'm yer guide for the next length of this grand adventure." Without waiting for a response, Saoirse grinned, revealing teeth just a little too sharp, and glided into the huddle of fae.

"We're going to do this carefully, and quickly," Finn said, addressing those gathered, his voice raised to carry to even the men at the ward-line. "As soon as the other guardi are here, I'm going to drop the wards. Everyone at the ward-line, you get to me as soon as they go down, no lingering, no stupidity, got it? Everyone else, stay together, as close as you can. We'll be going to Londonderry in two stages. Do not scatter at the first stop or so help me you will be left behind."

"Not enough time. We need to go *now*," Cuchi said as he took two strides away from the fae, his gaze locked on a twist of shadow under an old oak. "The tourist won't make it otherwise." Dawn was closer, but they were now in the half-light, when reality and fantasy melded and it was near impossible to distinguish light from darkness.

Mell nodded. "Whatever is out there is hungry, and it is *here*, not just close. I'm not sure we have minutes."

Finn's lips thinned then he nodded. "I'll take us a short hop, then. When my men catch up, we'll go the rest of the way." He locked gazes with Cuchi, then Dub. "*Now*."

He dropped the wards.

Chaos descended.

Femi grabbed Daniel and Old Mike and headed for Bat and the others grouped together.

Shadows darted from the underbrush, red eyes and yellowed fangs flashing from within. Tendrils of darkness reached for the human.

Pixies darted in, flashing between the streams of shadow and striking them with tiny blades, distracting.

Ari slipped into the place Old Mike and Daniel had stood, teeth bared, a *des* gripped in his right hand and razor claws spread wide with his left.

There was a whoosh, and three figures rose into the air beyond the line of hawthorn and oak at the edge of the property, barely visible against the gray sky. They hovered, the heavy beats of their leather wings sounding with thunder in the still morning, like far-off drums of war, a prelude to death.

Shadowed hounds continued to snap at Ari, and then Dub was there, his sword a flash of metal between teeth.

Femi, Old Mike and Daniel were a few yards away.

A shadow-hound slipped past Ari and Dub and headed for the trio as the figures in the sky dove, one minute thirty feet in the air and the next just above her grumpy not-man, their talons flashing dull gray in the lightening sky. Shar, an axe clutched tightly in his right hand and a long sword in his right, engaged the one on the right, drawing it away from his brother. Dub fought, the steel of this sword a blur as he pulled upon his Strength to increase the speed of his attacks.

The hound caught Femi's heel, pulling the man of ba to the ground and sending Daniel to his knees. Faolan dove for the shadow-hound, his own shadows tangling around it and his claws digging into its dark flesh. It twisted, snapping at him, and Faolan spun. The sluagh bent his knees then jumped, taking to the air with the hound held tight, then flung it away.

One of the flying beasts—other sluagh—cried out as Dub's sword caught its left wing, and it tumbled from the air. Killer trembled at her side, and Bat reached down. She didn't want her pup running into the fray. Already there were too many of her loved ones out there. They just needed everyone close enough they could activate the transport spell…

Cuchi ran to the fallen human, pulling him to his feet and giving him a shove in the direction of the huddled fae. Bat wanted to enter the battle, to shout to her gathered allies that it was time to fight, that the enemy was *here*.

But this wasn't the only enemy, was in fact not even a fraction of them, and this was not the battle that she needed them for. It did not match the vision she'd had. This was a skirmish, a mere delay in getting to the next step in the war that had officially begun.

Cuchi headed for Dub.

There were five very capable warriors out there, guarding the gathered allies. It would take Dub, Shar, Ari, Faolan, and Cuchi a measly few minutes to dispatch this contingent of the enemy. The guardi would here by then.

Old Mike reached them, slipping between two of the banshees. They stepped forward, eyes narrowed and lips pursed. One, her hair a bright red, opened her mouth, then shut it, a frown of frustration crossing her face.

Dub turned on the second flying beast just as it pulled back, its wings working to take it back up into the air. It spun to face Faolan and hissed, tongue flicking in agitated rage.

Femi had grabbed Daniel by the arm and continued to pull him along. Close, they were so close, and then the defenders could withdraw. Her heart pounded. They didn't even need minutes. *Seconds. They simply need a few more seconds…*

Dub cried out as three hounds descended on him. Two

were thrown back, but one slipped below the swing of his sword and buried its teeth in his calf.

Shar, his weapons weaving a deadly dance near as fast as Dub's, deflected a swipe of a clawed foot with the sword, and swung his axe up to bury it under the ribs of the sluagh he fought. It spun away, deep ochre blood spraying out to spatter against the green grass.

Daniel and Femi were two steps away. Cuchi reached Dub just as her not-man dislodged the shadow-hound and sent it tumbling end over end into the trees. The third enemy sluagh dove, its claws catching Cuchi's forearm and slicing the skin open through his sweater.

Armor. Where was the armor?

Femi skimmed between her and Finn, Daniel behind him by a half second. That was it. They'd made it.

"We're leaving!" Mell's voice rang out. "Get yer asses over here."

Faolan dove and landed beside the other sluagh that had come with him.

Dub's sword flashed and the last sluagh toppled to the ground, leg severed from its body. Shadow-hounds milled at the tree line, unwilling to attack without their masters.

They were still out there, their defenders, nearly fifty feet away. The battle had drawn them farther from the huddled group. Why weren't they coming back? The enemy sluagh had been taken care of. The human had made it to the allies.

Why were Shar, Dub, Cuchi and Ari lingering in the open?

Shar stepped back, his gaze still on the trees. He paused, head cocked as though listening to something.

Then he twisted his head, meeting Bat's eyes. He gave her a sweet smile that nearly broke her heart as words from two months ago came back to her. *Even if you were our doom, we would embrace you.*

Her throat closed. "Wait." Her words came out as a bare whisper. "Wait, Finn. Not yet."

A scream slashed through the morning air. It was deep, yet shrill, a million voices crying in pain—or crazed rage.

Mell's eyes slid closed. "Well fuck me."

Dub spun to face her, but he didn't look to her. He locked his gaze to Finn's, then nodded. Finn's lips thinned and he took a breath.

"What are you doing?" she asked, her heart pounding.

Finn ignored her. He raised his hands, palms down and fingers spread, then with a twist of his fingers, brought his palms together.

Her last sight before appearing in a green field bathed in the soft glow of dawn: a horde of grotesque and squat men in ragged red coats and hats spilling from the brush and leaping from the limbs of trees, all heading with dripping teeth and rusted blades toward her defenders.

The story Continues in The Final Melody...

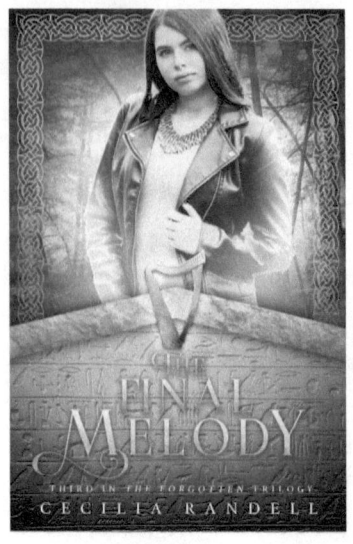

A Note From the Author

~

As with the book before, I had *way* too much fun researching the background for this story.

And, yes, I took more than a few liberties with the myths in this one.

One of the things I found so fascinating, though, was the parallels I did find. While there was actually more than one cauldron in Celtic legend, there was one that could bring the dead to life. And one of the Egyptian creation myths was of an egg on an island that rose from a sea of chaos... When I read that, I instantly asked myself "what if?"

This is another little detail, but again I found it so fascinating: the ancient Egyptian custom of wailing for the dead, and the legends of banshees...

One last thing, though this has nothing to do with the mythology. It simply has to do with Bat, and her own, personal journey. As I wrote this book, I could not help but think it was too angsty, she was filled with such doubt and confusion, where in the first book she was not. It bothered me, but I could not see another way to write her.

Then I realized I did not need to write her another way, for this was *her* journey. She had lived centuries with no hopes or goals, without examining her own past, without healing. And I have come to learn that in order to heal, you must face the pain, not ignore it. With pain comes confusion, and doubt, and changing your mind a million times.

All of this was simply part of her journey. Hopefully it was not too frustrating...

About the Author

Cecilia Randell was born in Austin, Texas and grew up in a home with her very own Cheerful Bulldozer. After some brief adventures in various places such as California and Florida, she returned to her hometown and took up a career in drafting.

A lifetime lover of words and stories, the transition to writing was two-fold: a comment from a relative and a short line from another author, saying to write what you want to read.

And thus the new adventure was born.

Now she can be found most days curled up in a comfy chair and creating new tales to share with others.